Gwynne FORSTER

Forbidden Temptation

Gwynne Forster

KIMANI
ROMANCE

 KIMANI PRESS™

ISBN-13: 978-0-373-86040-1
ISBN-10:   0-373-86040-4

FORBIDDEN TEMPTATION

Copyright © 2007 by Harlequin Books S.A.

www.kimanipress.com

Printed in U.S.A.

This month in
FORBIDDEN TEMPTATION
by Gwynne Forster

Ruby Lockhart had been looking for love in all the wrong
places. Until her one-night stand with family friend
Luther Biggens opened her eyes. Luther had always been her
rock, but that night he rocked her world. Had Mr. Right
and a possible happily ever after always been that close…?

Kimani Romance is proud to present

THREE WEDDINGS & A REUNION

THE LOCKHARTS—
Three Weddings and a Reunion
For four sassy sisters, romance changes everything!

* * *

IN BED WITH HER BOSS
by Brenda Jackson
August 2007

THE PASTOR'S WOMAN
by Jacquelin Thomas
September 2007

HIS HOLIDAY BRIDE
by Elaine Overton
October 2007

FORBIDDEN TEMPTATION
by Gwynne Forster
November 2007

Available from Kimani Romance!

Books by Gwynne Forster

Kimani Romance

Her Secret Life
One Night with You
Forbidden Temptation

GWYNNE FORSTER

is a national bestselling author of twenty-six romance novels and novellas, plus six novels and a novella of general fiction. She has worked as a journalist, university professor and, for a number of years, as a senior United Nations officer. As such, she was chief of research in (nonmedical aspects of) fertility and family planning, Population Division, United Nations, New York. In addition to her works published in the name of the United Nations secretary-general, she has, under her own name, twenty-seven publications in the field of demography. For six years she served as chairperson of the International Programme Committee of the International Planned Parenthood Federation (London, England). These positions took her to sixty-three developed and developing countries.

Gwynne holds bachelor's and master's degrees in sociology and a master's degree in economics/demography. Nine of her novels have won national awards, including the Gold Pin Award, which she won in 2001 for her romance novel, *Beyond Desire*. In 2006 *Affaire de Coeur* magazine elected Gwynne to its [writers] Hall of Fame, and in 2007 *Romantic Times BOOKreviews* honored Gwynne with a Lifetime Achievement Award.

Gwynne sings in her church choir, loves to entertain at dinner parties, is a gourmet cook and avid gardener. She enjoys jazz, opera, classical music and blues, and likes to visit museums and art galleries. She lives in New York City with her husband.

Dear Reader,

Thank you for reading *Forbidden Temptation*. It is my first experience with writing a story that is a part of a continuity series, and I very much enjoyed the challenge. I hope you have already read the three earlier books in this series and that you've been waiting to know what happens to Ruby and Luther (believe me, plenty!). If not, please look for them: *In Bed with Her Boss* by Brenda Jackson, *The Pastor's Woman* by Jacquelin Thomas and *His Holiday Bride* by Elaine Overton.

I've had so many wonderful letters of appreciation for Kendra and Reid's story in *One Night with You* that I'm behind in answering, but I will definitely reply to every one of them. My thanks to all of you for making the book such an outstanding success.

If you've read my bio, you know I've logged many air miles all over this world, but this past February I got my first look at Tulsa, Oklahoma. I was a guest of the Sisters Sippin' Tea Book Club, and let me tell you, those Tulsa ladies set the standard for literary interest as well as for hospitality. In late April I went to Houston (also for the first time) to receive a *Romantic Times BOOKreviews* Lifetime Achievement Award. I was also able to spend time with SWER (Sisters Who Enjoy Reading), one of my favorite groups of women, who live in and around Houston.

Finally, don't forget to pick up a copy of my latest Kimani Arabesque book, *Just the Man She Needs*. It's a cutting-edge romance, and when the principals get together, they really sizzle.

Warmest regards,

Gwynne

Acknowledgments

To my dear friend Carole A. Kennedy, who has given me
sisterly support, and who has always been there for me
when I needed her throughout the many years that I have
been blessed to know her. To my daughter-in-law, Meg,
whom I love and admire and whom I am blessed to have
in my family. To my beloved husband, who supports me
in every way that he can, brightening my life. As always,
I thank God for the talent he's given me in such generous
supply and for opportunities to use it.

Chapter 1

Ruby Lockhart rose early the day after Christmas. Her to do list resembled Santa's naughty-and-nice list. Unlike him, though, her work was just beginning.

She stretched as she got out of bed and braced herself for the day. In a few hours, her sister Opal's life would be forever changed. Little did she know, hers would be, too.

Yesterday's Christmas celebration had been memorable, with her sisters and the men they loved exchanging gifts and enjoying camaraderie after the festive meal that she'd spent two days preparing. As the elder sister of Opal, Pearl and Amber, Ruby hosted the holidays, a habit they'd cultivated after the loss of their mother five years ago. As tired as she had been last night, Ruby hadn't slept soundly. Last-minute details for the wedding occupied her mind throughout the night. Some would call her a control freak. She preferred to say she was proactive, doing her part to prevent any hitches.

She took the royal-blue jacket dress that she'd bought for the wedding out of the closet in her bedroom—the same room in which her parents had slept—and hung it on the back of the door. Amber, her youngest sister, always said she should avoid all shades of blue, because it didn't flatter her dark skin, but Ruby didn't care; she loved blue. Besides, people seemed to pay more attention to her light-brown, almond-shaped eyes than to her clothes or anything else about her.

She tried on the dress to be sure that the hem reached the top of her shoes, never a certainty at her height of her five feet, nine inches. Satisfied with the dress's fit on her trim, size-twelve figure, she called the bride-to-be and announced, "I'll be over in a couple of hours to check your dress."

"Thanks, but you needn't hurry. Pearl is here with me. Is Luther back yet? It's too bad he couldn't have Christmas dinner with us, but parents come first, especially on holidays."

"I don't know about Luther. I haven't spoken with him."

"You're not going to the wedding with him?" Opal asked, her tone incredulous.

"I never planned to. Anyway, he'll be there. You know he wouldn't miss it. Luther is as faithful as night and day," Ruby said, with the assurance of a preacher quoting scripture.

"Yeah," Opal said, "provided you're not thinking of Alaska where you can't always count on daylight. Pearl just said that you can put my hair up."

"Good. I'll be over shortly." In the meantime, Ruby could tick off a half dozen items on her mental to do list.

At five minutes of six and with her heart pounding in her chest, Ruby took her seat on the aisle of the third row in the Lakeview Baptist Church. When strains of "Here Comes the Bride" began, Ruby turned and saw Opal, so beautiful that she seemed to wear a halo. An odd sense of peace enveloped Ruby, and she relaxed for the first time in days.

"And by the powers vested in me, I now pronounce you man and wife." The Reverend Wade Kendrick's words brought tears to Ruby's eyes, and she smiled through the stream that bathed her face. She didn't think she had ever been so happy. D'marcus kissed Opal with the reverence of a man touching his newborn child for the first time. Ruby looked around, subconsciously seeking someone, anyone, with whom to share her happiness. Her gaze fell upon Luther who sat a short distance from her, and something quickened within her. Why was Luther looking at her with such a rapt expression on his face? Her eyebrows shot up, and he surprised her with a wink.

Ruby smiled at Luther, mainly because she always smiled at him, had since she was three and he was nine and she had followed him wherever and whenever he allowed. After the service, they met on the front steps of the church, and she hugged Luther as she usually did when they met. He stepped away from her quickly, and she gazed up at him with what she knew was a quizzical expression.

"I'll see you at the reception." He patted her shoulder and walked away with a limp that was barely noticeable.

"What's wrong with Luther?"

Ruby turned to see Amber standing beside her. "I don't know. He acted kind of strange." However, she didn't dwell on that. Luther was Luther, the Rock of Gibraltar, and she didn't doubt that he would always be that way, and always be there for her and her sisters.

"Wasn't it a beautiful ceremony?" she asked Amber. "I'd better get on to the reception," she said without waiting for her sister's response. She floated down the few steps as the sunset stared her in the face. Beautiful and powerful, the great disc colored the late December sky in shades of red, blue and gray and cast a fading glow on the wedding guests, enhancing their elegance. When she reached her car, she leaned against it for a minute thinking that even the light wind that freshened the air was careful not to disturb the women's fancy hats and hairdos. The guests' cars shone as if just waxed, and white carnations trailed up the posts around the church. Beauty surrounded her. She didn't think she would ever forget the feeling of contentment, of pure joyous satisfaction she had at that moment.

Luther Biggens's feelings about what transpired during the past hour and, especially, after the wedding ceremony did not conform to Ruby's. During the ceremony, she had caught him looking at her with an expression that even a child should have understood. Shock registered on her face. Yet, he doubted that she understood what she saw. A gracious woman wouldn't hug a man, knowing that he cared for her, unless she reciprocated his feelings. Ruby had hugged him as if he were her brother, and he'd barely been able to resist trapping her in a lover's grip. He had been in love with her since she was a teenager, but she'd obviously never considered that possibility, nor had she treated him as anything other than a big brother, which meant that loving him hadn't crossed her mind. Wearily, he got into his car and headed home to change for the reception that began at eight o'clock.

Luther had once dreamed of a life with Ruby, of a time when he would teach her to love him, and they would marry, have a family and grow old together. When he thought the time had come to pursue his dream, Ruby's mother died, leaving her with the responsibility of shepherding her three sisters through school and into relationships that became marriage. Ruby had focused on her sisters and her career, denying her femininity as if she weren't a woman herself, in need of a man's love and affection.

He parked in front of his house, went inside and the loneliness of his life glared at him like a bare electric bulb swinging from a ceiling. He'd lived for thirty-five years and what did he have that was meaningful to show for it? Certainly not the ribbons and braid on the jacket he'd once worn as a commander in the navy SEALS. Or his citation for bravery during the daring exploits in Yemen that had cost him his right foot and a good part of his right leg. Prior to that, he been self-assured and fun loving, but what woman would settle for a man with his disability? The navy didn't want him, and surely Ruby deserved better.

So he continued to love her from a distance and to be there for her whenever she needed him. All the while, wanting her.

He changed into a black tuxedo, white shirt and red cummerbund that he wore with a white carnation boutonniere. A pair of black patent leather shoes replaced his lizard-skin shoes and he slipped on his Oxford gray chesterfield coat and left home for the reception. He thought of calling Ruby to ask if she'd like him to accompany her, but realized that she would probably already be at the reception handling last-minute details. With God's help, he'd get through the evening without being miserable. At times, he wanted her so badly that the pain became almost unbearable.

* * *

As the doyenne of the Lockhart family, Ruby stood at the head of the receiving line, greeting guests and making small talk. She'd been standing there about fifteen minutes, enjoying the drone of chatter that had become increasingly loud and the laughter that could be heard above it. Relaxed and happy, she let her smile tell all around her of her pride in the occasion.

"Good evening, Ruby."

Her lower lip dropped, and she gaped at the man, helpless to do otherwise. "Luther, for goodness' sake," she exclaimed. "You…went home and changed." *What a stupid thing to say to a man, even if the man was Luther.* "Gee, you look like a million dollars." He winked, and tiny shivers raced through her. This was Luther? She managed to regain her aplomb and attempt to introduce him to the person standing beside her but suddenly couldn't remember that person's name or why the woman was standing there. As it happened, Luther was already acquainted with the woman.

Ruby watched Luther as he continued down the receiving line. Around six feet one inch and one hundred and ninety pounds, he carried himself so gracefully, no one would know he'd had that terrible accident.

And he was handsome. Why hadn't she ever noticed that his long silky lashes cast a shadow over his big brown eyes? And those dark eyes against the olive tones of his face… Oh, well, there was no reason why she should have noticed, she told herself. After

all, he was practically a member of her family. She
shook her head in wonder. At least she should have
noticed his mouth; that lusty bottom lip would win a
prize.

The best man's announcement of the bride and
groom interrupted her lustful thoughts. The lights
dimmed, and Mr. and Mrs. D'marcus Armstrong
danced the first dance. Just as Ruby removed her
jacket, exposing bare shoulders covered only with
spaghetti straps, Luther asked her to dance. She hadn't
known that he danced, and she wondered how she
should behave.

"Don't be so careful," he said. "I never attempt
anything unless I know I can do it."

"You look good," she told him. "In fact, you look...
uh...great."

"Thank you," he said, staring into her eyes. "I like
the way you look, too."

Why did he unnerve her? This was Luther, and she
had always felt safer with him than with anyone else.
"Thanks. Amber doesn't like me in blue."

A grin formed around the sensuous mouth that
she'd just noticed for the first time, and a smile made
his eyes sparkle. "Amber's a woman. What would she
know about what looks good on you?" He laughed,
and she joined the mirth, although she wondered why
she laughed when, in truth, she was thoroughly
confused.

He led her in a slow fox trot, and it occurred to her
that his disability made no difference. As they danced,

he clasped her right hand lightly, but his hand at her waist proclaimed power and authority. She relaxed in his arms, and let the music flow over her. When the music stopped, he stepped back and half bowed, a bit mockingly, she thought. With his hand at her back, he walked with her to their table for ten, sat opposite her and fastened his gaze on her.

"Champagne, ma'am?" the waiter asked her. She took a glass from the silver tray and thanked the waiter. "They'll be cutting the cake in a few minutes," he said. "Right now, we're preparing for the toast."

She drank sparingly, usually an occasional glass of wine with dinner at a good restaurant. She hadn't tasted champagne in ages. The best man offered the toast, raised his glass and invited the guests to join him. They had splurged on an expensive champagne, and after tasting it, she licked her lips approvingly and slowly drained the glass.

"This is good stuff," her cousin, Paige Richards, said. "Just the thing in this candlelit room with the orchestra playing this soft, romantic music. It's enough to make a woman say yes."

Ruby's gaze drifted to Luther, but she spoke to Paige. "Is that so? Then I think I'll have another glass."

Paige's eyes widened. "I'm not sure you should do that, Ruby. This isn't like you."

"Of course it isn't," Ruby said as she accepted a second glass of champagne from the waiter. "Now, if I put on an apron and went into the kitchen back there to help with the cleanup, that would be just like me, wouldn't it?" She took a long sip of champagne and the pit of her stomach immediately served notice that she shouldn't drink too much more of it. "I'm sitting here in front of this good-looking man, listening to this befuddling music and with nothing to do with myself, so why shouldn't I enjoy this champagne?"

Paige whispered something to Pearl, and Pearl leaned toward her older sister. "Ruby, maybe you shouldn't have any more of that champagne."

Ruby looked at Luther, raised the glass to her lips and let the wine drizzle slowly down her throat. Then she put the empty glass on the table. "Why can't we have another dance, Luther? These two old fuddy-duddies are cramping my style."

Luther got up immediately, put an arm around her waist and walked with her out to the dance floor. This time, he put both arms around her and moved in a slow drag. She put her head against his shoulder and let the champagne, the music and the aura of man encourage her recklessness.

When she missed a step, he held her a little closer. "Do you want to go back to the table?" he asked her.

"Nope. I'm perfectly happy right where I am."

"If I were you, I'd be careful of my words," he said.

She snuggled closer. "I'm always careful. Don't you know that *careful* is my middle name? Careful Ruby, that's me." She glanced around his shoulder and saw Pearl and Amber talking. "I'll bet they're talking about me."

"Who?" He stopped dancing and guided her back to their table.

"My guardians," she said. "Amber and Pearl." She took another glass of champagne from the waiter's tray, sat down and took a few long sips. "What are you two saying about me?"

"That you shouldn't drink any more champagne," Amber said.

"Oh, pooh," Ruby replied and, realizing that Luther had taken the chair beside hers, leaned over and kissed his neck. His eyes widened and he ran his fingers back and forth over his hair.

"Let her alone," she heard him say. "She deserves to have some fun. I'll take care of her."

She drained her third glass of champagne and looked at Pearl. "If this good-looking man was with you, you'd be having a good time, too. Come on, Luther, let's go see what everybody else is doing." Amber's gasp didn't concern Ruby. She was having the time of her life, and she didn't intend to let her sisters spoil her fun.

"Where are you taking us?" he asked her.

"Out here," she said, leading him to the anteroom that faced their table. At the door of the anteroom, she traced his bottom lip with her right index finger. "I've been thinking about this lip all evening. I don't know why I never saw it before tonight. It's so inviting. Maybe it's not real."

His pupils dilated, and he stared down at her with hot, stormy eyes. "Why are you playing with me?"

"I'm not," she said. "I just want to see what it tastes like."

Luther couldn't imagine what had gotten into Ruby when she reached up and sucked his bottom lip into her mouth, but he didn't hold back. He couldn't. He rimmed her lips with the tip of his tongue, and when she opened to him, fire shot through his veins and he plunged his tongue into her mouth, gripped her body to his and, mindless of their public posture, enjoyed the first sweetness he'd ever had from the lips of the woman he loved so desperately. He heard a gasp and set her away from him.

"What do you mean by starting that here in front of all these people?" he asked in a voice that trembled with the emotion that besieged him.

"There's nobody else in here," she said, but he could see that the kiss had discombobulated her, as well.

"I'm sorry that happened, Ruby."

"Well, I'm not. I loved it."

He shook her shoulders, though he did it gently. "Don't you know better than to tease a man the way you've been teasing me all evening? I'm a man with feelings, Ruby."

"Of course you are, and I haven't been teasing you. You look good, and I'm enjoying it." She looked around. "Where's that waiter with the champagne?"

"I think I'd better take you home. We'll take your car, and I'll come back and get mine. You shouldn't drive."

"You listen to me, Luther Biggens. I am perfectly sober."

"If you're sober, why did you kiss me?"

Her hands went to her hips, but she quickly removed them. "I kissed you because I wanted to, and I fully enjoyed it."

Luther couldn't deny he had, too.

"I'm not going home to that big empty house," she said. "If the wind blows the slightest bit, the whole place creaks. It's too big, too old and too dark. I don't like living there all by myself, and I'm not going there tonight." She folded her arms like a recalcitrant child, poked out her bottom lip and pushed out her chin. "I'm going home with you."

"Oh no, you're not," he said, feeling as if he were between a rock and a hard place. He wanted her alone with him in his house in the worse way, but he didn't want to spend the night struggling to control his rampaging libido.

She walked to the table with head up and shoulders back in her usual regal stride, and got her jacket.

"Where're you going?" Pearl asked her.

"Yes," Amber said. "Are you leaving already?"

"After all that I did yesterday and today, you'd think I'd be tired, wouldn't you?" he heard Ruby say, and as far as he was concerned, those were the words of a sober person. What the hell! If she wanted to go home with him, he'd take her there. Ruby tripped to the bridal table, kissed Opal, patted D'marcus's shoulder and walked back to Luther.

"I'll take you home, Ruby," he said, wanting to do the right thing. "If you're afraid to stay there by yourself, I'll sleep on the living-room sofa."

She laid her head to one side and looked at him with half-open, seductive eyes. "Didn't I tell you that I'm going home with you?" She reached out and took a flute of champagne from the tray of a passing waiter, and before Luther could stop her, she emptied the glass down her throat. "Delicious. Absolutely delicious," she said. "Come on. Let's go."

She didn't seem to need steadying, but, nonetheless, he walked out of the room with his arm around her. At the cloak room, he collected their coats, helped her into hers and took his time getting into his gray chesterfield. He was stalling for time while he did some thinking, but she locked arms with him, reached up and kissed his cheek and urged him to the door. If he lived to be a thousand, he'd never forget this night.

He loved her and he desperately wanted her, but did he dare make a move? What if he misread her, took the wrong step and ruined the most important friendship of his life?

"All right," he said to her when they got into her car with him at the wheel, "you said you want to go to my house, so I'm taking you there. But when you decide you want to leave, you only have to tell me."

"I know that, Luther," she said. "I've trusted you all my life. Sometimes I think you're closer to me than my sisters are."

For some reason, he didn't want to hear that. He wanted some assurance that, when she got to his house, she'd sprawl out on the sofa and go to sleep or, at best, she'd go to the guest room and stay there. He parked in front of his house, walked up the stone path to his front door and inserted his key. He opened the door, and she strolled in.

"Gosh, what a beautiful place," she said as she dropped herself on the sofa, crossed her knees and began swinging a shapely leg whose slope he knew so well that he could draw it from memory. "You wouldn't have any champagne, would you?" she asked him. "I've decided that I like it. Imagine living twenty-nine years and not knowing how good champagne is."

"I'm sorry, but I don't have any."

"Then could we have a glass of wine? After all, this is the first time I've been here since you bought this place. I like it."

"Since you're tired, perhaps you'd like to turn in? I'll show you the guest room."

"What about the wine? Don't you plan to be hospitable?"

"Look, sweetheart, it's almost midnight."

She didn't move. "I've been up this late before. Lots of times, in fact."

He took a deep breath, admitted defeat and went

to his kitchen for the wine. When he returned to the living room with two glasses of white wine, she had removed her coat and the jacket to her dress, exposing her beautiful brown shoulders and just enough cleavage to excite him.

He put the glasses on the coffee table. Damned if he was going to let her make a joke of him. "As soon as we drink this, I'm taking you upstairs."

He must have appeared foolish with his mouth agape as she picked up the glass, drank the wine, put the glass back on the table and said, "Okay. I'm ready."

She walked up the stairs ahead of him, and he could have told her to save the rear action; he'd been looking at it for years, and he knew it well enough to write a sonnet about it.

"To your left," he said, doing nothing to squelch the annoyance that crept into his voice. How was he supposed to deal with her? He didn't know this side of her, wouldn't have dreamed she had it, and seeing it made her even more enticing. "Not in there," he said as she strode toward an open door. "That's my room."

Without so much as a pause, she turned and entered his room.

"I said this is my room," he repeated. "You're sleeping across the hall."

"Okay," she said. "Where across the hall?"

He directed her to the guest room, and when she walked in, he stepped out, closed the door and slumped against it. "Thank God, I can breathe." Once inside his own room he removed his jacket, tie and shirt and sat on the edge of the bed to remove his shoes. Then he heard her knock. Now what? With a bare chest, but still wearing trousers, he got up, opened the door and gazed down at her.

He gulped. "What is it, Ruby?" The voice he heard must surely belonged to someone other than him; he'd never squeaked.

"Would you…uh…unzip my dress, please?" she asked him, managing to appear fragile and helpless. Oh, hell! Maybe it just seemed that way to him.

"Unzip your… Who usually unzips it?"

"Nobody. This is the first time I've worn it."

Instead of turning her back, she stepped closer, and he thought his knees had turned to rubber. "Please," she said.

"Turn around," he said gruffly. His fingers shook as he attempted to grasp the zipper, and he fumbled uncontrollably. Finally he managed to hold it, closed his eyes and pulled. He didn't hear the dress drop to the floor, and shock reverberated through his body when he realized that she had handed it to him. He opened his eyes and stared at the voluptuous beauty before him.

"My God," he uttered with a groan. He pulled her into his arms, let his hands roam over her breasts, arms, waist and buttocks until she reached up, clasped his face between her palms and parted her lips beneath his. He lost himself in her arms.

* * *

Ruby awakened and sat up suddenly, alarmed at the weight of a hand on her bare thigh. It didn't make sense. And why would a sledgehammer be pounding the top of her head? She looked to her left and gasped. Good Lord, that was Luther. What was…? It came back to her with blinding accuracy. At that moment he awakened fully and propped himself up on his left elbow.

"What's wrong? Can't you sleep?" He reached out to put his arm around her, but she slid farther from him.

"Wh-what have I done?"

"Don't tell me you're sorry or that you didn't know what you were doing," he said. "I'm having none of that."

She slid off the bed. "I'm sorry, and I apologize for…for…I don't know what came over me. Would you please close your eyes?"

"Why?" he said in an odd voice that didn't sound much like Luther's comforting baritone.

"Just please close your eyes. I want to dress." She got into her clothes as quickly as possible. "I'm going home. Do you know where my car is?"

He sat all the way up. "In front of the house. Are you telling me you don't remember me driving your car here?"

"Luther, please forgive me for any pain or inconvenience I've caused you." He started to get out of bed. "No, please don't. I don't want you to get up. I can find my way out. I...uh...thanks for everything." She wasn't sure why she was thanking him, but she hoped she would upon reflection.

She found her car keys on the table beside the living-room sofa, next to her coat. When she got into her car and put the key into the ignition, she glanced up at the house and saw Luther standing at the window.

"Lord, I must have been out of my mind to make love with Luther. He's like a brother, and...what can he possibly think of me? She rubbed her forehead in an attempt to ease the pain. "That's the last champagne I'm ever drinking. No. That's the last alcohol. From now on, I'm going to stay as sober as a judge."

She drove home, and after she walked in the door, her first thought was of the lonely echoes of her steps as she headed upstairs. The flashing red light on the phone beside her bed told her that she had messages. No doubt from Pearl and Amber. Tomorrow would be time enough to deal with them.

"What do they think?" she said aloud. "And Lord, what was I thinking? I had no business going to Luther's house that time of night. I must have been out of my mind." She showered, put on a nightgown and prepared to get a few hours sleep. She hadn't been in bed five minutes when the memory of the moments in Luther's arms came back to her as clear as a bright summer morning.

The man sent her through the stratosphere. For the first time in her life, she had exploded in orgasm after orgasm. And oh, how he had loved her. He'd worshipped every inch of her, kissed her from forehead to feet, and when he finally got inside her…the earth had moved, and it wouldn't stop. She sat up in the bed and let out a sharp whistle. Then she blinked rapidly; she hadn't known that she could whistle. She wondered what he'd thought of her wildness, her completely uninhibited behavior. If only she didn't have to see him again. Well, he would learn that she didn't plan to chase him. Never!

Luther stood at the window of his bedroom and watched as Ruby pulled away from the curb. What had he done to himself? An ache settled inside of him, more painful than any he'd ever experienced in the years of longing for Ruby. He'd known all along that, if he got a taste of her, he'd need her more than ever, but he hadn't been able to stop himself. She had stood before him, almost nude, with her lips parted and that look of expectancy, that invitation to madness on her face. He couldn't stand it. Her gaze had roamed his face and settled on his lips, and he'd pulled her body to his and plunged his tongue into her waiting mouth.

He turned, limped back to the bed—his limp was always most prominent when he was unhappy—and sat down on the edge of it. What a woman she was! She had come to him like a nail to a magnet, responding to his every touch, every kiss. And oh, man, when he'd finally got inside her, she'd gone wild, matching him stroke for stroke and bump for bump, exploding in multiple orgasms that he could feel, gripping his penis until he thought he'd lose his mind. She suited him as no other woman had.

He fell over on the bed, but sat up quickly when the musty odor of their lovemaking aroused him. "What do I do now?" he asked aloud. "She couldn't get away fast enough. This prosthesis turned her off, and she was in such a hurry to leave that she didn't even take the pains to hide that from me." He knew he wouldn't sleep, so he showered, changed the bedding to remove that reminder, went to his den and turned on the television. On the coffee table sat the two glasses he had placed there earlier, hers empty and his untouched.

"It's a lesson I won't forget," he said. "Neither Ruby nor any other woman who's likely to interest me will settle for a man with one leg. I might as well accept that and get on with my life." He went into the kitchen to make coffee, turned on the tap and stopped with his hand suspended in the air. "Maybe it wasn't my leg. Maybe I was mistaken. I thought I gave her all that a woman could ever want, but maybe I was so carried away with what was happening to me that I got it wrong. Yeah, that's it. My prosthesis doesn't look that bad. Oh, I don't know. I'll learn to live without… Oh, hell!"

In his semidark living room, Luther sat in the early-morning quiet, thinking of his life, of the woman he loved and had possessed but couldn't have, of the family he wanted so badly. He had to fight back the threat-ening depression. He couldn't let it sink him. And why should he? His mind brought back to him the story of Derek LaChapelle, who had won eight varsity letters at Northbridge High in Northbridge, Massachusetts, while playing with a prosthetic left leg. Derek had lived with it from childhood, Luther said to himself. At least he'd grown up with both legs, and nobody who didn't know would guess he had a prosthesis.

He punched the sofa pillow and said to himself, "Heck, I'm going back to bed."

Several afternoons later, while sorting out a problem in her office, Ruby answered a telephone call from Pearl.

"Paige and I are going to paint our bathroom and kitchen," her sister said. "This yellow on the walls now was Opal's suggestion. She loves yellow, but I've got-ten to the place where I can hardly stand it. D'marcus will see so much yellow in his place that he'll think he's got jaundice. Say, why don't you come over and help us?"

"Okay. I can leave here around five-thirty, but I'll have to run home and change."

"Good. Paige bought some frozen quiches, and we can make a salad. See you later."

Ruby hadn't been in the apartment Pearl shared with Paige more than half an hour when Luther walked in with containers of paint, two rollers and some paintbrushes. She stared at her sister. "Why didn't you tell me he'd be here?"

Her face the picture of innocence, Pearl merely shrugged. "He who? You can't be talking about Luther. Anything wrong with you two?"

"Of course not," Ruby said, so quickly that Paige's eyebrows shot up. "I mean, what could possibly be wrong with Luther and me?"

"Nothing," Paige said. "The two of you left Opal's reception when it was still going strong, and my tongue almost dropped out. Arm in arm is what I saw with my own two eyes."

"You're imagining things," Ruby said.

"Maybe she was, but I wasn't," Pearl said. "I also didn't imagine all that champagne you drank. I know you were happy for Opal, but you didn't have to drown yourself in it."

"Now, look here. I— Oh, hello, Luther."

Pearl and Paige stared at Ruby. "Did you two have a fight?" Pearl asked without looking directly at either of them.

"If we did, I don't remember it," Luther said, his gaze piercing Ruby with an unmistakable and unspoken accusation. "Why do you ask?"

"'Cause you're acting like you just met," Paige said.

"Where do you want me to put this stuff?" Luther asked Pearl. "If I'd known you planned to paint this evening, I'd have worn something appropriate. If you can hold off till Saturday, I could do most of it myself."

He went to the refrigerator, opened it and poured a glass of orange juice. "I love orange juice," he said. "If I thought I could tolerate the local politics, I'd move to Florida."

"Thank God you can't tolerate them," Pearl said. "I don't know what we'd do without you."

"You'd manage," he said. Suddenly, Ruby realized that both Pearl and Paige were staring at her. Wasn't she the Lockhart who was closest to Luther? Yet she hadn't reacted to his suggestion that he preferred Florida to Detroit. Her second slipup. The first was not hugging him when he walked in.

Luther seemed preoccupied and in a hurry. "I'll just set this stuff in the pantry, Pearl. If you need me to help you with it, give me a ring."

"You going?" Pearl asked him, obviously astonished.

"Yeah. Call me if you need me."

"Something's gone wrong," Pearl said to Ruby after Luther left. "You two are always like two peas in a pod. Did he give you a hard time about drinking all that champagne and playing up to him at Opal's reception?"

"I didn't play up to him," Ruby said.

Paige rolled her eyes. "Girl, if you think you didn't, then you really did have too much to drink."

"Right," Pearl said. "And if you don't *ever* get kissed again, he sure laid one on you when you led him out to that little anteroom. Darned if I would have thought he had it in him."

A frown distorted Ruby's face. "I don't believe a word of that, and if you two don't stop putting me on, I'm going home."

"My advice to you is lay off the drinks," Paige said. "If you don't remember *that,* you don't know what you did after you left there."

"Your imagination is getting out of hand, Pearl," Ruby said, wondering why she hadn't stayed home. She didn't even like quiche. "Get off my case, or I'm leaving."

"I haven't said a thing," Paige said. "It didn't used to be so easy to yank your chain, Ruby."

"Leave her alone," Pearl said. "When I wake up tomorrow, I don't want to see anything yellow. Let's get started."

Ruby wrapped her hair in a hand towel, grabbed a pair of rubber gloves, a roller and a can of paint, and went to the bathroom to begin painting. Luther had hardly acknowledged her presence. Would a man be so cool if he thought you were good in bed? She doubted it. And especially not Luther who, for almost as long as she could remember, had encouraged her in everything she did. Maybe she hadn't satisfied him. She couldn't remember how he'd reacted in the end. She only knew that he'd made love to her as if she were the queen of his heart, and she had seemed to float on a cloud, and then go higher and higher until she exploded in relief.

A tear fell on her hand. *How could I do that? I'm*

*so ashamed. He doesn't want to be around me. I drank
so much champagne I don't know what I did to... Why
did Luther make love to me?*

"What about Wade?" Ruby heard Paige ask her
sister, interrupting Ruby's thoughts. "Maybe he won't
like the gray you're putting in the bathroom."

"You can't get more conservative than gray," Pearl
said, "and you know how conservative Wade is, bless
his heart. Gray walls, silver shower curtain, silver
frames on the posters, gray carpet and gray and green
paisley towels. That'll be cool, right?"

"Works for me," Paige said. "By the way, let's see
if we can get Ruby into something other than black
and navy blue for your wedding reception."

"You have to admit that the royal blue she had on on
Saturday night was an improvement. I'm going shopping with her tomorrow. I'll find her something to wear."

"We've almost finished here," Paige said. "Let's put
the quiches in the microwave, and you start on the
salad."

"Maybe we should call Luther and ask him if he
wants to have supper with us. We certainly have
plenty."

"Okay," Pearl said. "He was so nice to pick up all
this stuff for me."

Ruby put the paint roller on the tray and sat down
on the closed commode. Did her family think her
dull? She didn't have anything against bright, fashionable colors. She'd simply been so busy since their
mother died trying to be a role model for her sisters

that she hadn't given much thought to being fashionable and to making a life with a man of her dreams. No wonder she hadn't been able to please Luther. But she had no intention of withering like a rootless plant in the hot sun. She would always be grateful to Luther for teaching her her sexual potential, but now that she knew what she was capable of, she wasn't going to be timid about exploring it.

Ruby pulled off the rubber gloves and brought the paint and roller to the kitchen. "Where do you want me to put—" She broke off when she saw her sister on the phone. "Who're you calling? Are you talking to Luther?"

"Just a minute, Luther," Pearl said. "I think Ruby wants to speak with you."

"I do not. I didn't say I wanted to—" Pearl shoved the phone to her face. "Uh…hello, Luther. Actually I didn't tell Pearl I wanted to speak with you. I asked her if she was speaking with you."

"So I heard. I never did find out why she called. Let me speak with her." Ruby listened for a few seconds, long enough to realize that he wouldn't say anything else, and handed the phone back to Pearl, who, with her mouth agape, nearly dropped it.

"I'm going to skip the quiche," Ruby told Paige, since Pearl was still speaking with Luther. "I'd rather shower than eat. Tell Pearl I'll meet her at Saks tomorrow at five."

She couldn't get out of there fast enough.

After Pearl's wedding she told herself she'd take a

nice long vacation. That would make it impossible for
her sisters and their cousin Paige to pester her about
her behavior during and after Opal's wedding reception. Frankly, she was sick of hearing about it, because
she was sure she hadn't done anything dishonorable.
She'd always heard it said that a person wouldn't do
anything when inebriated that she wouldn't do sober.
"I'm definitely counting on that," she said to herself
and walked into her house. Actually, it was the family
home, and she'd give anything if her sisters would
agree to sell it and share the proceeds. But no, they
wanted to gather there on holidays and special occasions with her substituting for their parents. She didn't
mind, because she loved her sisters.

The phone rang as she walked in. She didn't have
to look at the caller ID; she knew she'd hear Pearl's
voice.

"Hi, Pearl," she said. "What's up?"

"Hi, Ruby. This isn't Pearl. This is Trevor Johns.
Pearl and Wade sent me an invitation to their wedding,
and I…uh…would you allow me to accompany you?"

Well, maybe her life was about to become interesting. "Why, yes. I'd enjoy your company," she said, seeing an opportunity to show Luther that he had nothing
to fear from her, that she didn't expect anything of him
more than usual. "But I have to be there a little early,"
she added.

"That doesn't matter," he said. "Just tell me what
time to come for you."

She told him, adding that she would look forward

to seeing him. She didn't plan to mention the date to her sisters. Oh, they'd have something to say, but she wouldn't hear them. She hoped Luther would notice that she wasn't without a date at the reception. He hadn't even said goodbye to her when they spoke on the phone, so he wouldn't ask her to go along with him. Let him wonder about Trevor Johns and what he was to her. She just couldn't figure out why Trevor had asked her when Detroit was full of younger and flashier women. If he had an agenda, she'd know it quickly.

Chapter 2

Ruby went to meet Pearl and Amber at the famous department store somewhat halfheartedly that afternoon. Reasonably satisfied with herself, she saw no reason to remake herself to suit anyone, including her beloved sisters. But a kind of restlessness pervaded her, and she couldn't put her finger on the why or what of it. Granted that, after what Luther did to her, an eagerness to discover more about sex and to make up for lost time seemed to have gotten a solid hold on her. Still, that didn't seem to be reason enough to dress according to Amber's sense of fashion. Or Pearl's, for that matter.

She strode into the store and headed for the bank of elevators where her sisters waited for her. "Sorry I'm a little late, but the traffic was awful."

"I thought maybe you'd decided to let us mind our own business," Amber said.

"Don't think it didn't occur to me," Ruby replied.

"I saw a beauty in last Sunday's paper," Pearl said. "I hope you'll like it, 'cause I think it's perfect for you."

When they wandered into the section containing evening gowns, Ruby stopped at the first rack. "That one's pretty."

Amber rejected it. "It's blue and doesn't have a bit of sex appeal. Try living dangerously for once, and wear something that flatters your figure. If I had your height and figure, I'd dress like Halle Berry and Tyra Banks. Give 'em something to whistle at."

Ruby couldn't help laughing. Amber knew how to make a case for the ridiculous. Something to whistle at, indeed! "I'm not wearing anything that has my nipples showing. Half of these dresses don't leave a thing to the imagination, neither above nor below the waist."

"Put one of 'em on, and I bet you won't leave that reception alone," Amber said.

Ruby wasn't going alone, but she didn't plan to tell them.

"How about this one?" Pearl said, holding up another gown. "It's dazzling, and you can wear it."

"It's red," Ruby said, wrinkling her nose and making a face. "Attention is supposed to be on the bride."

"Oh, I'll get enough attention," Pearl assured her. "I just want you to look great. Try it on."

"Yes, indeed!" Amber said. "That dress is to die for. Go on. Try it."

Ruby hated pulling off her clothes, and liked even less trying on clothes in stores. But she knew when to give in. "I'll be back in a minute."

"Uh-uh," Amber said. "We're going in there with you."

Resigned, she found a size ten and a size twelve and took both into the dressing room. She tried on the ten first and let out a gasp.

"What did I tell you?" Amber asked in a voice that held more than a note of triumph. Superiority was more like it, Ruby thought.

She had to admit that she'd never looked that good in anything. "But what about my shoulders?" she asked, hoping to finding something wrong with the strapless, draped sheath in brick red.

"What about 'em?" Pearl said. "This dress is perfect on you. Wrap it up, girl, and let's go. Wade's waiting for me. We have a date tonight." She winked at Ruby. "In this dress you'll get one, too."

On New Year's Eve Ruby wore the same royal blue dress and jacket to Pearl's wedding that she'd worn to Opal's the week before, but with her hair up in a French twist and Amber's "Jezebel earrings," as Wade called them. She looked much better. Even she had to admit that last week the dress didn't do a thing for her. Except get her into trouble with Luther.

After the ceremony, she rushed home to change

into the red evening gown for the reception. She stood at the mirror admiring what she saw and appreciating, at last, her sisters' pleas to stop looking so dowdy. From now on, she vowed, there would definitely be some changes made. She slipped on her black satin shoes, got the matching purse and added her perfume—something else she intended to change. After wearing the same fragrance for over ten years, she could use a different scent. Yes, indeed, she told herself as she walked down the stairs, anybody who expected the same old Ruby was in for a surprise.

She let Trevor Johns ring a second time before she opened the door. He stared at her, and she'd swear with her hand on the Bible that his eyes doubled in size.

"Ruby?"

She squelched the laughter, but a grin broke out on her face nonetheless. "Hi, Trevor. Come on in while I get my coat."

"You sure look pretty. Even prettier than you looked last week at Opal and D'marcus's wedding. You ought to wear red all the time." He handed her a bouquet of yellow roses. "I didn't get red ones, because they're supposed to be for intimate relationships, but I sure wish I had."

She decided not to comment on that. If he was working up to something, she didn't think she was ready to hear it. Not that he wasn't interesting in some ways. He towered over her, and that was in his favor, as were his good looks. And the brother knew how to put on clothes; he looked almost as great in that tux as Luther did in his. Luther… She was not going to allow him to cross her mind. She put the roses in a vase on the table in her foyer and handed him her coat.

He helped her into her coat without allowing his hands to touch her bare shoulders—another point in his favor—and she let herself relax. The evening would be all right.

"I wonder what's keeping Ruby," Luther said to Opal and D'marcus, who had delayed their honeymoon in order to attend Pearl and Wade's wedding. They stood near the door at practically the same spot where, only one week earlier, he'd kissed Ruby for the first time. It seemed as if years had passed.

"I think she's with Pearl," D'marcus said. "You know Ruby has to check everything out. I expect she'll be out here in a minute or two. After all, she's at the head of the receiving line, and it's time for the reception to begin."

Luther hoped they considered it normal for him to express concern about Ruby. He was worried about her; maybe he'd killed any chance that he could have a relationship with Ruby. He didn't expect her to accept him as a lover, her behavior since rocking him out of his senses was proof of that.

What the hell! He stared in disbelief as Ruby—it *was* Ruby, wasn't it?—approached them arm in arm with a six-and-a-half-foot turkey dressed up in a penguin suit. He shook his head in dismay. He wasn't being fair, but he couldn't help it. The knife stabbed his gut and then turned when she looked up at the guy and smiled.

"Hi," she said airily, as if she hadn't created a stir. "The place is lovely, isn't it? And so romantic."

"Hello, Ruby," he said, struggling to keep his voice low and calm. "Well, I suspect you're ready to begin receiving, so I'll see you later."

"Oh, Luther!" she said, as if he were an after-thought. "You're supposed to be in the receiving line right after Amber and Paul. Where do you think you're going?"

He wanted badly to tell her he was going where he wouldn't see *her,* but instead, he said, "Where did you think I was going?" and headed down to where Amber and her new husband, Paul Gutierrez, shared a laugh with Paige Richards. He didn't wait to be introduced to Ruby's date. Indeed, he didn't want to meet the man or even to remember what he looked like. And he prayed to God she wouldn't drink any champagne. In all the time he thought about it, he hadn't been able to figure out any other reason why she'd made love with him last week. She had appeared to be stone-cold sober, and he prayed that she had been, but then, why did she reject him? He shook his head. He wasn't going into that again; he'd suffered enough about it.

"Who's the guy with Ruby?" he asked Paul.

"Damned if I know, man. I hardly recognized her. Talk about a siren! She ought to come out like that all the time."

"Tell me about it. Where are the bride and groom?" he asked Amber, effectively getting the conversation away from Ruby.

"They'll be in as soon as the best man gives the signal, and he has to get it from Ruby," Amber said. "Reminds me of Ford's assembly line. Thank goodness Paul and I skipped all this formal stuff."

Luther looked from Amber to his friend Paul, and for the first time that evening, a feeling of warmth and happiness enveloped him. When he'd sent his buddy to rescue Amber from Dashuan Kennedy—a no-good man if ever there was one—he didn't dream that Amber and Paul would fall in love and marry. But as he thought of it now, it couldn't have been otherwise. They seemed to suit each other the way pods suited peas. Perfectly.

He waited until Pearl and Wade entered, heard the toasts and gave his own toast as was expected of him. He was about to leave when D'marcus moved to the microphone.

"We have a little news for you," he said with his arm tight around the waist of his new wife. "We hunted half a year for it, but today we found our dream house. I just wanted to share that with our families and friends and to let you all know that we'll be staying right here in Detroit."

"Well," Pearl said when the applause died down, "congratulations, Opal and D'marcus. I'm happy you'll be staying here, because I've decided not to audition for that record label in Nashville. I got a call from a label right here in Detroit, and I'm going for it. I can pursue a singing career and stay right here with my husband and my family."

Luther gazed around him at the hugs and smiles of joy. The Lockharts had been a part of his life since he was a boy. They were grown now with men of their own, and they didn't need him. His gaze locked on Ruby, dazzling in that red dress and those shimmering earrings, with her hair pulled back to expose her high cheekbones and sculpted face. Against the soft candlelight, she bloomed like an American beauty rose, her skin glowing above the strapless gown. He sucked in a breath. In his mind's eye, he envisaged her escort with his mouth on her sweet breast. Damn! It was time he got on with his life.

He hugged Pearl and shook Wade's hand. "Have a happy, you two. If you need me, you know where to find me."

Then he thought twice about leaving so early, as anger stirred in him. He wasn't an old shoe to be discarded with the advent of a new style. It was New Year's Eve, three minutes to midnight. Damned if he'd let that guy kiss her at the stroke of twelve. He walked over to her and took her hand, delighted when her eyes widened and her lower lip dropped.

"May I have this dance?" he said. He didn't wait for her to answer, and began the dance.

"It was a nice wedding reception, wasn't it?" she asked him as they moved in the slow waltz.

"I dislike meaningless small talk, Ruby, just as I

hate every other kind of superficiality." She seemed to recoil from the blow of that comment, but he didn't care. At least, she was still perceptive.

"Happy New Year," someone yelled. Impulsively, he locked her to him, pressed his lips to hers, and when, in her shock, she parted them, he plunged into her. Caught off guard, she pulled him into her, loving him in return. His heart skipped a beat and then took off, as all of his blood seemed to head in one direction, straight to his groin, burning his veins with the heady heat of desire He stopped, almost pushing her away when fire roared through him. He'd meant to punish her with that kiss, but it was he who received the chastening.

He could feel the tremors that shook her, but no matter, he stepped farther away from her. "Happy New Year, Ruby." Without looking at anyone or letting anybody catch his eye, he walked out. Not even the biting cold air sobered him mentally or tempered his desire. He got in his car and just sat there, listless, unable to will himself to start the motor and drive. He'd been alone plenty in his life, but he didn't remember having been as lonely as he felt right then.

After nearly a quarter of an hour, he inserted the key into the ignition, revved the motor and headed home.

Ruby stood as he left her, catatonic, unable to move. What on earth had possessed Luther to do that in front of all those people? She looked around, expecting that she'd be the center of attention, that everyone would be staring at her, but it seemed that no one had noticed it, and she realized that others had been sharing New Year's Eve kisses and hadn't seen her exchange one with Luther. None, except Trevor Johns.

He strode over to her, took her arm and walked with her to the anteroom. "What was that about? What's that guy to you?"

She didn't like being questioned, although Trevor had escorted her to the reception and probably thought he had a right to know why she'd kissed another man in his presence.

"I didn't expect that any more than you did," she said. "If I ever find out why he did it, I'll tell you. Right now I'd like to drop it. I'm sorry if it embarrassed you."

"I'd been hoping that you and I might get something going," he said, "but... Look, you kissed him back. I mean, you didn't fool around."

"Look, Trevor, I've known him since I was two or three. Think nothing of it."

"If you say so. But can you kiss me the way you kissed him?"

Her face twisted into a frown. This man was too possessive. "I haven't known you as long as I've known him," she said and whirled around to go back to join her family at their table.

"Having a problem?" D'marcus asked her.

"Thanks. I can handle it." If she'd driven her own car, she'd be on her way home right then.

"If you decide you want to go home, let me know," D'marcus said. "This is what brothers are for."

"Thanks, bro," she said. "I'll remember that."

Later, after deciding that she didn't know Trevor Johns well enough to trust him, she said to D'marcus, "Why don't you and Opal drop by for a glass of wine or a cup of coffee on your way home?"

"I'm driving, so I'll skip the wine," he said, "but I'd love a cup of good coffee."

Ruby had to tap Trevor's forearm to get his attention. "I'm ready to go. Ruby and D'marcus are coming by for coffee. Are you ready?"

His expression of surprise suggested to her that he had either expected her to leave without him or that having her brother-in-law and sister for company had derailed his plans. "Is this some kind of family custom?" he asked her. "I mean... Well, hell. Let's go."

His response tempted her to tell him good-night then and there, but she restrained herself and forced a smile. "We're ready, D'marcus."

Trevor parked in front of Ruby's big Tudor house and turned to her. "I'm really not in the mood for coffee."

"Thanks for the pleasant company," she said, allowing herself to sound insincere, and opened the door. However, Trevor hurried around to assist her, and she was glad he did, for she could barely maneuver in the slim sheath. When he walked with her to the front door, she told herself that inviting Opal and D'marcus for coffee was one of the smartest things she'd done.

She opened the door and, without entering, said to him, "Thanks again. Good night." She extended her hand, but he ignored it.

"Good night, Ruby. It isn't often I get to escort the belle of the ball. Be seeing you."

She let out a long sigh of relief when Trevor met Opal and D'marcus on the walkway and nodded, but didn't hesitate.

"Still want to make coffee?" Ruby asked her.

"Sure. Come on in."

"He's a decent enough guy," D'marcus said. "What happened that caused you to dump him like that?"

"He got too possessive."

"Maybe he got uptight when Luther kissed you," Opal said. "Of course, it's none of my business, but what was Luther mad about? He didn't seem affectionate. And last night, you two acted like you hardly knew each other. I don't get it."

"Neither do I," Ruby said and headed for the kitchen, grateful she had to make the coffee. When she returned to the living room with a tray, she stopped and stared at the newlyweds locked in a sizzling kiss. It hadn't take them long to switch their minds off her and Luther, she thought. She put the tray on the coffee table and cleared her throat.

"I hope you and Luther straighten out whatever's wrong between you," D'marcus said, picking up the conversation where they'd left it. "He's a great guy, and this family is very important to him. Who knows? Something could even develop between you two."

Didn't she wish! But Luther wanted no part of her, and he'd made that clear. Even when she'd shamelessly kissed him back tonight, hoping to let him know how he made her feel, he'd pushed her away. He'd done it gently, but he'd done it, and that told her more than words could have. Why did he have to be the man to teach her what lovemaking was all about, to cherish her as if she were the rarest gem and to make her explode again and again in orgasm? He wasn't the first, but he was the only one who mattered.

She sipped the coffee and remembered D'marcus's comment. "Me and Luther?" she exclaimed. "I was pie-eyed about him when I was three. I'm grown up now." She looked at her brother-in-law with one raised eyebrow. "Wouldn't that be a humdinger!"

Ruby slept late New Year's morning and awakened feeling lost. For the first time in her memory, she didn't feel like calling Luther to wish him a Happy New Year. Her reluctance to talk to him sprang from her fear that he would reject her gesture. How times had changed. Luther had been her solid rock, and now she feared calling him. Who would ever have imagined it?

She scrambled out of bed, showered, dressed and went downstairs to cook her breakfast. "If this is what the remainder of the year will be like," she said to herself, "I'm not looking forward to it."

After breakfast she decided to do her laundry. Nostalgia gripped her when she took the bedding from the hamper, remembered her lovemaking with Luther and thought how ephemeral happiness could be. She sat down on a stool in the laundry room and mused about her chances of finding that feeling with someone else.

I want to find out more about it while I'm still young and I can enjoy it, and I'm going to. Luther wouldn't have noticed me last night if I hadn't been wearing that sexy red dress, so I'm going shopping.

She spent the remainder of the day purging her clothing, most of which was better suited for a woman twice her age. The following Monday morning she called the Salvation Army. Then she went shopping.

She didn't have to be told that the fashionable clothes, shoes and accessories she bought raised eyebrows, and with her hair cut in a pixie style and three-inch-heeled suede boots on her feet, she attracted a lot of glances. As she strolled through Twelve Oaks Mall, she couldn't believe the amount of male attention she received.

A few evenings later when she walked into her house, the telephone began to ring and, thinking that the caller was one of her sisters, as was usually the case, she dashed to the phone.

"Hello?"

"Hello. This is Lawrence Hill. I hope you remember me. We met at the Harvest Ball the day after Thanksgiving, and I remember how well you dance. I'm calling to ask if you'd go with me to the local Kappa dance Saturday. I'd be honored."

"Yes, I do remember you," she said. "Let me think

about this a little bit. Call me tomorrow evening. It's formal, isn't it?"

"Black tie. I'll call about this time tomorrow, if you don't mind, and I hope you're going to say yes."

"We'll see. Thanks for calling, and have a pleasant evening." They said goodbye and she hung up. You bet, she remembered Lawrence Hill. Who could miss him? The man was a stud if she'd ever seen one, but she'd turned over a new leaf; she was no longer the family wallflower who stood by while her sisters found their mates, fell in love and married. Not that she wasn't happy for them. Lord knows she was, but there had always been that little voice inside that asked, "Why not me?" Maybe she'd go out with Lawrence Hill, and maybe she wouldn't. If things were normal, she'd phone Luther and ask his views on the matter, but life was lopsided there right now, so she called D'marcus instead.

"Do you happen to know Lawrence Hill?" she asked him.

"If it's the guy I'm thinking about, he's a fraternity brother. Seems nice enough if you can handle a stiff dose of ego."

"He asked me to go to the frat dance with him Saturday after next."

"Must not be the same Lawrence. I don't know of a Kappa dance coming up anywhere near here."

She didn't press it. "Thanks. Must not be the same guy," she said, but she knew it was the same man.

She gave it to Lawrence Hill straight when he

called and asked her, "Well, what will it be? I've waited impatiently all day for your answer."

"I can't imagine why, Mr. Hill. I spoke with my brother-in-law who I think you know. D'marcus Armstrong. He said the local Kappa fraternity isn't having a dance on Saturday. Goodbye." She hung up without giving him a chance to speak. Was he planning to say the dance had been postponed and then suggest that they go some place else? She wished she hadn't been so hasty. It would have been fun to watch him wiggle out of the hole he'd dug for himself.

If this was a sample of the current dating game, Ruby didn't want any part of it. With her sisters married as her mother wished, she could at last focus on her career, and that was what she planned to do.

Fine particles of snow dusted her face as she stepped out of her house and strode to the waiting taxi, her form of transportation until her car was serviced. She loved her work at Everyday Opportunities, Inc., and with her family responsibilities behind her, she was in a position to develop the consulting firm into a huge business. After all, small businesses employed more people than corporations did. In an expansive mood, she overtipped the taxi driver and marched with buoyant steps into the building that housed the consultancy, greeting employees and building attendants as she went. She hung up her coat and headed for her office, the company's second most spacious accommodation.

"Looking good this morning, Miss Lockhart," one

of the clerks told her, his white teeth sparking against his nut-brown face.

Her new shoes, with the pointed toes and spiked heels, didn't feel good on her feet, but apparently they made her look good. She gave the clerk a bright smile.

"Yes, indeed," said her secretary, who happened by at that moment. "With those legs, Miss Lockhart, you ought to pitch all your flats straight into the garbage. 'If you got it, flaunt it.' That's what my brother always said, God rest his soul."

Such comments gave Ruby courage to accept as normal that men found her interesting and wanted her company, though it was a new experience. She kept that in mind when Joel Coleman, owner and operator of Diet Sensibly, Inc., a small business that she counseled, invited her to dinner. She accepted.

"Who's the new man in your life?" Joel asked her as they waited for the first course.

She scrutinized him for a second to see if his question implied a hidden motive, decided that it didn't and relaxed her face into a slight smile. "Why do you think there is one?"

"We've known each other for about four months and suddenly you're a changed woman. That usually means a new love interest."

"If that's the case, why am I having dinner with you?"

Joel leaned back in the chair, poised, with a self-possessed air, and smiled. "I didn't have the nerve to ask that question. Why *are* you having dinner with me?"

She realized that she hadn't given the man his due. He was not only a clever businessman, he had a mind that served him well. "I thought you'd be a pleasant date. Was I wrong?" She added the latter in order to level the playing field; the man was sharp, and she meant to let him know that the trait wasn't confined to him.

His left eyebrow rose slowly. "In other words, back off. Right? I try to be as pleasant as possible." A few seconds passed, and he added, "Whenever possible."

"Hmm. I don't think I'll ask about the occasions when it's not possible to be pleasant."

His shrug and half smile suggested that nothing could be gained by pursuing the matter. While they consumed as good a meal as she'd had in a long time and she discovered that they had much in common, she sensed a restlessness, an undercurrent of edginess in him that put her on guard. There'd be no invitation to come in for coffee when he took her home, she promised herself. This brother could be too difficult to control.

"Would you like to go to a night spot?" he asked her as they left the restaurant. "Brock Madison's Trio is performing nearby."

"I'd love to, Joel, but I have to get up early in the morning."

"If you're sure," he said.

She couldn't help being on edge. She hadn't wrestled with a male since her early teens, the age at which the boys she knew confused *no* with *go ahead*.

She imagined that some never got the responses straight in their heads.

"Since you have to get up so early," Joel said as they stood in her open front door. "I don't suppose I can expect a nightcap. But I would like a kiss."

Like a thunderbolt the realization hit her that she didn't want Joel or any man other than Luther to kiss her. She turned away just as he came in for the kiss.

"That's what I suspected. Thanks for a pleasant evening." With that, he strode down the walk whistling the "Toreador's Song" from the opera, *Carmen*.

She closed the door, thinking that, if she had hurt his feelings, he certainly intended her to see that her rejection meant nothing to him. She could do without Joel Coleman, Lawrence Hill and Trevor Johns. In fact, she could do without any man who didn't spell his name L-u-t-h-e-r B-i-g-g-e-n-s.

But she couldn't imagine a future with the man she'd known almost all her life.

Deciding that it was past time he got on with his life, Luther drove slowly along Ford Road, organizing his thoughts and formulating the arguments he would need to convince his family to accept his proposal. He reached his parents' home in Dearborn, Michigan, a few minutes before noon on the second of January.

"Happy New Year, everybody," he said as he strolled into the den where his parents, his sister Glenda and his brothers Charles and Robert sat around the fireplace roasting nuts and enjoying the still-sparkling Christmas tree. They all jumped up when he walked in, but stood back until Irma hugged her oldest son first.

"We thought you'd never get here, son," Jack Biggens said. "Your mother's got the bread ready to bake, but she knows how you like to walk in and smell it perfuming the place. Come on over here and have a seat."

He hugged his father, handed him a bottle of Scotch and greeted his siblings. "Mom, are you baking the bread here in the fireplace as usual?"

"Beats the oven anytime," she said. "It'll be ready in about forty-five minutes, just in time for lunch."

He sat down and began cracking pecans, his favorite nut. "We got a lovely poinsettia from Ruby," Glenda said. "I haven't seen her for a while. How is she?"

He didn't come there to talk about Ruby, and he didn't intend to. "Ruby's fine, as far as I know. When are you going back to school, Charles?"

"Classes start the tenth, so I'll be leaving Friday."

Their conversation roamed over a myriad of topics and, as usual, he enjoyed the love and camaraderie with his family. After lunch he decided that the time had come to tell them what he wanted. He waited until they'd left the table and were back in the den.

"I've been managing the dealerships ever since I recovered from that accident and left the service," he began. "Dad's ready to retire, Glenda doesn't live anywhere near a dealership, Robert's got his own thriving company, and Charles has never been interested in the automobile business. I hired an accountant to estimate the worth of the business, and I want to buy you out." He heard the gasps, noted that they didn't come from his parents and continued.

"I'll buy five-sixths of that amount from you, and you can split it among yourselves as you see fit."

"That wouldn't be fair, son," Jack Biggens said. "Since you've been the manager, you've increased the holdings and the profits. I think you should get a quarter, and that's what I'm proposing."

"You mean we're going to sell to Luther?" Charles asked.

"Why not?" Jack said. "He busts his butt at it every single day, and you don't give him a hand when you're in town. I say we take a vote."

"No vote's necessary. I say we just do what's right," Irma said. "If the five of us split three-fourths of the proceeds, it's just and right."

Luther knew that, when his mother put her foot down, his siblings would fall in step.

"Thanks," he said. "I'll send the contract over before Charles goes back to the university. It's a load off my shoulders."

As he headed home, an icy mist threatened to make driving impossible, and he stopped several times to deice the windshield. He didn't make New Year's resolutions, but as he walked into his house, he promised himself that he would get over his almost lifelong passion for Ruby Lockhart. Pain lodged in the region of his heart when he let himself recall how, on that one night when she was his, she'd moved beneath him, rocking to his rhythm like an ocean wave undulating beneath the moon.

"It hurts," he said aloud. "But she'll never know how much."

He wasted no time drawing up his plans to modernize the business and, before he went to bed that night, he knew where and how he'd start. "I'll have my hands too full to think about Ruby, much less see her."

However, Luther's role in Ruby's life remained basically as it had always been.

As she sped down the Edsel Ford Parkway three days after New Year's, a blue SUV swiped the left side of Ruby's car and sent it spinning into the right lane. She'd never prayed so hard in her life as she did while struggling to control her car. When it finally stopped on the right shoulder of the highway, she got out, wrote down the plate number of the offending vehicle and stood beside the driver's door of her car waiting for the driver of the SUV. A big, lumbering man got out of the SUV half a city block away and started toward her but, unsure of what to expect, her nerves rioted throughout her body, and she took out her cell phone and dialed the one person she always relied on.

"Hello."

"Luther, it's Ruby." The words rolled out of her at a rapid-fire rate. "I'm on Route 12, and somebody just hit my car. He's a huge man, and he just got out of his SUV and he's headed this way. Maybe I should just—"

"Get in your car and stay in it," he said. "Lock the door and roll down the window just enough to speak with him. Did you call the police?"

"I forgot. I'll call them now. Look, the man's almost here, so I'd better hang up."

"You'll do no such thing. Keep that phone open and right where he can see it. Where are you on twelve?"

"Just past the intersection of Route 94 headed to Detroit."

"I'll be there in fifteen minutes."

She hurried back into her car, closed and locked the door, rolled down the window about two inches and dialed the police. It hadn't occurred to her to be afraid or even especially cautious, but she trusted Luther as she always had, and when the big man reached her car, huffing and puffing for air, she was on her guard.

"When did you get your driver's license?" he yelled. His breath gave her the real reason for his having nearly run her off the highway.

"I've been driving for...let's see...about thirteen years, and I've never had an accident. Please let me see your driver's license."

"Oh, yeah? You're out of your mother-loving mind, lady. You hit *me*."

"No matter who hit whom," she said keeping her voice low and calm, "we have to exchange information, don't we?" She didn't dare rattle the man, and she wanted to keep him there until the police arrived.

She was beginning to wish she hadn't called Luther, because the man's belligerent manner suggested that he'd use any excuse for a fight.

"Look," she said, "we have to settle this. I'll write my information out and give it to you." She reached into the glove compartment, got a small pad and a pencil and handed it to him through the slightly open window. "You write your info out for me on that little pad, and we'll be on our way."

"You're a slick one," he said. "I wouldn't trust a woman as far as I could throw her. It'll cost me four or five hundred bucks to get my car painted. You can give me the cash or a check, I don't care which. But if the check bounces, expect to see me again."

In spite of the cold wind blasting her through the partly open window, perspiration beaded on her forehead. She couldn't move the car without hurting him, and he had only to shove her car with all his strength and she'd be lying in the little ravine at the edge of the highway. As her mind raced for a solution, a car pulled up behind hers, but from her rearview mirror, she knew at once that it wasn't Luther's car. Her breathing accelerated, and the man at her car window turned to see who had parked behind her.

She noticed that his hands began to shake, turned around and saw a uniformed patrolman get out of the unmarked car and said a word of thanks.

"What's going on here?" the patrolman asked. She jumped out of the car and handed the officer her license and registration.

"I was in the middle lane going fifty, officer, and he passed me on my left and knocked me all the way to where my car is. I spun around several times, till I thought I couldn't get control of my car."

The officer walked around the car, looked at the tires and the scratches on the left side of the car. He stopped in front of the other driver. "You had to be going pretty fast to do this. Both of her right tires are split. Let's see your papers."

"I....uh...she hit *me*, Officer."

"Your papers, buddy."

"They, uh...they're in my car."

"I'll walk with you."

Luther drove up as the two men walked off, and she didn't think she'd ever been so happy to see anyone.

"Are you all right?" Luther asked her.

"I'm fine," she said, although she wasn't. He showed no warmth, neither in his voice nor his demeanor. After walking around the car, he took out his cell phone and called a tow truck. "You can't drive this till you replace these tires and check the wheel alignment. I'll bet that joker doesn't have a dollar's worth of insurance."

The patrolman returned with the man, wrote out a report, handed each a copy and told her, "He doesn't have any personal insurance, but you may be able to recover your costs from his employer, who owns the car. Here's the information. I wouldn't drive your car till it's checked."

"Thank you, Officer," she said.

"If you have anything in this car that you don't

want to lose, let's put it in my car," Luther said. They emptied her glove compartment and the trunk and put all of it in Luther's car. "Go sit in my car. It's too cold to stand out here," he said.

The tow truck arrived minutes later. Luther gave the driver instructions, got a receipt and handed it to Ruby when he got into the car. "You ought to have your car back in a couple of days. If you need help, give me a ring."

"Thanks. I don't know what I'd do without you."

He didn't look her way as he started the car and eased into the traffic. "You don't say."

Ruby felt his words like a punch to the stomach.

It didn't seem right to be at odds with Luther, the one person who had always been there for her. If only she could think of something to do or say that would get them back to the warm camaraderie she'd had with him nearly all of her life. If only she hadn't made love with him. No, she couldn't be sorry for that. He was the man who'd given her her birthright. But she didn't want it to end there. She was smart enough to know that there was more, and she wanted it. Yet, Luther was serving notice that she wouldn't get it with him.

Well, she told herself, glancing at his steely face, *we'll see about that.*

Chapter 3

Luther could feel the heat emanating from Ruby and knew she sensed the desire that seemed capable of running away with him. "Don't lose that receipt, now," he cautioned again, mainly because the silence was almost more than he could tolerate. Unfriendly, abnormal relations with Ruby chilled him like an icy grip on his heart, and he shuddered to banish the feeling. He stopped in front of the big Tudor house, a symbol of the Lockharts' better days.

"I'll take this stuff inside for you," he said, but he meant to get out of her house quickly. Being alone with her would invite memories of her sweet surrender and reduce him to begging for her love. He was damned if he'd crawl no matter how much he needed her.

"Thanks," she said. "Would you please put it over there near the stairs to the basement?"

He did as she asked and noted that she stood between him and the front door. He didn't know if she'd positioned herself there on purpose, but it didn't matter; on his way out, he gave her wide berth.

"Thanks for helping me, Luther," she said, and he thought he detected a plaintiveness in her voice.

"It wasn't much," he said as he reached for the doorknob. "You know you're welcome."

For the first time in his life, Luther fled from Ruby. In his preoccupation with her, he'd almost forgotten the woman who was coming to his house for an interview.

Now that he was sole owner of the dealerships and would make all decisions without his father's help, he'd probably be at it eighteen hours a day, so he needed a housekeeper or someone who'd take care of his house, do the marketing and at least cook his dinner. He had to get home in a hurry. He had interviewed one on the telephone earlier that day but she lacked good references. The woman coming to his house tonight seemed to have just the right credentials, but he needed to see her and talk with her.

He opened the door to a middle-aged woman who wore a gray felt hat and a gray coat. No points in her favor; he hated seeing dark-skinned women in grays, browns and blacks. She smiled as if she'd known him all of her life, and he couldn't help responding to her.

"Thank you for coming, Mrs. Yates."

"Glad to be here. Just call me Maggie, Mr. Biggens. Nothing fancy 'bout me."

He walked with her into his living room and asked her to sit down. "I'd like to see your references," he said, accepted them, glanced briefly at them and put the paper on the coffee table. "I want a woman who will look after my home as if it were her own, and that means cleaning, marketing and cooking. I send my shirts to the laundry."

"With just one person to look after in this house," she said, gazing around, "you better let me iron your shirts. I can do 'em as well as any laundry."

"All right. We'll try it. Punctuality is important to me. Unless there's a blizzard or a hurricane, I'd expect you to be here on time. You'd have Thursday afternoons and Sundays off. You get five-fifty a week, plus transportation and your meals. I pay all of your Social Security and if you want to wear a uniform, I'll buy them. If you don't, fine with me. If we hit it off, you'll get a raise." He looked at her for a reaction.

"Sounds fine, Mr. Biggens. If you don't mind, I'd like to ask you a few questions."

His left eyebrow shot up. "Why, of course."

"How do you get along with your mother?"

He gaped at her. "My mother? Never thought about it. She's my mother; I love her, and I'd do anything on earth for her."

"Do you look after her and go to see her?"

Where was this headed? "I see my parents at least once a week. They don't need anything, but if they did, I would provide it without being asked. I honor my parents. I'm the oldest child, and I don't take that responsibility lightly."

"In my life, I've found that a man who honors his mother, honors all women. I think you're a good man, and I hope you'll decide that I can come to work for you." She thought for a minute. "Just please don't ask me to cook no chitterlings, Mr. Biggens. I can smell 'em a block away. Awful!" She made a face.

He squelched a laugh. "Let that be the last thing you worry about. I'll check these references, and if you're home around five tomorrow, you'll hear from me."

"If that's all that's standing between me and the job, I'll be seeing you. The folks I work for always love me, and you will, too."

Somehow, he didn't doubt it. Common sense told him to check the references, but unless she got a really bad report, he'd hire her. He'd liked her on sight, and that didn't happen too often.

As predicted, her references were impeccable. At five o'clock, he telephoned her. "How soon can you start?"

The next morning, he told Maggie what he liked and didn't like to eat, gave her a key, a housekeeping budget, told her what kind of accounting he wanted and went to work. No more breaking the speed limit to get to the deli or the supermarket before it closed. In his first act as owner of his own dealerships, he made plans to partition the showroom and to build an attractive and comfortable room in which to discuss the cars, show videos of them and offer the customers complete comfort while they made up their minds.

"I'm not going to think about her, and I am not going to need her," he said as he measured the space in the display room for the furnishings he would need. "I wish to hell I'd never touched her. She's fire in my blood, and— Oh, hell!" Knowing it was a losing battle, he pitched the yardstick across the room.

Ruby hadn't planned to go to the office that morning. She had appointments with the owner of a small knitting company and, later, with the manager of a florist shop. She'd spent the previous evening brushing up on the wholesale florist business, especially on the amount of waste a florist could absorb and still make a reasonable profit. She answered her ringing cell phone as she got into her car.

"Marva's sick, and it's serious." The receptionist at work didn't waste time with small talk. "You'd better come in. Several items on her desk require urgent attention."

She cancelled her appointments, then headed to the office with the feeling that her life was about to change. And indeed it was: Marva Wright, the CEO, was hospitalized with a stroke.

For the first time in her memory, she worked all morning without coffee or a Danish. A stack of problems faced her, problems with which she had no experience, and each time she reached for the phone to call Luther and share her joy about the solution she implemented, she nearly wept. She knew she could do the job, but being unable to share her ideas with Luther, to boast about the smart things she did and to laugh with him about the silly things she contemplated doing hurt badly. The misery of it lodged in the pit of her stomach like a painful sore.

She answered the phone and heard Paige's voice. "Say, girl, how about being one of my bridesmaids?"

"What? Girl, you get outta here! When? I want details." Paige had been dating Lyman Epse for a while, but she'd never let on that she and the Detroit Chargers forward were that serious.

Paige chuckled. "Last night. I'm looking at this great big diamond on my finger right this minute."

"You go, girl. Sure I'll be a bridesmaid."

"You don't have much time. Lyman gave me all the money I need to pull the wedding off. He's on the road so much, he's left it all up to me. He's going to Europe in February to play on some kind of a goodwill tour, so he wants us to get married before he leaves, and he'll take me with him. Can you be at Jane's Bridal Salon in Dearborn at five-thirty this evening?"

"Sure thing." Ruby hung up and slumped in her chair, feeling as if all the air had been sucked out of her. Paige was her favorite cousin, and Ruby was happy for her. But she couldn't suppress the feeling that it would never happen to *her,* that she would grow old without Luther. Oh, he'd come whenever she called, but that would be the end of it. It wasn't enough.

She pulled herself up and resumed the task of stepping in as CEO of Everyday Opportunities, Inc.

"Your sister Opal is on line one, Ms. Lockhart," came a voice through the intercom.

She wasn't used to having a secretary answer her phone. She picked it up. "Hi."

"I won't keep you," Opal said. "I was wondering if you knew Luther bought out his family and is now sole owner of Biggens Ford Family Cars."

"What? When did that happen?" *I need one more shock today. Just one more.*

"In the last few days, I guess. D'marcus was talking to him, and you know Luther. He never makes a big deal out of anything. He told D'marcus that he couldn't meet him for lunch because he'd just undertaken a big job and had to do a lot of the work himself. Turned out he's renovating his showrooms. My husband had to squeeze it out of him that he's now the sole owner. I knew you'd want to know, so you could call and congratulate him."

"I will, as soon as I can. Marva had a stroke this morning, and I'm acting as CEO, plus doing my own work. All I want to do right now is keel over in bed and sleep." Ruby wasted no time; she said goodbye to her sister.

With her left hand holding the receiver in the air and her right hand poised above the cradle ready to dial, she wondered whether Luther would welcome her call. She didn't handle slights well at best, and since she wasn't accustomed to getting them from

Luther, maybe she shouldn't call him. She hung up and the phone rang.

"Remember me—Trevor Johns?" the voice said. "I was wondering if you got over being mad at me and whether we can see the town tonight."

When she could close her mouth, she said, "Of course I remember you, Trevor. I was never mad at you, but I do remember well why I decided that you and I mix like oil and water. Let's forget about dating."

"Well 'scuse me, babe. I don't need no chick with her ass on her shoulder."

"Really?" she said. "I'm sure you'll find what you need if you head straight for a dark alley in the nearest slum district. Bye." She hung up, and in her mind's eye she saw his frustration at her comment; Trevor Johns liked to dominate a woman, and he liked to have his way. If he were only like Luther, gentle, sweet and…

Without thinking about it, she dialed Luther's cell phone number. "Hi, Luther. This is Ruby."

After a few seconds, during which time she knew he was dealing with the surprise, he said, "Hi."

"Opal told me you're now sole owner of Biggens Ford Family Cars. I called to congratulate you."

"Thanks." The silence that followed was tantamount to his splashing ice water on her.

She tried again. "Why don't you come over this evening, and I'll fix you dinner and we'll celebrate. It's an important milestone in your life." She hadn't meant to say any such thing, but…well, so be it.

"That's nice of you, Ruby, but I just hired a house-keeper, and she'll have dinner ready for me when I get home."

What the heck! He didn't offer an alternative and she didn't want another slap in the face. She struggled to control the quivering of her lips. Maybe she just didn't understand men. "I'm sorry, Luther. Congratulations on owning the dealership."

"Thanks. I...uh...I'll call you as soon as I get things straightened out here. Goodbye."

Ruby hung up. He was kind even when he was being mean. She knew he didn't plan to call her. She had to do something to take her mind off him. That was hard enough when she was at work, but in the evenings alone at home, it was all but impossible. She couldn't call her sisters and chat on the phone; they were newly married and would want to spend the time with their husbands.

For several months, she had considered volunteering one evening a week at the community center in Morningside. She didn't doubt that every shopkeeper in the area needed advice, so she made an appointment to give a talk there the following evening on the management of a small business with limited cash flow.

"I'll have fliers out all over the neighborhood within the next hour," the excited social worker told her. "And maybe I'll see if a radio station that supports us will make a few announcements. This is the first good program I've had here in ages."

"Glad to do it," Ruby said.

Especially if it took her mind off Luther Biggens.

* * *

"All you shopkeepers and small business tycoons out there in Morningside or anywhere else in Greater Detroit, listen up," the radio announcer said. "Ms. Ruby Lockhart, acting CEO of Everyday Opportunities, Inc., will lecture tonight on managing the ups and avoiding the downs of operating a small business. Be at the Morningside Community Center at six sharp this evening. It's free, and you'll get coffee and doughnuts with the advice."

"Well, what do you know about that?" Luther said to himself as he headed to his office. "I'm not sure she'd consider my dealership a small business, but I'll bet I can learn something." The disc jockey read the ad two more times before Luther got to work. "Yep," he said aloud, as he entered his showroom, "I'll just do that." He didn't bother examining his real reason for attending the lecture.

He phoned Maggie. "Will it upset you if I don't get home till eight-thirty tonight? I'll drive you home or call a taxi for you. I want to attend a meeting that should be over by eight."

"Mr. B, you're the boss. If you want to eat your dinner at ten, all you have to do is tell me, and I'll take a late-afternoon nap so I won't mind being up late. No problem. 'Course, I don't suppose you'd stop somewhere and bring home a quart of pistachio ice cream, would you? I picked up the wrong kind, and I'm not happy if I don't have my ice cream."

"What kind did you get?"

"Butter pecan, and it don't look a thing like pistachio."

"Butter pecan's my favorite. I'll bring the pistachio. See you this evening."

He couldn't remember a day that moved along so slowly. Every ten minutes he looked at his watch thinking that another hour had passed. It seemed an eternity till he left for Morningside.

At three minutes to six, Luther parked a few doors from the center, found the conference room and sat on the last row a few feet from the door. He wouldn't mind if she didn't see him, and if the room was crowded, maybe she wouldn't.

He listened intently for the hour and a half to one of the most professionally delivered lectures he'd heard in a while. Pride suffused him as she talked, answered questions and broke down complicated concepts and problems into easily understandable terms.

At about five minutes of eight, when she'd answered questions for half an hour, she told the packed room, "I'll come back another time, but right now, folks, my tummy is telling me that I'm mistreating it." Her audience laughed and stood as one to applaud her. From the clothes she wore, to her manner of speaking, her ready smile and occasional joke, she suggested that she was at one with her audience. A smart woman, one he hadn't previously known.

He stood to leave, with the intention of getting away before she saw him. However, the cold and damp weather had brought on a stiffness in his right leg and knee, and he managed to stand only slowly and with difficulty. As he straightened up, she bypassed the people who clamored for her attention and came straight to him.

"Hi. I was so happy to see you here, Luther. At first, I thought I was hallucinating. I'm so glad you came."

Her smile illumined her face. She stood there, calm and cool as if he wasn't a man who had kissed every inch of her, as if he hadn't thundered inside of her, gripping her in a powerful storm and driving her to orgasm again and again, while she thrashed beneath him begging for more. And yet...

"Why did you do it?" he heard himself say. "Why, Ruby?"

She stared at him through the deep frown that covered her face. "Why did I do what?"

He couldn't believe it. She didn't know what she'd done to him. He wanted to shake her until she saw the love in his heart, until she could feel how he hurt. Without another word, he swung around, limping far more than usual, and left. He thought he heard her call his name, softly as if she barely dared to, but he didn't stop. The farther away from her he got, the better for both of them. He got into his car and sat there for a few minutes, gathering his thoughts.

Why am I blaming her? I was as much a participant in it as she, and I haven't even bothered to find out her reaction to our lovemaking. Maybe she's hurting, too. Oh, hell! And maybe I'm being soft as usual where she's concerned. He pulled away from the

curb. After a short while, he saw a deli and remembered the pistachio ice cream, bought half a gallon,
and headed home.

For a few minutes, the lights shining from his
living-room and dining-room windows alarmed him.
Then he remembered Maggie. When he walked into
his house, the aroma of roasting pork, spices and
baking biscuits reached him, and he felt a mulelike
kick in his gut. So this was what he was missing in
not having a wife to come home to.

*Get it together, man, and be thankful for what you
have.* He hadn't felt such discomfort in his right leg
in more than a year. Wondering if the weather alone
accounted for it, he made a note to see his doctor.

"That you, Mr. B? Come on back here. It's cold out
there. I got some hot cider waiting for you." She met
him at the kitchen door with a mug.

He gave her the ice cream, inhaled the fragrant brew,
took a long sip and looked at her with one eyebrow up.
"This is good. It doesn't have any alcohol in it, does it?"

With her hands on her hips, she leaned her head to
the side and grinned. "Do tell, Mr. B. If you don't
drink alcohol till I give it to you, you'll be a model of
sobriety. Go wash your hands. Dinner will be on the
table in three minutes. I'm hungry."

It didn't register until he was walking back down
the stairs that she had delayed her dinner in order to
eat with him. "You shouldn't have waited for me," he
said. "I appreciate not having to eat alone, but I don't
want you to deprive yourself on my account."

"Tell you the truth, Mr. B., I never did like eating alone."

She said grace as he was putting the first forkful of garlic mashed potatoes into his mouth. He sampled the roast pork. "Maggie, if you cook like this every day, I'll soon be overweight. This is fantastic." He bit into a biscuit and stopped himself just before he whistled. "This is wonderful."

Somehow, enjoying a delightful meal in his own home, a meal that he didn't cook, enlivened his spirits and lightened his mood. "Do you have any children?" he asked Maggie.

She shook her head. "My husband and I weren't blessed like that. And after cigarettes did him in, I decided not to risk another marriage. That one was more hurt than happiness."

She went to the kitchen with as many soiled plates as she could carry, and he followed her with the remainder. "Wasn't he nice to you?"

"Yes," she said over her shoulder. "When he was there. Him and his women. Lord, I got so sick of it."

He resisted putting a comforting arm around her shoulder, although to do it seemed so natural. "I'm sorry to hear that. You deserved better. Much better. Get your coat. I'll take you home."

"I noticed you walking with a limp tonight," she said. "Did you hurt your foot?"

"If it hasn't been obvious to you already, Maggie, that means it's less noticeable than I've always thought it was. I lost my right foot and part of that leg when I was an officer in the navy SEALS. I got in the way of a land mine."

She walked up to him, her face clouded like that of a mother in pain for her child. "How do you walk so...so noblelike, Mr. B?"

This time, he did pat her shoulder. "I wear a prosthesis."

"Well, that's one big word, and I don't know how it hooks up to your leg, but maybe it's irritating your leg. Why don't we go to the emergency room and have it looked after?"

He stared down at her. "Are you kidding? It's ten-thirty."

"You don't want to get an infection. I do declare. Men don't have no sense whatever about taking care of themselves. You want me to drive?"

He rubbed his chin, not because he was angry or irritated, but because the woman really cared.

"Thanks," he said, "but I can drive. Let's go."

He was glad they did, because he got relief from the nagging pain.

"This pad's about worn out," the doctor said, "and you're irritating the flesh every time you put pressure on it. It'll be fine now, but you want to watch it."

"You're an angel," he told Maggie later, as he got out of his car and walked her to the door of her apartment, although she insisted that he didn't have to do that. "Thanks. My leg's fine now."

"You're welcome. See you in the morning."

He drove home thinking how much easier it would

be for Maggie if she were his live-in housekeeper. The house was so big, he'd never know she was there.

He'd built the house when he still hoped for a family with Ruby. He knew now that would never happen, and as he pulled into the driveway, the big house reminded him of the futility of his dreams.

What caused her to behave as she did? He'd give anything if he could stop torturing himself about it!

Ruby remained near the door of the community center staring at Luther's back as he hurried away. Maybe if she understood him, she could bridge the gap that had recently seemed to widen whenever they met. Why had he come to her lecture? He knew more than enough about running a business. And she wished she knew what he meant when he asked why she did it. She released a long breath, glad she had the presence of mind not to leave without finding the social worker and thanking her.

With the frigid wind slapping her face, she hunched her shoulders for warmth and hurried to her car. Maybe if she had a roommate, she wouldn't need Luther so badly. No, she couldn't do that; her sisters would start feeling sorry for her.

She stepped into the dark foyer, turned on the light and climbed the stairs to her bedroom. It was useless, she knew, but she still checked her phone in case Luther had called. "I owe myself a better life than this," she said to herself, "and I'm going to have one."

The next morning she dressed in her gray knee-

skimming crepe skirt, red and black scoop-neck cashmere sweater and black suede stiletto-heeled boots,
then added her coat, gloves and scarf and headed for
an appointment with a new client.

"What seems to be your basic problem?" she asked
the man. "I can see that you're overstocked, but what
else—"

He interrupted her. "Uh, how long have you been
doing this kind of work?" the man asked her, his beady
eyes seeming about ready to pop out of his head.
"You...uh couldn't be the boss of a big company.
Babe, you got it everywhere it counts."

She glared at him. "Don't forget how much you're
paying for this consultation," she snapped. "If you
want to waste the time, fine with me!"

"I was expecting your boss."

"I *am* the boss."

And so it went. Three consultations, and instead of
worrying about their business problems, the men worried about the ache in their groin. She hoped for a different reception at her last consultancy of the day. The
woman had a bakery that thrived on a small scale,
wanted to expand and needed advice on financing the
expansion.

"For as much as I'm paying your company," the
sixtyish woman said, "I expected somebody more experienced, not a fashion plate with her skirt up to her
behind."

Ruby rolled her eyes. "Mrs. Henry, I have a degree
in business management and five years of experience

as a consultant to small businesses. I know what I'm doing. If you're not satisfied, don't pay. Shall we get on with this, or not?" Ruby noted the woman's reaction and concluded that her client understood attitude.

"All right, Miss Lockhart, let's get started."

The following day brought similar reactions to Ruby's new image. "I like the way I look," she said to Opal in one of their phone conversations, "and I am not going to change to suit somebody's bias."

"Yeah, but we're talking money here," Opal said. "Your clients are older people, and they don't trust anybody who doesn't wear Oxford gray."

"The women, maybe, but the men see a roll in the hay. Let 'em sweat. I like the way I look, and I'm not changing it."

"Tone it down a little bit. Maybe leave the boots home. If you look as stunning in those new clothes you bought as you did at my wedding reception, I can't blame those guys."

"Oh really, Opal. I didn't have a single date all last year. I cut my hair, shortened my skirt and lowered my necklines, and men show up like bees after honey." *All but the one I want.*

For almost thirty years, people had looked through her as if she didn't exist. If wasn't her fault if the average person didn't seem to be able to distinguish between character and cleavage. "I'm not remaking Ruby Lockhart to suit them," she said to herself after hanging up.

However, after several new clients cancelled appointments, Ruby had no choice but to concede failure. Dejected, she stopped wearing makeup, put the fashionable boots in the back of her closet and went to work wearing pant suits, cowl-neck sweaters and flat-heeled boots. She hated the way she looked, but she welcomed the added warmth against the blasts of frigid Canadian air.

Without a more attractive alternative, she struck out for the Detroit Institute of Arts that Saturday afternoon. After admiring some eighteenth-century masterpieces, her gaze caught the silhouette of a man who stood before a portrait by Gilbert Stuart. It couldn't be. Without giving thought as to why she shouldn't approach him, she walked over, reached up and tapped Luther on the back of his shoulder.

"Hi."

He turned around, and his eyes lit up when he recognized her. But as quickly, they clouded over with indifference. "Hi. I almost didn't recognize you." He didn't smile, and after a second or two, he turned back to the portrait that had previously captured his attention.

She started toward the room in which the Rembrandts were displayed, but suddenly had no taste for them, and left the museum. She looked more or less as she always had, yet he alluded to the change in her appearance that had begun after Christmas. She didn't know what to think. Maybe he was saying she should be herself. She sighed. Why should she care what he thought? All right, so he found her sexually uninteresting. A fine time to let her know it after rocking her out of her senses. Well, she'd show him!

That night she went to Paige's first wedding rehearsal as the "new Ruby," dressed in a long, wide-tiered black suede skirt and a scoop-neck cashmere sweater, with large gold bangles in her ears. Her spike-heeled boots pinched her feet. "Why are you having the rehearsal so early?" she asked Paige, who parked behind her in front of the church. "Aren't you supposed to have the engagement party first?"

Paige took Ruby's arm and started toward the church's front door. "All of Lyman's ushers are professional basketball players, except one, and this was the only time he could get them all together. Come on, Lyman will have a fit if I'm not there holding his hand."

Ruby's heartbeat took off when she saw that Paige had invited Luther, though she wondered in what capacity. Seeing the groom's friends, nearly all of whom were basketball players and apparently eligible, she decided to give Luther the space he seemed to want. And when Craig Murphy, the most famous of the group, singled her out for attention, she did not ignore him.

"Are you Paige's sister? he asked her and then answered his question. "No, you're not. She doesn't look a bit like you." A smile flittered across his face. "Too bad for her. I hope you like basketball."

"I liked it when I played left forward on Howard University's varsity team." His eyes lit up, and a grin exposed his glistening white teeth. *This man is infectious,* she thought. *I'd better watch my step.*

"Maybe you can give me some tips," he said. "I also play left forward." She threw her hands up, palms out as if in surrender. "If you're hanging out with Lyman Epse, I'm sure there're no flies on you, Craig. I couldn't teach you a thing."

As soon as she said it, she knew she'd left herself open for a witty jibe, and he didn't disappoint her. "I'll bet you could, and I'm sure I'd enjoy the lesson. If you live here in Detroit, I'd like to see you again."

She didn't look in Luther's direction, but she could feel his gaze burning her. She nodded. "If you really want to," she said, trying to decelerate Craig's pace, "you'll call me."

"Are you giving me the brush-off?" he asked her.

"No. I'm giving myself time to think about it. I suspect I'm older than you, and—"

"What difference would that make? I'll bet you went to graduate school."

"I got an MBA at the University of Michigan, and I work as a consultant to small businesses."

"Interesting," he said. "When I break a leg or something or get too old to play basketball, I want to operate a round-the-world tour company. I love to travel."

"The wedding party's lining up over there," she said, almost relieved to be able to terminate the conversation. Every glance in Luther's direction found him looking at her.

"Since my parents are gone, Luther's escorting me,"

Paige told them. "Opal is my matron of honor, and Craig is Lyman's best man. Everybody line up according to height. Luther, honey, would you escort Ruby, please."

Luther didn't seem happy about that prospect, Ruby thought. "Don't worry," she said to Luther from the corner of her mouth. "I'm not likely to fall down, so you won't have to touch me."

"What do you mean by that?" he whispered. "What's gotten into you lately?"

She looked at him then, unwilling to treat as trifling something that pained her so deeply. "I miss the wonderful relationship I've had with you for most of my life. But I no longer mean anything to you, and I've decided that I'm not going to care. You do your thing, and I'll do mine."

A shadow that could have reflected pain flashed in his brown eyes and he frowned as if he'd missed the point. But true to his nature, Luther stood taller as if to say, *I refuse to hurt.* What he actually said was, "Let it lie. This is a time for pleasantness, for happiness."

"Yes," she said, dripping sarcasm, "let's not spread any gloom by being honest."

He grabbed her arm. "Why did you go to bed with me?" And then his lower lip dropped, for he had evidently shocked himself by his frankness.

She raised her head in that aristocratic way that Amber always described as arrogant and said, "Because I wanted to. Because I always wanted to. Subject closed." Let him digest *that.* She ignored his widened eyes and the gaping hole his mouth had become. "Maybe you ought to figure out why you *took* me to bed." When she saw that he was at a loss for words, she couldn't remember when she'd felt so good.

"Don't forget your places now," Paige called out, relieving Luther of the need to answer Ruby's challenge.

Following the rehearsal, Ruby hugged Paige and her sisters, dashed out a side door, rushed to her car and went home, avoiding both Luther and Craig Murphy. However, Craig evidently did not plan to be rejected.

"How did you get my phone number?" she asked him when she answered the phone less than ten minutes after walking into her house.

"What's the problem? I asked Paige. Can we have dinner tomorrow evening? Or lunch tomorrow if you're busy in the evening. You're not getting away from me, lady."

She thought about it for a few seconds. "How old are you, Craig?"

"Twenty-six, and I don't care how old you are."

"Aren't you playing somewhere tomorrow night? This is the height of the basketball season."

"Day after tomorrow. I'm off tomorrow."

"Hmm. Okay. Lunch." He gave her the name and address of the restaurant. "See you at one." She rationalized that she had to eat, so it wouldn't hurt to eat with Craig.

After hanging up, she kicked off her shoes and went to the kitchen to make a sandwich. "I wonder what's on Luther's mind now," she said aloud. "I gave him plenty to think about."

Luther thought about her words through most of the night, and by sunrise, there only seemed to be one logical conclusion: *His prosthesis repelled her.* She had been sober, or so she claimed; she'd wanted to make love with him; and he gave her complete satisfaction. He knew it, because at the moment of release, she'd gripped him so powerfully that he nearly lost control and, in the end, he gave himself as he'd never done with any other woman. If she wanted Trevor Johns, Craig Murphy or any other man, he couldn't do anything about that. Maybe she felt she needed a whole man. She was entitled to one, and that excluded him. With a sad shake of his head, he pounded his right fist into his left palm, thinking back to the days when he commanded eighty navy SEALS, the toughest men in the service. Sometimes, life was hell!

With two employees out, thanks to the sleet, he got to work early and assumed the job of salesman, something that he rarely did. His only customer that morning was a knockout, a woman who would command attention no matter how many Jennifer Lopez and Halle Berry types surrounded her.

"Are you going to give me a nice, big discount on that one?" she asked, pointing to a sedan.

"We'll see. It depends," he told her.

"On what? I'm used to getting whatever I want,"

she said, tracing the row of buttons down the front of his shirt with her right index finger.

Well aware that he could get a woman's blood to flashpoint if he wanted to, he let a grin float across his face and closed his left eye in a slow wink. "The car's for sale, babe, but I'm not."

"What a pity," she said, regret lacing her voice, "and such a nice package, too." She put a down payment on the car, crossed her knees and swung her legs. "What are you doing this evening?"

He had very little tolerance for overly aggressive women, and easy sex had never interested him. This time, he didn't bother to grin. "Sorry. This evening, I'll be at home with Maggie." Let her arrive at whatever conclusion suited her.

"Maggie's a lucky woman," his customer said, uncrossing her legs. "Let me know when my car comes in."

"You bet."

He hadn't been tempted, although he admitted that the woman had given him a much-needed ego boost. He flexed his right shoulder in a quick shrug, sat down and began checking inventory and sales in his other shops. Women could be so cruel even when they didn't plan to be. Best not to let them get next to you. He thought of Ruby and hoped she didn't realize that she'd hurt him. From now on, he intended to leave her and other members of the opposite sex alone.

Chapter 4

Ruby sat in Hanson's Gourmet Restaurant getting angrier by the second. Her lunch date was over half an hour late. She had half a mind to leave, but decided instead to wait and see Craig Murphy when he got what he deserved. He arrived fifteen minutes later with a smile blooming on his face. She forced herself to smile in return.

"Sorry, sweetheart, but I had a run to make." He let out a long, laborious sigh. "One of those things."

She continued to smile, but when he sat down at the table, she stood immediately. "See you around," she said and strode out of the restaurant. She heard him call out, "Where are you going?" but she kept walking. Her office was a short distance from the restaurant, but she hailed a taxi and glanced back through the rear window as he stepped out of the restaurant, put his hands on his hips and let his shoulders droop.

"Good riddance!" she said.

"What's that, ma'am?" the taxi driver asked her.

"Nothing. I just learned a lesson, and so did that guy back there."

She bought a ham sandwich and a bottle of cranberry-apple juice at a deli next to her office building and ate lunch at her desk. Afterward, she phoned Opal. "What did you do after the rehearsal? I had to leave."

"So we noticed. Luther seemed put out. What happened between you two that you're...well, you don't seem to be friends."

"Luther's bossy," she said, refusing to tell the truth. "I'm almost thirty, too old for a guardian."

"Hmm. That doesn't sound right, Ruby. You've always seemed to look up to Luther, and you never minded if he was bossy. By the way, Craig Murphy acted as if you'd bewitched him."

"That man is full of it." She told Opal about the luncheon date. "Now he knows there's at least one woman who'll thumb her nose at him. I never did like strutting turkeys."

The sound of Opal's giggles reached her through the wire, reminding her that hearing Opal laugh her distinctive laugh had always been one of the joys of her life. She decided to throw her sister into a laughing fit when she said, "Yah, da brovva do love he pretty self." Opal laughed until she seemed about to lose her breath. "You'd better stop laughing like that. Before you know it, you'll pull something loose."

"A fine one you are to talk," Opal said. "You say things just to make me laugh." She took a deep breath. "But seriously, what are you going to do about Luther? He seemed really out of sorts, really down, after you left."

"What makes you think it has anything to do with me?"

"Because you're putting on an act trying to make me believe you don't care what happens to him. What *did* go on between you and Luther after you left my reception? After all that champagne you drank, maybe you don't remember."

She remembered, all right. And Opal was getting a little too close to the truth. "That's right. I don't, and as long as I woke up the next morning in my own bed and Luther woke up in his, I don't need to give it a thought."

"What's gotten into you, Ruby? Luther's our friend. If he's unhappy, you ought to care."

"What are you so shook up about?" Ruby asked her, irritation beginning to surface. "Being married is making a mother hen out of you. Look, I gotta get to work. Talk to you later."

She'd hardly cleared away one small pile of paperwork when Pearl called. Ruby hadn't spoken with her since she'd gotten back. "I can help you and Wade move, if you need me," she told her sister after Pearl lamented about the packing.

"Thanks, but Wade got tired of fooling with it, and he's paying the movers to finish up." She barely took a breath before she launched into the next topic. "Would you believe I've already selected six of the twelve songs for my first album? Ruby, I'm so excited. I'll be rehearsing with the studio band day after tomorrow."

Ruby listened as Pearl talked on and on about her new career and how all of her dreams were coming true. "Imagine three of us getting married within weeks of each other," Pearl said. "Mama would be so happy, and you know how Daddy loved to hear me sing. I think he'd want me to do this." The happiness in her voice rang out as clearly as the sound of temple bells chiming on an Asian breeze.

"Oh, I know he would," Ruby said, "and you'll be great."

"You'll be next," Pearl said, "and soon, I hope, because you've sacrificed so much for us. I don't know what we would have done without you after Mama passed."

"You're my sisters, and you're all precious to me. If you'd been the oldest, you'd have behaved exactly as I have."

"All the same, you're a very special person."

"You're making me weepy." Ruby blinked back a tear.

They talked a while longer, then Ruby had to get back to work. The conversation stayed in her mind for the rest of the day. Time was when she would talk with

Luther like that for long periods of time, half of a Saturday or Sunday afternoon. Some of the best ideas she'd had for Everyday Opportunities, Inc., had emerged during her talks with Luther. And no matter what she needed, he was always there for her. She had often wondered if he divined her need of him. She couldn't imagine life without him.

Ruby couldn't know of Luther's decision that the best way to protect his pride and his heart was to avoid women, especially her. When Wade invited him over, Luther couldn't have been more relieved.

"What's the idea of staying away from everybody?" Wade asked him. "You could at least come over and have dinner with Pearl and me one evening. I know you love roast pork, and we have a rotisserie that does it to perfection. How about it, man?"

"How about Sunday? I drive over to Dearborn to see my parents in the early afternoon when they get home from church, but I could get over to your place around five. How's it going with you and Pearl?"

"Great, man. Sometimes I think I've died and gone to heaven."

"I can't tell you how happy it makes me to hear that. Give Pearl my love. I'll see you Sunday."

He sold two cars that morning, one to an old woman who had no business driving and the other to a thoughtless woman who bought the red sports car for her seventeen-year-old son. Luther reasoned that if he didn't give them what they wanted they'd get it somewhere else, and he couldn't afford to turn his back on opportunity. Since it was Thursday and Maggie's afternoon and evening off, he stayed late in the shop, dawdling about, unable to focus on any one thing.

"What's wrong with me? I've never been this way." Resolved to shake the mood, he went home, and when he walked into his house, he realized the source of the problem. Every man he knew belonged with a special woman, was a part of a couple, and he was beginning to feel conspicuous, the odd man out. He didn't mind being alone; he just hated feeling lonely. And that's what the company of lovers—married or single—did for him.

He also hated not having the loving relationship that he'd enjoyed with Ruby since before he entered puberty. He had grown to love her, but he'd had to bide his time while she grew up, finished school, cared for her ailing mother and then cared for her three sisters. Just when he'd thought it was time to reveal his feelings for her, that land mine changed his plans. She was twenty-four, beautiful and in full bloom, and she was his heart. But after the accident he was no longer the man he'd been.

So, he occupied himself with work. But for what and for whom? His niece and nephews? He had enough money to live comfortably, a sizeable pension for a cushion, and most of the time, he enjoyed his work. The average man would say that Luther Biggens shouldn't complain, and he didn't, not even about the loss of a foot and a part of his leg.

He found his dinner in the refrigerator along with one of Maggie's creative notes on how to warm it. She'd certainly set her heart on taking care of him. The thought gave him a good laugh, and with that, his mood lifted. He warmed his dinner in the microwave oven and sat down to a meal of crab cakes, braised mushroom caps, grated potato cakes and spinach sautéed in garlic and olive oil.

"Good gracious," he said as he ate, "if she were ten years younger, I'd take her out of circulation just to assure myself of a meal like this one seven nights a week for the rest of my life." He thought about that for a few seconds, threw his head back and laughed at the top of his voice.

Straighten up, man. You're the guy who always went after whatever he wanted...and usually got it. If you hadn't had that accident, you'd probably be married to Ruby right now. So who says you can't get her?

Luther told himself if he got inside of her again, she'd be his. But who knew how she'd behave later when the picture of him with this damned thing hooked on to his leg flashed through her mind. He was not opening himself to that pain again. Not unless he knew she loved him, as a man. Maybe then he'd take the chance.

He welcomed the ring of the telephone. Anything that took his mind off Ruby.

"Hi, Luther. I'm so glad I caught you. This is Opal. Pearl's giving a practice concert in the studio tomorrow night, and D'marcus and I are hoping you'll come. It'll be wonderful support for Pearl, and you know how glad she'll be to see you."

After making a note of the address and the time, he said, "Thanks for letting me know. I'll see you there."

He reached up above the refrigerator and turned on the radio to listen to some music as he usually did while he cleaned the kitchen. He rinsed the dishes, put them in the dishwasher and stopped as the sound of Andres Segovia playing Dittersdorf's Concerto for Guitar reached his ears. While he was in the service, his guitar had been his salvation and his sanity. After the accident, he'd put it away, just as he seemed to have put away his optimistic attitude toward life.

After the piece ended, he went to the den where he looked at his guitar for a long time. Finally he took it out of the case, tuned it and began to play the music he loved. Although his fingers lacked the strength and dexterity they'd once had, they had not forgotten the music. Hours later he put the instrument away. He would remember that evening as a turning point in his life.

The following night, Luther sat in the last row of the recording studio's small concert chamber. Ordinarily, he'd have circulated with the Lockharts or checked to see if all was in order, but he didn't feel the need to do that. It was as if someone had poured strength into him, not physical toughness, but a mental vigor that enabled him to perceive his real self and to deal with that self. He saw Pearl enter the room from a side door, and waved at her. In the past he would have gone up, wished her luck and asked if he could help in any way.

Pearl waved back, leaned down and said something to Ruby, who turned and looked in his direction. He nearly laughed after he raised his right hand, smiled and wiggled his fingers. He'd perplexed her, no doubt about that. When Pearl rose, he knew she'd come back to him and, forthright as ever, she hugged him and spoke her mind. "Hi, Luther. What're you doing back here? You ought to be up there with the rest of the family."

"Thanks, but there are only a dozen rows of seats, so I can hear you perfectly well back here. Besides, the closer I am to the door, the less walking I have to do."

She seemed surprised. "I forget about your leg. It's not noticeable, especially since you always wear those nice lizard-skin shoes. Does it bother you? I mean, is it uncomfortable?"

"It has its moments, Pearl. I don't suppose I'll ever get used to it. I endure it."

"You deserve better." She touched his arm. "You're sure you want to stay back here?" At his nod she added, "Oh, for goodness' sake, Luther. You and Ruby are beginning to make everybody uncomfortable."

"I can't imagine why. See you later," he added as a group of men with instruments settled on the stage. Someone signaled to her, and she kissed his cheek and went up on the stage.

After a few nervous first notes, Pearl showed what she could do as she wrapped her velvet voice around the words of an old familiar gospel song, singing it as it had never before been sung. He couldn't have been prouder if he were listening to his own sister.

After the applause, the producer stood, glowing like a happy parent, "She's got a lot more of those, and we'll begin recording on Monday. I haven't had a hit this big since the Motown days."

"I'm not a hit yet," Pearl said.

"You're money in the bank," the producer said. "Stick with me, and in a year, you'll be a household name."

Luther hoped the man knew his business.

"How about stopping by for a drink or coffee?" D'marcus said to him, walking along beside Luther as they left the studio. "We don't see much of you these days."

"And I can imagine how that upsets you," Luther said, certain that his face was the picture of innocence. "Who ever heard of newlyweds worrying about their friends?" He enjoyed the man's sheepish expression. "I don't drink if I'm driving, but I'll stop in for a cup of coffee."

"Great. Opal made a caramel cake yesterday that was so good it talked. Ever know a woman who could bake like that but still ruins scrambled eggs every time?"

Luther released a few hearty chuckles. "Man, this

world is full of mysteries, and most of them begin with women."

"Tell me about it." He handed Luther a card. "Here's our address in case you lose me in traffic."

He'd forgotten that the Armstrongs had already moved into their new home. He'd take the opportunity to consider an appropriate housewarming gift. And he'd forgotten something else, too. Ruby would no doubt be there, as well, and in those close quarters, the two of them would be the center of attention.

What the hell! He'd give them something to talk about, and he'd give Ruby something to think about. Heck, he wished he had his guitar. In an expansive mood as they were about to get into their cars, he looked over toward Ruby, winked and enjoyed her apparent shock. If she asked why he had winked at her, he would definitely tell her that the devil made him do it. He suppressed the laugh that bubbled up in his throat. Life was beginning to be fun again.

Ruby got into her car, slammed the door and started the motor. She had a good mind to go straight home. What on earth possessed Luther to wink at her, and with that wicked grin of his? She decided to ask him and remembered that he hadn't answered the last question she'd put to him.

When she got out of her car at the Armstrongs' home, it seemed as if the wind undressed her and pelted her flesh with its icy bluster. She tightened her coat, and as she glanced up at the star-filled sky with its clear, frosty moon, Luther's hand touched her elbow, and her stiletto boot heel caught in a crack of the pavement. For a second, she knew again the feel of his arms around her, and she didn't rush out of them.

She also didn't try to avoid Luther after they entered Opal and D'marcus's house for she knew that, in his current mood, he wouldn't cooperate.

"I thought you two were on the outs," Wade said, when Luther took Ruby's arm as they walked into the living room. "Looks like I was wrong."

"Whatever gave you that idea?" Luther asked him. "We've been buddies since I was nine." Thank God Ruby stepped on his good foot. He felt the vibration all the way up his thigh.

He grinned down at her. "Why would you do an evil thing like that? I only have one foot, and you tried to maim it. Shame!"

"You think you're being clever, don't you? If I get mad enough, I'll stand right here and tell everybody what this is all about."

"Really?" His grin set her blood to racing. What was it about the man? "If you do that I'll have to defend myself," he said, "and that would mean explaining that you didn't know how to unzip your evening gown, and you asked me to do it, and then you let it fall to the floor and turned around and faced me wearing nothing but a two-inch strip of red cloth." Her gasp didn't stop him. "Not a man here would blame me for getting inside of you and making you beg for mercy."

"I didn't do that." She wouldn't admit it for money.

He cocked an eyebrow. "The hell you say. And while we're at it, let me tell you, sweetheart, you really dialed my number."

"I don't know what that means." At least he didn't say she wasn't adequate.

"Oh, you get my meaning, all right. You asked why I did it. Now, you know."

"Y'all want coffee or something else?" Opal asked them. "You're acting so serious over here."

"Coffee," Luther said.

"A dry martini," Ruby said, although she'd never drunk one in her life. "Or maybe you have some champagne?" she asked, hoping to tantalize Luther. Apparently she managed. His large brown eyes rounded, and his Adam's apple bobbed. "Don't you drink champagne, Luther?" she asked him, relying on her sweetest, most affected childlike voice to ring his bell.

But he didn't back down. "Drink all the champagne you want, Ruby. I'll take *good* care of you. You know that."

Her blood heated her face.

Opal returned with the martini. "Here you are, but I wouldn't drink too many of those, Ruby. D'marcus makes 'em strong."

Ruby looked from her sister's departing back to Luther, whose grin became a laugh that he enjoyed more and more. "You're nuts if you drink that," he said. "And next time, don't try to show how clever you can be." He was no longer laughing. "You can't drive home if you drink that stuff. It's lethal."

She wished he weren't right, and she wished she had the guts to drink it down straight. And while she didn't mind waking up in his bed a second time, she didn't like the prospect of his ignoring her afterward again.

She handed the drink to Luther. "Here. Try it. You may like it."

He looked hard at her. "You couldn't ruin my foot, so now you want me to get behind the wheel of my car and break my neck. You're a cruel woman." His gaze roamed from her feet to the top of her head and back. Very slowly, as if cataloguing her assets and enjoying the view. She shifted from one foot to the other, getting warmer by the second. "And that's not all you are," he said, more to himself than to her.

After ignoring her for days, Luther was noticing her again. But he wasn't quite the old Luther. She wasn't sure she liked it. As long as he put a wall between them, there was a chance that he'd ignored her because he was hurt and maybe felt something for her. But this happy not-quite-buddy-as-usual Luther was not the man she wanted to see.

"What happened to that shot of fire?" Opal asked Ruby, carrying a tray of hot biscuits and ham. "You look like you drank it."

"I didn't drink a drop of it," she said. "I gave it to Luther."

Opal's eyebrows shot up. "Luther didn't drink that, and if you didn't, why are you so flustered?

Oops! None of my business." She passed the tray to Luther, her eyes flashing mischief, and headed back to the kitchen.

I'll be damned if they're not trying to hook me up with Ruby.

Luther said good-night and excused himself, claming a busy day tomorrow.

What on earth had happened to give the impression that he and Ruby had more than a sister and brother relationship? Well, if the family thought it possible, why not? He didn't want to get his hopes up, but he knew that if he tried he'd give it everything he had. He parked in his garage and entered his house through the kitchen door. *If she could love him, he'd be king of the world.* But he knew it wouldn't happen.

He got to his parents' home around one-thirty Sunday afternoon, minutes after they arrived from church. He never did see why that preacher thought he had to repeat things a dozen times. Maybe the man thought you weren't a Baptist unless you spent two and a half hours in church every Sunday morning.

He helped his mother with lunch, which was always the same, chicken that she fried the night before and heated in the oven, string beans, macaroni and cheese, stewed collard greens, apple pie and coffee. His mother didn't cook on Sunday. She always said it was her day of rest. He warmed up the food while she set the table.

"How's Charles getting on?" he asked her.

"All right as far as I know. Lord, I got my fingers

crossed till he finishes. I want all my children to graduate from college, and Charles has so many other pri-
orities that I'm afraid he won't make it."

"He'll finish, Mom. Charles wants a soft job, and
he knows that means a college degree at the least.
Hard work is not in his DNA."

Her joyful laughter gave him a good feeling as it
always did. "Yeah," she said, "and studying beats
working. By the way, how's Ruby? We don't see her
at all these days. I used to think you and Ruby would
get together. She was always...well, kind of crazy
about you."

Now, where did that come from? "Mom, I was her
knight in shining armor when she was three years
old."

"And when she was twenty-three," Irma Biggens
said. "Tell your father the food's ready."

*I wish these people would get off my case. Don't
they know it takes two?* If they started that at Pearl's
house that evening, he'd be leaving early. It was bad
enough that he was always by himself. If he wanted
women, he'd have a few, but he wasn't willing to pay
the price.

He went to find his father.

"How'd you like what I did with the showroom,
Dad? I hope to do the same at the other three shops."

"You keep calling them shops. No shop was ever
that big. It's a wonder we didn't think of it earlier. The
showroom reminds me now of a living room. Gives
the place elegance. I liked it a lot. Wasn't it expensive?"

"It could have been, but I did most of the work my-self. I had a builder put up the wall and install the restroom. I wanted a place where women would be comfortable."

"Well, it's as nice as any lounge anywhere. Did Ruby help you pick out the carpets and furniture?"

Ruby. Always Ruby. "I don't think she even knows I've done it. Give me credit for having some taste, Dad." He draped his arm across his father's shoulder. "I learned a lot right here at home."

"I guess you did."

Luther took a deep breath. If he was lucky, neither of his parents would bring up the subject of Ruby for the remainder of his visit.

However, when he reached Wade and Pearl's house, the first thing he saw was Ruby's car in the driveway.

"Fancy meeting you here," he said to Ruby when she answered the door. "Anybody else home?"

"Try to control your sarcasm," she said. "Wade's out back firing up the grill, and Pearl's in the kitchen. If I'd known you'd be a smart aleck, I would have let you wait out there in the freezing cold."

He took the liberty of tweaking her nose, which beat keeping his hands off her altogether. "I appreciate your thoughtfulness. Must be all of six degrees out there," he said and headed for the kitchen. He didn't need to be alone in close quarters with Ruby Lockhart. As it was, she heated him up from across the room with no effort. She managed to breeze by him, her hips swaying as she preceded him down the long hall, the scent of her seductive perfume trailing in her wake. Liquid began to accumulate in his mouth. If he thought she did that deliberately, he'd make her pay for it.

"What kind of perfume are you wearing?" he asked her when he entered the kitchen, where she sat on a high stool with her long, mind-blowing legs swinging. Fearing that he'd have an erection, he turned and faced the big clock that hung above the refrigerator.

"Fendi. I just started wearing it. I decided I needed a new perfume to go with my new hairstyle."

"And your short dresses and four-inch heels." He decided to let her have it. "Oh, yes, and high-fashion makeup. I suppose all that calls for new perfume. Nice scent."

"Now, don't you two start," Pearl said. "Friday night, you were acting so civil that I thought you'd made up. I sure wish somebody would tell me what's going on. All my life, I could depend on the two of you sticking together like two peas in a pod, and all of a sudden, you're like the Hatfields and the McCoys. It's making me nervous."

He turned around, but Ruby's legs hadn't stopped swinging, and all he could think of was the way those long shapely legs had hooked around his hips while he drove into her. Why in the name of kings did he come here? He should have gone home.

"Could I have a glass of water, Pearl?"

"Sure." She got a glass from the cabinet above the

sink and handed it to him. "There's a bottle of water on the bottom shelf of the refrigerator."

He gulped down a glassful and handed the glass back to Pearl. "Thanks."

"Wade'll be inside in a minute. He's grilling the roast. It doesn't take long on that rotisserie. I gotta run downstairs to the basement, but I'm scared to leave you two up here by yourselves."

"What do you think we'd do in your absence?" he asked her, struggling to keep the grin off his face and the humor out of his voice.

"Only the Lord knows," she said.

"Luther's a gentleman," Ruby said. "He'd never do anything a woman didn't want him to do, would you Luther?" His head jerked up, and Pearl stumbled, nearly dropping the meat that she was taking to the freezer in the basement.

"I'd sure like to know why that sounded like sarcasm," Pearl said.

"So would I," Luther grumbled.

"Sarcasm? I've never been more serious in my life."

Pearl headed down the stairs, and he managed to retrieve his breath and calm himself. "So what I did to you the night of Opal's wedding was what you wanted?"

She uncrossed her knees and cupped them with the palms of her hands. "Absolutely. Didn't I act like it?"

He'd never lost his temper with her, but he knew he was on the verge of it. "Don't play with me, Ruby. I'm not your toy. And your recent metamorphosis doesn't cut any ice with me. I never thought you'd be a woman who enjoyed playing with a man's feelings. Get a hold of yourself." He opened the back door and joined Wade on the porch. If they'd been alone in that house, he didn't doubt that he'd have made her eat her brazen words.

He inhaled the aroma of pork roasting in what must have been a marinade of herbs and garlic. "Smells great, man," he said calmly to Wade, as if Ruby hadn't irritated him almost beyond measure only minutes earlier. "I have a feeling I'd like to have one of those," he said, admiring the stainless steel grill. "It looks pretty handy."

"Yeah, man. Except for the lack of a sink, it's a little kitchen. My parishioners gave it to us for a wedding gift." He checked the pork.

"Say, I'm glad you came out here. Pearl was teasing Ruby about you earlier, which is fine, but Ruby didn't confirm or deny a relationship between the two of you. I think it would be wonderful if you two got together."

"Ruby and I have always had a special relationship, since we were kids, in fact. So I don't understand this sudden speculation about us. True, it's the season of Lockhart marriages, but don't waste your mind on it, Wade."

"Actually, I wouldn't if you two hadn't started behaving differently toward each other. But I'd be the last one to make a friend uncomfortable."

"Thanks. So Pearl's about to begin a recording

career. I knew she could sing, but I never dreamed she was so good," Luther said, steering the conversation away from Ruby and himself.

"She's got a glorious voice, and I'm thankful that she wants to sing gospel songs. I'm a Baptist minister, you know, and the church frowns on blues and such." He stopped basting the pork and looked Luther in the eye. "If you love her, man, go after her. There's nothing on this earth that equals coming home at night and walking into the arms of the woman you love."

What could he say to that? He hated lying, so he said nothing. That was one hope he could not afford. He had lived that dream for one fleeting hour, and then she awakened him with a shock that he'd never forget. No thank you.

He appeared to take added interest in the fragrant roast. "Hmm. Man, that baby must be pretty close to done. The smell is making me hungry."

Wade speared the edge of the roast and handed Luther a sliver. "Taste this. It's hot, now."

"Mmm-*mmm!*" Luther almost groaned, the meat was so good. "You wouldn't give me the recipe for that rub would you?"

"Nothing to it. Mix up some rosemary, thyme, garlic, salt, pepper and paprika in olive oil. Rub it in and let it stay in the refrigerator overnight. Everybody'll think you're a genius. Ask Pearl for a platter, would you? I'll grill up these veggies, and we'll eat."

Luther took the opportunity to ask Wade a question that plagued him. "How did you know that Pearl loved you?"

"It wasn't anything in particular. I felt it. She... gave herself over to me. I don't mean sex, that's important, but it's not all. One day I realized that she trusted in my love for her, and that it made her happy, that I was necessary to her. She needed me. And the way she responded to me made me feel like the king of her world."

Luther went into the kitchen to ask Pearl for a platter and his gaze landed on Ruby standing at the sink peeling a red onion while tears streamed from her eyes. "Let me do that," he said to her. "I never cry when I peel onions."

She handed him the paring knife. "Why not?"

He plugged the sink and half filled it with water. "I don't cry because I peel the onions under water."

Ruby wiped her teary eyes. "Do you have any more clever tricks like that?"

"You bet I do, and I'll be glad to show them to you."

Pearl entered the kitchen, wiping her hands on a paper towel.

Wouldn't she walk in just as he had Ruby in a corner. With only the two of them present, she would have been forced to answer. He took the platter to Wade and went back into the kitchen.

Pearl called out to him. "I've been meaning to ask you, Luther. Do you know a good pianist? I need a new one for the recording session."

"One of my former navy SEAL buddies is a fine pianist and he loves gospel music. He's...uh...disabled, but he can still sit at a piano and play." He cast a side glance at Ruby for her reaction. She stood with her back against the counter and her arms folded, and he couldn't read her facial expression.

"You could try him," he said to Pearl. "He's a gentleman. If you weren't satisfied, you wouldn't be obligated."

"Thanks. You're a good musician yourself, so you should be a good judge. Call him and see what he says." She seemed to muse over something. Then, she said, "You know, Luther, you always come through for us. I can't imagine you not being a part of my life."

He wasn't sure how he felt about that statement or what it implied. "Oh, you'd get along just fine without me. All of you would."

Wade walked in with the results of his labor perfuming the kitchen and went directly to the dining room. "Come on," he called over his shoulder. "Dish up the greens," he called to Pearl, who brought a bowl of stewed turnip greens, and sat down to eat.

"Let's hold hands and bow our heads," Wade said. "Lord, we thank thee for this food. Bless each of us with its nourishment, and bless our love for each other. Amen."

Ruby's soft hand remained locked in his. He looked at her, but she was staring down at her plate. He wanted to hold it indefinitely, but seeing the looks that passed between Wade and Pearl, he released her hand. Something did not add up.

The next day when he telephoned Roger Perkins

and asked if he would consider working as Pearl's accompanist, he couldn't know that that call would change his life.

Chapter 5

Luther hesitated before dialing Roger Perkins's telephone number. He hadn't seen the man since he'd left the hospital, and he didn't know Roger's mental condition after losing part of his leg. Like him, Roger had been single and in love with life when a land mine had altered the course of his future. By twenty-three, he'd become an accomplished pianist and he'd joined the navy hoping to save money to attend Julliard School of Music. Luther doubted that that part of Roger's dream would ever come true. But the man showed brilliance when he sat before a piano, and Pearl deserved the best. He lifted the receiver and dialed.

Roger knew him at once.

"Luther! This is a real surprise. How are you, man?"

"Great. You sound prosperous. How's it going?" Luther asked him.

"Not as prosperous as I'd like to be," Roger said, "but considering what I've come through, I wouldn't dare complain. I'm alive, man."

"I know what you mean. This life takes some getting used to. Look. If you're not too busy, I have a dear friend, a gospel singer, who needs an accompanist. She has a recording contract and the most beautiful, smoky and sultry voice you want to hear. Can you spare the time? She lives right here in Detroit."

"Spare the time? How permanent is this position? I get a gig here and there, but that's barely enough to keep me going. I haven't been able to get work with a music group. Maybe they think I can't run to catch planes."

"If the two of you gel, I suppose it's as permanent as you want it to be. She's just starting, but the label is paying you."

"I'm in. Say, why don't you come to the club sometime? It isn't gloomy, and a lot of your guys are here and would love to see you. We shoot pool, play cards. And this is one place where nobody gazes at you with a long face feeling sorry for you."

"I think I'll drop by there tomorrow evening. I wouldn't mind seeing some of my old buddies."

Luther walked into the officers' club lounge the next night and looked around at the fifteen or twenty men, some in uniform and some in civilian clothes, who sat reading, drinking coffee, playing cards or participating in other sedentary activities. He saw a man approaching with the aid of two forearm crutches.

"I was waiting for you, Luther," Roger Perkins said with a big smile that lit up his face. "It's sure good to see you moving around like this. Would you like to go down to the game room? We can get some coffee."

"Five years haven't done any damage to you," Luther told the younger man.

"Well, no. In fact, my attitude has taken a big leap forward. This place does that to you." Luther couldn't see how associating with a group of disabled men could brighten your outlook.

They took the elevator to the lower level. "I called Pearl Kendrick. We had a good talk, and I'll meet her at the studio tomorrow. If her singing voice is equal to her speaking voice, it should be warm and lovely. I can't thank you enough, Luther. A sympathetic accompanist can make her sound even better than she is, and I'm going to do some special arrangements for her."

Luther liked what he was hearing. "I couldn't forget how you play, man," he said to Roger.

"What about you? Do you play much these days? We have some real jam sessions here sometimes."

They got off the elevator, and he walked slowly to accommodate Roger, who seemed unaware of his slow pace.

"This is Luther Biggens, everybody, my former

commander. He's retired. Got roughed up like the rest of us."

Luther walked around greeting the men, some of whom had served under his command. "I'm glad to see all of you," he said and stopped in front of a lieutenant who wore a metal prosthetic arm and hand. "Logan! My Lord, man, I've been wondering whether you made it out of there. I can't tell you how many times I've awakened calling your name."

They embraced each other, and Logan wiped the tears from his face with his left hand. "I was about three feet from you, sir. I kept calling you, but you didn't answer, and I couldn't see a thing. I'm so glad you made it."

"How've you been?" Luther asked him.

"Couldn't be better. After I came out of the hospital, I met and married a fantastic woman, and she's given me twin sons. Like I said, life couldn't be better."

Luther regarded the man carefully. "I thought I was bad off without my right foot and half of my leg, but you're telling me I'm damned lucky."

"Your foot, eh? In here, that hardly counts. And you don't need your foot in order to make love to your woman, but keeping her happy with one hand and a metal claw takes a hell of a lot of skill on my part and patience on hers. But I didn't let it stop me." He winked at Luther. "It works. What matters in this business, man, is love." He wrote his address on a piece of paper. "Come over sometime. I want you to meet my family."

Luther ran his hand over his short kinky hair, hoping that his skepticism didn't show. Logan hadn't impressed him as a Pollyanna; indeed, while under his command, the man had exhibited a crusty edge and a toughness that marked him for leadership. He noticed that Logan wrote out his address with his left hand and not with the prosthesis on his right arm.

"I remember your being right-handed, Logan."

"You do what you have to do, man. How about joining that game of rummy? It's just starting."

"Haven't played since I left the service, but…why not?"

"Oh, you needn't worry," Logan said. "We don't play for money. It wouldn't be fair to Christopher. He can't see."

Luther took the seat that faced Christopher and looked at the other four players whom he hadn't previously met. Two were missing arms, Christopher couldn't see, and Luther couldn't detect the other man's disability, but he knew he had one. Maybe he'd wake up any minute and discover that Logan was not the Angel Gabriel giving him a lesson in thankfulness for what he had. He'd never considered it a blessing to be missing a foot and part of a leg, but in view of what he saw around him, he could damn well rejoice.

Christopher shuffled his special deck of braille cards and dealt a hand to each of his companions and himself. Luther had what could have been a winning hand, were it not for his having forgotten the game's fine points.

"If I'd had your hand," Christopher told him, "I'd have cleaned up."

"You've got an awesome memory," Luther told him.

"You would too if you had to depend on it as I do. You don't cultivate your memory capacity. I do, and it allows me to jerk people left and right, especially when they think they can trick me."

"I suppose when you lose one ability, you gain one to compensate for it," Luther said to no one in particular.

"You go, man," Christopher said. "My hearing's superior, too. Say, Commander, what did you lose and where?"

Feeling as if he hadn't earned the right to be among those seriously disabled ex-service men, Luther downplayed what he'd done, the medal he received. "I just lost a foot and a small part of the leg."

"No kidding," one of the vets said. "You don't walk like it. Let's see what they gave you."

Luther's eyes widened, and his bottom lip dropped slightly. He ran his fingers over his hair as he always did when surprised. He'd never intentionally shown that leg to anyone other than a doctor or other health personnel.

"Come on, man. You barely limped when you walked in here. This I got to see," a soldier remarked.

Luther pushed away from the table, rolled up his left pant leg and pulled off his lizard-skin shoe.

"Well, I'll be damned," the soldier said. "Would you look at that! They even painted it to match your skin color." Luther hadn't thought about the advantage of having his prosthesis the color of his skin. He unrolled his pant leg and put on his shoe.

"They told me the advantages and disadvantages of the different types, and I chose this one," Luther explained, trying to push aside his feeling of guilt that he was better off than the others there.

They talked about the differences in types of aids and the recent developments in the field of prosthetics. One of the men yawned, and Luther looked at his watch. "Good grief," he said. "Do you guys know it's almost midnight? I was going to stay here for an hour. I'm an early riser. See you again soon." He walked around to where Roger leaned on his crutches shooting pool. "I'll call you in a day or so, Roger, and maybe we can get together."

As he drove home, he thought of the men there, making the best of what was left of their lives, and especially of Logan. One day, the man had had the world on a string—tall, handsome, young and blessed with brilliance and courage. And then, that land mine had changed his life forever. Changed all of the survivors.

He parked in his garage, and entered his house through the kitchen. Maggie had noticed that he did that at night, and she left the kitchen lighted. He laughed when he saw the oatmeal and raisin cookies on the table and a note beside them. He knew the milk was in the refrigerator, and he also knew she'd poured a glass and covered it with aluminum foil. She'd told him she wanted him to find a nice girl, as she'd put it, but she made it convenient for him to postpone the task.

A check of his voice mail revealed calls from Pearl and Amber. It was too late to call either, but he'd get to it early the next morning.

"Do you know this hotel Paige reserved for her engagement party, Luther?" Amber asked him when he called. "Paul said he'd rather stay some place else if it's not five-star."

"It's five-star, all right," Luther said. "If it's not, you'll never see one. Lyman Epse is superrich, and he told her to do whatever she likes. That's why she's having a three-day party. Imagine! That guy rented the hotel for two nights and three days. That blew my mind."

"I can't wait to see it," she said. "It'll be like a family reunion. How's Ruby?"

Now, he knew the real reason for her call. Why would she ask *him* about her sister? Amber had some notion that he and Ruby belonged together. Maybe they did, but if everyone except Ruby thought so, their thoughts didn't mean a damned thing.

"I haven't seen her recently, Amber. You know more about her than I do."

"Gee," she said. "That's too bad."

After hanging up, he telephoned Pearl but didn't get an answer. He thought of calling Ruby. If Logan could find happiness with a woman who didn't know him when he was a whole, vibrant man, why couldn't Ruby accept *him*, a man she'd known and cared about most of her life? And a man who had thrilled her, who'd fired every nerve in her body, and who had flung her to the heights of ecstasy? She'd lie if she said he didn't, and she knew he'd do it again if she gave him the chance. How could she be so shallow?

Ruby was not in the office when Luther called, but in the Morningside district with a talented woman who made doll clothes as a means of supporting herself and her three children. Ruby hadn't planned to give free individual counseling in that district, but the woman needed help. By the time Ruby left her, she had convinced the woman to make children's clothing instead and had worked with her on the design of a catchy flier that would serve as an advertisement. She returned to her office, called the human interest editor of a local paper and asked her to interview the woman.

I've got her life on track, Ruby thought. *Now, if I could only do the same for mine.*

Her intercom light flashed, and she pressed the button. "Yes?"

"Mr. Biggens called," her secretary said, "but he didn't leave a message. Shall I dial him for you?"

"Thanks, but I'll get to him later."

She pondered the wisdom of calling him, but decided that his call must have been important, because he hadn't called her since that night. She closed her office door and dialed his number.

"Hello, Luther, this is Ruby. You called me?"

"Hello, Ruby. It was a moment of impulsiveness. You weren't there, and the moment's gone. How are you?"

"Right now, I'm confused. You called me, but you didn't have anything to say to me. That it?"

"Pretty much."

"Luther, I'm losing patience with you."

"Did you ever have any? Since I came back from the Middle East, I mean?"

"Exactly what does that mean? I had enough patience with you to let you… Oh, what's the use? Have a good day. Goodbye." She hung up, and for the first time since her mother had died, she sobbed uncontrollably. After a few minutes, she went to her private bathroom, washed her face and looked at herself in the mirror.

He finds a dozen ways to let me know he doesn't want me. Damn him! I deserve better. She turned away from the window and walked with lead feet back to her desk. *I wish I could get interested in another man. Really interested, so much so that Luther Biggens wouldn't exist for me.*

The light flashed again on her intercom, and she pushed the button. "Yes?"

"Mr. Biggens on two, Miss Lockhart."

Now what? "Hello, Luther."

"Hi. I have to go over to Penwood, near Royal Oak,

and I was wondering if you would ride over with me and drive my car back." They'd done that any number of times, and it seemed natural that he'd ask her. She knew he'd bring someone's car back and that he didn't trust anyone else to do it. "I can't leave the shop unattended, and I have only one man there today."

"When do you want to go, Luther?"

"As soon as you can get away."

"I'm the boss now, so I do as I like. I'll drive home, leave my car in the garage and wait there for you. Give me about forty-five minutes."

"That's great. I appreciate it. See you soon."

Little Ruby running behind you as usual. All I need is my damned yellow and brown blanket, and you wouldn't know I was a day older than three years. She was annoyed with herself. Would she never get over that man? She'd go with him and drive his car back, but would he ignore her the next time he saw her?

She hurried home and changed into warm clothes. When she saw Luther's car drive up she headed out to meet him. He wouldn't be able to say she got him into her house in order to try seducing him. She remembered how carefully he'd avoided getting near her the last time they were alone in her house.

"Aren't you taking the highway?" she asked him as he headed for one of the back roads.

"The woods are still pristine white from that last snow we had. It's my favorite drive, winter or summer. You know, when I was in the service, I thought about my family, you, your sisters and the way this drive looks in spring and after a fresh snow. I've loved it since I was a boy, and I'd ride my bicycle out here some Sundays. It's idyllic anytime of year."

She noticed that he drove slowly, allowing himself to enjoy the tall pines that peeked out from the snow. The narrow road curved along like a slowly winding river, and a sprinkling of snowflakes dusted the windshield.

It is so beautiful, she thought, unaware that she'd said the words aloud, until he said, "I thought you'd like it. If I had my way, you'd like everything I like."

A peculiar pinching in her stomach was the only evidence of her sudden nervousness. "What do you mean?" she asked when she settled herself.

"If you need an explanation, I don't think you'd understand. You know, I went to the officers' club last night for the first time since I was…you know…since I came home from the service. All the men that I saw there were disabled, and I was amazed at the way they handled it. I couldn't get over some of them."

"Are you going back?" she asked him.

"Yeah. I told them I would. They have a string quartet and a jazz combo. I think I'll take my guitar and sit in with some of them. One of the men may become Pearl's accompanist. At least, I'm hoping it'll work out for them. He's a fine man, a terrific pianist, and he needs the work. A lot of people can't stand being around disabled people, and that kind of stupidity is the reason why that gifted man needs a job."

"If he's good, I'm sure Pearl will hire him."

He glanced at her and spoke softly. "Would you?"

"If I sang well with him, of course I would. Why are you asking me that?"

"Perhaps because I…I don't know you anymore, Ruby."

She folded her arms and prepared to give him what for. "You know me as well as I know you. Maybe much better. Sometimes I think I don't know you at all."

"I'm not sure the time for us to air this is when I'm driving in what looks like sleet. If you want to talk about us, let's do it when neither of us is behind the wheel of an automobile."

She pushed out her bottom lip and hated herself for being childish. He had no idea how she felt about him, and at the moment, he didn't seem interested in finding out. "If you find yourself in the same room with me, you'll probably run," she said, not caring what his reaction to that would be.

He slowed down, and she feared that he'd park and give her what for, but when she looked at him, the sadness of his facial expression shocked her. "What… what's wrong?" she asked him.

He shook his head slowly and, she thought, sadly. "I can't count the times that you and I made this trip together, and for the same purpose. It seemed such a natural thing to do, so I called you and, as you've always done, you agreed. I didn't want us to battle during the trip. Oh, hell, Ruby. I don't know what I wanted."

She put her hand on his right one, and he flinched,

thought it was barely perceptible. "Let's not fight anymore. When we get there, I'll buy you a cup of coffee and a slice of cheesecake," she said.

He turned his palm up to join with hers, though he didn't look at her. "Thanks. You *would* remember that I love cheesecake."

"That isn't all that I remember about you, Luther."

"I'm afraid to ask what else." He released his hand from hers, reached over and flipped on the radio to a station that offered easy listening music. "Let's not ruin this good moment. We don't have many of them these days."

She wanted to ask him to clarify that, but she couldn't risk his thinking that she was being provocative. She told herself to focus on the fact that he hadn't moved his hand from hers, but had turned it over, giving her a rare moment of sweet intimacy with him. She knew she couldn't count on more than that, for the man she thought she knew like the back of her hand had become an enigma.

"You always loved cheesecake," she said softly. "That's why I learned to make it. I think I was about fifteen the first time I tried it."

"Yeah. I remember you came over with it one Sunday afternoon, and I'd never seen anybody look so proud. I didn't have the heart to tell you you'd screwed it up."

"I know. You actually ate it with all those nuts ground up in it."

"I expect I'd have eaten it if you'd put a cup of salt in it instead of sugar. That was really touching."

"I got it right the next time, though. Didn't I?"

"Yeah." He sounded so wistful that she turned to see if she could read his facial expression. "And for the rest of the summer, till I went to the academy, you brought me a cheesecake every Sunday. To this day, nobody's cheesecake tastes as good as yours."

She noticed that the grains of snow had become flakes, drifting down lackadaisically as if they had all the time in the world. She said as much to Luther and added, "Gosh, wouldn't it be wonderful if life was as tranquil as this picturesque environment. I'd love to stroll through those woods right now."

"It seems idyllic, but that's because we're in this warm car. It's freezing cold out there and windy, too. But if you want me to stop, I'll—"

"Thanks, but I think I'll enjoy it from here." Maybe she shouldn't say it, but she felt it so deeply that she didn't want to keep it to herself. "You've always been willing to help me do whatever I wanted to do, even when you thought I was a little off the wall, and you haven't changed in that respect. I wish—"

He interrupted her. "Let's not reminisce anymore, Ruby. If we do, we're going to ruin the most pleasant time I've had with you since the day after Christmas."

Hot blood stung her face. She didn't know what he was referring to, and she didn't plan to ask him. He obviously hadn't found her a good lover, or he would have wanted them to make love again. Furthermore, she'd made up her mind to forget about him, hadn't she?

As if he knew he'd jarred her sensibilities, he said, "We're almost there, and don't you forget you promised me coffee and cheesecake."

"Not to worry. If I promise you something, you can put your life on it."

"I know," he said, parking the car in front of Lena's Parfait, their usual haunt. "That's not my worry. The problem is what you're careful *not* to promise." He ignored her gasp, got out and walked around the car to help her out.

"Thanks. You're a darling."

"Glad to know it. Looks as if the snow has stopped, at least for now. I was worried about you driving in that stuff."

"You shouldn't be. I drive in heavy snow. Boy, I can already taste Lena's caramel cake." Without thinking she took his hand and started toward Lena's. He squeezed her fingers, and she cautioned herself to think nothing of it, that he was just being Luther, friendly and dependable.

"You are not paying for anything," she told Luther later when he reached for the bill. "I told you I was treating you to cheesecake and coffee, and you agreed."

"But I ate three slices."

"So what? Deal with that when you get on the scales tomorrow." For reasons she didn't dare question, she reached across the little table and tweaked his nose. "Such a handsome face! For goodness' sake, wipe that scowl off it."

He stared at her as if she were a recent arrival from Mars. Stared and stared until shivers raced through her and she had the feeling that her blood had begun to run backward. She grabbed the sides of her chair to steady herself. Uncomfortable with the silence, she said, "Don't you have to be at that place at a certain time?"

He didn't answer, but stood, not taking his gaze from her. "Let's go."

She reminded herself to be careful with him. Lately, he'd gotten to be so mercurial. A few minutes ago, he was playful. Now, he was moody. Oh, what the heck. He seemed dead set on keeping her at a distance, but that wouldn't kill her.

He parked on Lanier Street in the heart of Penwood, a village of about twenty-five hundred people. "Let's meet at my shop. I'll drive behind you, okay? Be back in a few minutes."

About five minutes later, the sound of a horn behind her got her attention, and she saw from her rearview mirror a white stretch Town Car. She flashed her lights, and he flashed in response. *My, my. The brother's got a rich customer.* She pulled away from the curb and headed for the main highway that led to Detroit. He hadn't said she should take the back road, and she didn't intend to. Besides, the last thing she needed sitting alone in that car was a romantic environment. It hadn't done any good earlier when she was in the car *with* him. She'd give anything to know what moved Luther Biggens. *I sure as hell don't.* She refused to examine that thought, merely laughed at it.

They arrived at her house around dusk, and, after having fought with herself about it from the time they left his showroom, she decided not to invite him in. She didn't handle rejection well, and even if she did, she didn't want anymore of it from him.

He walked her to her front door, she opened it and looked him in the eye. "I had a wonderful time with you. Bye." She reached up, kissed his cheek and turned to go inside. His grip on her left wrist startled her.

He stared down at her, his eyes ablaze with she didn't know what. Anger? It couldn't be passion. He didn't feel that kind of heat for her. He stopped her apology before she could utter it.

"A kiss on the cheek is the last thing I want from you." Without another word, he whirled around and, with his limp more obvious than usual, he left her standing there. She didn't remember him leaving her outside of her door once in the twenty-six years she'd known him.

She went inside and closed the door. "Men! I wish I understood them…or at least that one." *I think I saw pain in him when I tweaked his nose and again when I kissed his cheek. Lord, I hope not. I wouldn't hurt him for anything.*

At home that evening, Maggie presented Luther with another gourmet dinner, the centerpiece of which was a roasted duck with orange sauce. "If you continue to cook like this, Maggie, I'll soon be dirt poor," he told her, savoring the tasty food.

"Betcha won't," she said, enjoying her own cooking. "Check my book over there on the sideboard. I do intelligent planning, and I'm spending only sixtythree percent of what you told me to spend on food. I just ain't buying hot dogs, potato salad and coleslaw from the deli the way you used to do, and I make the bread and the deserts, 'cause homemade tastes better, is cleaner and healthier. Say amen to that, Mr. B."

He showed his teeth in a wide grin. "Amen to that, Miss M."

"You quit laughing at me. You hear?" She tossed her head in the manner of a woman who knows what she means to a man, looked at him and then lowered her lashes. "I cooked for some other corporate giants in my day, and ain't a one of them that won't have me back tomorrow if I was stupid enough to go. I haven't smelled a drop of hard liquor since I been here, and the first thing to hit my nose when I entered those houses was liquor. You're a fine man, Mr. B, and some girl somewhere is gonna discover that." She sucked on the bone of a duck leg. "At least I hope. Reminds me of a fine canoe floating on the water and deteriorating from nonuse. I do declare."

His fork clattered against his plate. *"What did you say?"*

"No use asking. You heard me." She enjoyed a

heaping forkful of garlic mashed potatoes. "And the longer that canoe stays out on that lake, the less use it'll be to anybody."

Feeling defenseless, he said, "You are one irreverent woman."

"Am I telling you anything your mother wouldn't tell you?"

He flexed his right shoulder in a slight shrug. "Not really. But she doesn't pester me about it, Maggie, because she knows I don't have much tolerance for that."

"Humph. I know it, too. But I'm not your mother. I'm your friend. Want some ice cream on your apple pie?"

"You bet. And if you don't stop spoiling me, no woman will want me."

She got up and headed for the kitchen. "The sex ratio ain't that lopsided yet," she said over her shoulder. "Women love sweet men. All you got to do is open your eyes and pay attention to what you hear."

"Do you ever make cheesecake, Maggie?"

"I used to, but people are so worried about cholesterol these days that I stopped making 'em. I can make you one if you like."

"I guess not," he said, and didn't bother to hide his disappointment. "It's just my favorite thing to eat. I had three big wedges this afternoon at Lena's Parfait over in Penwood."

"Can't blame you. Everything she makes is first class...and very rich. I wouldn't do that on a regular basis if I were you."

He got up and took his plate and two serving dishes to the kitchen. "I'm going to the officers' club. How soon can you be ready? I'll drop you off on my way." He scraped the plates and put them in the dishwasher.

"Thanks, Mr. B. This won't take me but about fifteen minutes. Then, I'll just grab my hat and coat, and we can leave."

He went up to his room, checked his answering machine and got his guitar. The thought of joining a small group of musicians appealed to him, and it would assure that he practiced regularly. He leaned against the doorjamb and inhaled deeply. He'd always been honest with himself and others, and when he was in war zones, that honesty had saved his life on more than one occasion. He faced the truth, and it was not a happy moment.

He was going back to the club because he was comfortable there. It was the one place in which he gave thanks for his blessings instead of cursing his misfortune. He dropped Maggie off at her house and headed for the officers' club.

"Hey, man, I see you brought your instrument," a captain he'd met on his previous visit said. "Feel like playing a spell? I have my violin. What do you like?"

"Classical, jazz or blues, but since I haven't played recently, let's stick to jazz."

"Works for me. Hey, Perkins, how about joining us for some jazz?"

"Count me in," another said.

"Let's go over there, Luther," Roger said. "Linden

plays the cello, but he can't move it around much. Hope you don't mind."

"Of course I don't mind," Luther said. "He doesn't seem to—"

"He can't lift five pounds," Roger whispered. "Imagine, a man can't even hold his child. Still, he's so personable and great fun to be with. Sometimes you forget he's disabled."

Jazz turned to blues, and it was hours later when Luther drove home. That evening was just what he needed. He'd been living exclusively among people who made themselves forget that without this prosthesis he'd be hobbling around like a three-legged pup. He had enjoyed being with men like himself, men who faced their lot unapologetically, making a life for themselves and their families. Compared to them, he could hardly consider himself to be disabled.

He entered his kitchen whistling "When the Saints Go Marching In," ate the cookies Maggie had left for him, drank half of the glass of milk, went to bed and slept soundly. Tomorrow he had a new goal—to find out exactly where he stood with Ruby.

Chapter 6

After supper Ruby sat down to work out her next lecture at the Morningside Community Center. She hadn't dreamed that her lectures would be so popular. The local TV station would be interviewing her and broadcasting a sixty-second clip of the lecture, and news accounts of her second lecture had brought new business to her consulting firm. No matter how she struggled to make the lecture new and interesting, no useful ideas came to mind.

Luther's last words when he left her at her door continued to plague her. If he didn't want her kiss on his cheek, what did he want from her? Nothing? All of a sudden, she rejected that thought with stunning finality. *When she'd covered his hand with hers, he'd encouraged her, she recalled, even caressed her hand. That was a far more intimate act than her kiss on his cheek. Deep in thought now, she rubbed her forehead. Something wasn't right. The man had been giving her mixed signals lately, innuendos, too, as if she didn't know a come-on when she saw or heard one. He didn't want her? Or he didn't want her to know he wanted her?*

She closed her laptop, jumped up and walked to the window that overlooked the back garden, bleak now from the ravages of winter. Had she and Luther imagined those snowflakes that lulled them into sentimental reminiscences? She slapped her right cheek with the palm of her hand. "I've been stupid!" she said aloud. "When did I ever want something and not go after it?"

She raced down the stairs and into the kitchen. "Where the devil did I put that cheesecake recipe?"

The phone rang as Luther headed into the house from the officers' club. He grabbed it right before the machine picked up. It was Paul Gutierrez.

"Paul! How's it going, man?"

"Couldn't be better. Amber and I want you to come out to L.A. We're having Joachim christened, and we don't want to do that unless his godfather is present."

"I'm honored, Paul. Who's the godmother?"

"Amber can't decide which of her sisters it should be, so Joachim will have three godmothers. Crazy, but man, you know these Lockhart women. They're to-getherness personified. Problem is that even with three godmothers, none of them can make it. Amber doesn't seem to mind too much. Each of them sent a letter confirming her willingness and ability to raise Joachim if need be. That's enough for us. Can you come out this weekend?"

"Wouldn't miss it."

Two days later, he held the happy, energetic child and spoke the vows that bound him to the little boy for as long as they both lived. As an adult, he hadn't spent much time around small children, and hadn't realized that he would derive so much pleasure from interacting with an infant. He didn't want to release the child for his nap and feeding, and followed Paul to the nursery.

"Having my son with me has changed my life," Paul told him. "Watching him grow and noticing how he learns things, copying what he sees. It's…I can't explain what I feel when he's with me. And Amber is a born mother. When I met her, that was the last role I would have cast her in, but she's wonderful."

"I can see that, and I'm proud of her."

"I heard you dropped by the officers' club. How'd you like it there?"

"Long story, man," Luther said. "I look at myself, at my…I can't even call it a disability anymore, considering what most of those men are dealing with. I'm fortunate. And I'm playing the guitar again. You don't know how good a feeling that is. Life is good."

Paul draped an arm across Luther's shoulder and led him toward the living room. "That's the best thing

I've heard in a long while. I'd hang out there regularly, if I were you. Next time I'm in Detroit, I'd like to go with you. Yeah, that's great news."

Amber walked in and looked at them with an inquiring expression on her face. "What's great news? Luther, how are things with Ruby?"

He cocked an eyebrow. "What things? What do you mean?"

Amber sat down on the sofa. "From the time I first knew you, Luther, you and Ruby were as tight as could be. You went together like cheese and crackers. What happened?"

How could he tell her the way in which he had screwed up? He couldn't. He took a long, deep breath and blew it out slowly, an act that sharpened their focus on him. "I think back on those days when she and I were such good friends, when she was closer to me than anyone in my family except my mother. That was an era of innocence, a time when life was sweet, and we had no idea how sweet it was. I suppose it's over." He hadn't meant to sound dramatic or sentimental, but he couldn't help it. The feeling came from the pain in his heart.

"It doesn't have to be that way, man," Paul said. "If I'd put up with Amber's nonsense, I wouldn't have her this minute." He looked at his wife. "Am I right?"

"Yes, you're right," she said, "but when you made up your mind, you played hardball. I'm not sure I could have gotten away from you if I'd wanted to, and

I didn't. You moved me from the minute I set eyes on you, but I didn't let on."

"How'd you know you loved her?" Luther asked Paul.

"It was everything, man. I couldn't get enough of her, couldn't stay away from her, and I thought of her all the time. When she became more important to me than anything or anyone, and when she needed me and let me know it, and I realized I didn't want another man to have her, I capitulated. The jig was up, man."

Luther listened quietly, refusing to admit to them that Ruby possessed his heart. Would the day ever come when he and Ruby could discuss their games with each other? Was she pretending not to care for him? He didn't dare hope. Besides, if she cared, would anything about him, including his prosthesis, repel her to the extent that she would run away from him as she had the night after Christmas?

"Life doesn't stand still," he said to Amber and Paul, feeling like their elder, "and sometimes it doesn't pay to look back. 'Long ago' isn't worth a wink."

As he flew back to Detroit the next morning, he wondered at his own words. He didn't want to restore the past. The last thing he needed was a brother-sister relationship with Ruby. He couldn't handle that, feeling about her as he did. Once he had made love with her, he could no longer treat her platonically. And of all the people who knew them both, he believed that Amber had guessed his true feelings for her oldest sister.

He sensed that by going to California, he had burdened himself unduly. Being there with Paul, Amber and Joachim brought to the surface longings he'd kept buried for five years. The desire for a family. For a woman who loved him and who gave him children that he could nurture and love. He wiped a tear. *I'll be damned if I'll give up.*

Ruby didn't bother to telephone Luther, because she wanted all the advantages, including being able to see his face and judge his reaction when he saw her. She also decided to go to his showroom rather than his house. When you were dealing with Luther, you had to lock all your gates, dot your *i*'s and cross your *t*'s, because he had shrewdness down to perfection. She didn't want him to think she was aiming to be alone with him. She wanted *him,* not a one-night affair.

"Ruby! What a surprise!" She hoped he was glad to see her, but the frown on his face suggested the opposite, and she had never figured out what he was thinking when he narrowed his left eye as he did then.

"Hi," she said. "I was thinking about the fun we had the other day in Penwood, and I made you something." She handed him a parcel. He took it and continued looking at her until, in a fit of nerves, she ran her hands up and down her sides. "What's the matter, Luther? Shouldn't I have come?"

"Oh, yes. Yes. Come on in." He led her into the lounge. "What's in here?"

She could see that he'd guessed the package's

contents for his eyes sparkled with anticipation, the way a child's eyes do at the sight of a new toy. "I should have brought you some coffee," she said, suddenly self-conscious. Wanting Luther in the way a woman wants a man seemed strange at times.

He put the package on the coffee table. "If this is what I think it is, you may be in trouble."

She crossed her legs and leaned back in the big leather chair. "What kind of trouble? Is it trouble that I'll enjoy?"

He stared at her for a second, then casually picked up the bag and opened it. "Tell me this isn't cheesecake?" he said. "If it is, I am definitely not responsible for the way I behave." He took the cake out of the bag, put it on the coffee table and fished in the bag until he found a knife, fork and napkins. She watched him cut a slice and taste it, savoring it as if it were the most delicious thing he'd ever tasted. He left the room, returned with two cups of coffee, gave her one and drank half of the other.

He cut a small slice of the cake for her. "Here, have some. It's unbelievable." Suddenly, he put the cup on the coffee table, walked over to her and picked her up from the chair.

Opportunity knocks but once, she told herself and looped her arms around his neck. For a few seconds, he stared into her eyes. She was praying that he wouldn't let his awesome willpower rule him. He sucked in his breath, and she met his lips when he lowered his head. She didn't know whether it was his moan or hers that filled the room, and she didn't care. She parted her lips, begging for more, and she could feel his hesitation just before he plunged his tongue into her mouth.

It felt so good. Feeling his tongue dance in and out of her mouth the way his penis had shocked her into orgasm was almost more than she could stand. She gripped him tighter and tried to wrap her legs around his hips. If he'd only put her on that sofa… A shudder raced through her, and she thought he attempted to push her away. It was then that she heard the telephone. He released her reluctantly, but that didn't pacify her.

"Biggens."

She didn't listen, mortified because he had tried to break the kiss that she felt she had initiated. She grabbed her pocketbook and dashed out of the showroom. What did he think of her now? She gathered her aplomb as best she could and kept the three consultation appointments on her calendar for that day. But oh, how she dreaded going back to the big Tudor house to be alone there. Alone with her thoughts. Could Luther kiss her like that if he didn't feel anything for her? And how far would they have taken it if the telephone call hadn't interrupted them?

Luther would have pondered the same question if he'd had time. "What do you mean Charles has gone to court?" he asked his lawyer in reference to his youngest brother. "What the hell's he got to feel cheated about? The family took a vote, and every one of them, including Charles, agreed to sell me the dealership. He got his share of the money, which was a lot more than he deserved, since he's never done a day's work at either of the three showrooms. A fight with my own brother is all I need."

"What do you want me to do?" the lawyer asked him.

"Tell him to meet me in court. He's wasting my time and his money." He hung up and called his father.

"I told Charles not to do that," Jack Biggens said. "He thinks he was entitled to more than he got. I built up the business and worked in it every day, and yet I agreed that his share would be equal to mine, although he never did a lick of work at any of those showrooms. Go ahead and take him on. It'll teach him a lesson."

Luther hung up, looked around and saw that he was alone. When did Ruby leave? It was the second time that she'd set him afire, given him hope and then run off when he wasn't looking. When he'd gazed into her eyes, he'd seen complete surrender. He'd swear it. And she'd kissed him as if she'd die if she couldn't have him. He stopped his left foot just before he slammed it into the closed circuit television he used to demonstrate his cars. He looked down at the cheesecake and couldn't help laughing. At least she'd had the wisdom to leave his cheesecake. He poured out the cold coffee, got a fresh cup and sat down to enjoy the best cheesecake he'd tasted in years.

"Be careful, girl," he said between forkfuls. "If you don't want to be consumed, stay away from the fire, 'cause you'll get no help from me." The phone rang, and he let the answering machine take care of the call. After consuming half of the cake, he put it away. He'd never been afflicted with greediness, but he could eat every morsel of that cheesecake. And he could also love her senseless.

"I will, too, dammit, if I get the chance." He let enough time pass, then called her on her cell phone. "This is Luther. I've eaten half of this cheesecake, and I stopped because I didn't want to make myself sick. It's wonderful, the best I've had since the last time you made me one."

"I'm glad you're enjoying it."

She didn't sound like herself, but he didn't intend to probe. "How are you going to get your plate back?"

"I'll come by for it one day," she said, still with more diffidence than he normally associated with her.

"I could be a gentleman and bring it to you."

"Uh, I wouldn't want to put you out."

He was having none of that. "It didn't put you out to make the cheesecake and to bring it to me in twenty-three-degree weather, so it won't put me out to wash the plate and take it to you. Subject closed. I'll let you know when I can bring it over, and don't bother dropping by here for it. When this plate gets back to your kitchen, I'll be the one who puts it there."

"All right, if you want."

"Why did you run off while I was talking with my lawyer?"

"I didn't want to hang around your place of business. What if a customer came in?"

He didn't laugh; she was too transparent to be amusing. "Was there some reason why I couldn't have two customers there? Why did you kiss me?"

"I didn't kiss you. You kissed me."

"Really? And what were you doing in the meantime? Woman, I thought you'd burn me to ashes. I never had a woman take from me the way you did, and God knows you gave. I'm still wondering what would have happened if my lawyer hadn't called."

"Look, I have to go. I'm glad you like the cheesecake."

"You're chicken, eh? You think you have the right to kiss me like that and leave me to deal with it as best I can? Don't you care?"

"Luther, you're trying to start a fight."

"Not on your life. I have a big enough fight on my hands with my brother."

"Your brother? Not Robert. What's the problem?"

"No, it isn't Robert. It's Charles." He told her about the suit Charles had filed against him.

"Why that lazy mama's boy," she shouted. "How does he dare do such a thing? Where is he?"

"He's home right now, but he'll be back in school Tuesday."

"The nerve of him! If he doesn't learn the value of work, he's going to stay in trouble," she fumed.

"I know. We all do."

"I have to go, Luther. If you want cheesecake every Sunday, just say so. No strings."

"Yes, I want cheesecake, and you couldn't be that naive. Nothing in life comes without strings of some kind. I'll call you when I'm bringing the plate. Bye." He had embarrassed her. Good. A woman too shy to acknowledge her sexuality deserved that and more. She hadn't heard the last from him.

Finished with her lecture, Ruby walked out of the community center. It had been a success. She wished she could say the same about her encounter with Luther. She cared deeply for him and, if she hadn't already known it, their kiss would have alerted her to that fact.

What had that call interrupted? She thought of it long after she kicked off her shoes, changed her clothes and put a frozen pizza into the microwave for supper. Why would Charles take Luther to court? The more she thought of it, knowing Charles's selfishness as she did, the angrier she became.

She finished her supper and went to her room. For a few minutes, she looked out on the wintry garden and then walked back to her bed. "What's wrong with me?" she asked herself as she returned once more to the window. Well, she could get at least one thing off her chest, so she sat down and dialed Charles's phone number.

"Charles, this is Ruby."

"Say, what's up? You've been scarce around here."

"I'm fine, Charles. I called to ask *you* what's up. Luther told me you're taking him to court. How can you do this to him, Charles? He loves you so much, and he's always looked out for you. You've hurt him, Charles, and you ought to be ashamed of yourself. He doesn't deserve this from you."

"Look, Ruby, I don't have to justify my behavior to you, but I am entitled to what's mine."

"You think you're entitled to more than your father received?"

"If he didn't fight for his rights, that's him. I want what's mine."

"Luther said you voted with the others and that you all got equal shares. Now you're breaking ranks with your family. You're being disloyal to your brother."

"Ruby, if this was any of your business, I'd state my case to you, but it isn't. You'd do well to look at yourself. You use Luther as if he were a piece of rubber that you can pull, twist and manipulate to your satisfaction. Whenever you want anything done, you call him. Luther do this, Luther come here for me, go there for me, be my little puppy. And you do it because you know he's enamored of you."

"What?"

"Don't pretend with me, Ruby. You know how he feels about you, and you string him along for your convenience."

"Not one word of what you say is true."

"No? Take a good look at yourself, and clean out your own closet before you start cleaning out mine."

"You're accusing me, because you know you're wrong. Unless you want to waste a lot of money on lawyers and court fees, you'd better withdraw that suit, Charles. With your entire family as Luther's witnesses, you can't win. Try to repair some of the damage you've done."

After she hung up, a heavy cloud dropped over her. Had she abused Luther? Her belly contracted sharply, and her heartbeat seemed to have slowed to a crawl. She made a cup of green tea, took it to her bedroom and sat in the middle of the bed, strung out with worry and a fear of self-examination.

She ruminated about her behavior toward Luther from the night of Opal's wedding reception. She didn't remember ever having as much self-confidence as she'd had that night. She knew she'd flirted with Luther, and she couldn't understand why, because until that night she hadn't been interested in him or, if she was she hadn't been aware of it. The champagne certainly didn't clear her head, though she'd lie if she said she was drunk. She knew what she was doing when she asked him to unzip her dress. Or at least she thought she did. But why? Why did she do it?

Had Charles told her the truth? Did she use Luther? Was she so used to his doing whatever she asked that she'd seduced him because she knew she could? But Luther made the experience real, unforgettable, and forced her to lay herself bare to him. Wasn't that why she left him as soon as the moment of reckoning came?

She held the bedspread to her face, and let it catch her tears. Now that she knew she was attracted to him and wanted him, he was wary of her, and she didn't blame him. How could she have been so stupid and so blind for so long? Even if Luther was enamored of her, as Charles claimed, with his Herculean strength and determination, he would ignore her if he believed she'd mistreated him.

With her hands locked behind her, she walked from one end of her bedroom to another, battling the urge to call Luther. She needed to hear him say that she hadn't hurt him, even though she knew that would be a stretch. Finally, she crawled into bed long after midnight.

He's been so good to me. If I'd only realized what he could mean to me. He deserves so much better than I've given him.

If Charles's comment shook her up, Amber's call the next day did nothing to relieve her stress. "Would you believe what Luther asked Paul when he was here this past weekend?" Amber asked Ruby during their conversation.

"Not much surprises me these days, Amber. What did he ask Paul?"

"He asked my husband when he realized that he loved me. That surprised me. It didn't seem a bit like Luther. Maybe he's interested in somebody. He's awfully good-looking, you know, and he's not a bit poor. I imagine women like him. That limp is hardly noticeable. I used to think something would develop

between you two, but…uh…you don't seem interested in him. I guess if you've known him since you
were little more than a baby, he doesn't seem like a
man, but a friend. You know what I mean?

"Sis, you should have seen Luther with Joachim.
Luther was enchanted with him. Somehow, I'd never
associated Luther with babies, but he and Joachim got
along like bread and milk. Luther didn't want to give
him up, and Joachim didn't want to leave Luther. That
told me a lot about Luther Biggens. "

"If you've got a point, Amber," Ruby said, becom-
ing irritated for no good reason, "please make it."

"I just wondered if Luther had said anything about
having a woman he's…uh…making it with. I've never
seen him with one, but if a man wants to know how
to be certain he's in love, he must be taking stock of
things. Oh, yes, I'm forgetting something. Luther
asked Paul that question immediately after we asked
him how you were. Instead of answering he remi-
nisced about how sweet life was when the two of you
were close. I say that's a heck of a time to question
whether you're in love."

"Amber, honey, don't be so full of melodrama. He
wasn't determining whether he's in love, but how Paul
knew *he* was in love with you. Don't mutilate the
facts."

"Okay. Pay me no mind, and you'll be sorry. I'll
see you in a couple of days when we come for Paige's
engagement party. Imagine marrying a brother who

can buy out a five-star hotel for two nights and three days! Mr. Epse is da man!"

"Tell me about it. I'm so happy for Paige," Ruby said. "She's had a difficult life, and I hope that's a thing of the past."

"I expect it is. The brother's carried away with her. They'll have a home in the Detroit area, but she's going to travel with him. Imagine going all over the world and traveling first class while you're doing it. Way to go, Paige. All she has to do is keep it between the lines," Amber said, "and that goes for you, too, sister dear. See you at the party."

Ruby shook her head slowly. She wasn't foolish enough to ignore Amber's sentiments. Amber may be the baby sister, but Ruby would bet she understood men a lot better than Ruby herself did. She just wished she knew where to start.

Direction came from an unlikely source.

Ruby had never liked her manicurist, apart from the work she did, because she considered her too frivolous, but when she kept a noontime appointment that day, she found herself listening to the woman's chatter as she gave advice to all who would listen.

"Unless a woman is totally unfeminine," the manicurist said, "she can get any man she wants. First, she has to let the man know she wants him, but in a subtle way, and pretend she doesn't want him to know it. Expose some of the goodies, but just a little bit, and do it often enough. His ego and his libido will do the rest."

Ruby could hardly believe her ears as she listened
to the conversation that followed and the examples
some of the women gave of their success with men
using that or similar methods. And here Ruby thought
it came about as a result of a natural attraction. Those
women declared war and set out to win. But she
wasn't sure she wanted to do that. However, when she
was back at her desk searching for an excuse to telephone Luther, she conceded that her method was no
more honest than the one proffered by the manicurist. "At least I have options," she said to herself. "If I
can't work it one way, I'll try the other."

Luther had also arrived at some important decisions. He would no longer behave apologetically for
his disability. He was born with two perfect sets of feet
and legs and lost one set in the service of his country.
Anybody who didn't want to see the result didn't have
to look. He was finished wearing hot, uncomfortable
long pants in the heat of summer. He bought three
pairs of Bermuda shorts, and three bathing trunks that
amounted to little more than G-strings. He dumped his
purchases on his bed, and had an indescribable feeling
of relief, as if he'd just been released from a dungeon.

He packed the items for his weekend at the hotel
to celebrate Paige's engagement to Lyman Epse. The
invitation had requested that all guests stay at the
hotel and announced a Friday-evening barbecue and
entertainment, a Saturday-afternoon pool party and a
Saturday-night gala.

Ruby had better not try anything cute, because he'd let her have it straight. He was getting tired of this cat-and-mouse business, although he knew he helped her instigate it. She came at him with her fresh, sassy cracks, and wanted him to think she was teasing. Sometimes she was and sometimes she wasn't, and he knew the difference. She'd never got fresh with him until he took her to bed and showed her what it was all about. Tomorrow she'd see so much of his prosthesis that it would cease to repel her. And if she was the woman he hoped she was, she'd look at him with mature eyes and mature feelings and not with the values of an adolescent looking to be swept off her feet by a knight on a white horse.

He went down the stairs whistling. "You get Friday and Saturday off, Maggie," he said when she peeped at him from the kitchen door. "And you get a fifty-dollar raise."

"Thank the Lord," she said. "You just keep right on whistling, Mr. B." Her laughter seemed to shower the house with warmth.

"I appreciate your reverence for the Lord, Maggie, but I'm the one who's giving you that fifty-dollar raise. Don't I get a thank-you?"

She rubbed her hands together. "Lord, Mr. B, I do declare if you're not the funniest sometimes. You know I thank you. I'm the only person I know who can't wait to get to work. The Lord's gonna bless you. You hear?"

Ruby checked into the hotel a few minutes before noon, unpacked and went to the second-floor lounge where Paige's guests were to register and collect favors and additional instructions. She hoped Paige hadn't invited Trevor Johns. Ruby didn't want anything to get between her and Luther, and Trevor was just insensitive enough to spoil the whole weekend for her. She collected her bag of information and goodies, went back to her room and switched on the TV.

"I wonder what time Luther's getting here," she said to herself, just before she dozed off.

At a quarter of five, she awakened with a start, wondering where she was. The phone was ringing repeatedly, and after fumbling around, she located it. It was Opal. She was in the lobby and Luther had arrived and was asking for her.

So Luther was looking for her. Good. She dressed in the first black leather pants she'd ever owned, a red long-sleeved shirt, put silver hoops in her ears and slipped on a pair of spike-heeled black boots. She applied her favorite perfume and pulled a red scarf through the belt loops of her pants. After locking her purse and other valuables in the safe, she put her door key in her pocket and headed for the party.

"Nobody ever saw me dressed this way," she said to herself, "but if *this* outfit shocks 'em, tomorrow night their hair will stand up."

She loitered near the entrance to the ballroom where the predinner drinks were being served, looking over the crowd. After a few minutes, she saw Luther and headed directly to him. Before she took twenty steps, Trevor Johns attempted to detain her.

"I'm with someone," she told him, hardly sparing the man a glance.

"But—

"Sorry." She kept walking. By the time she reached Luther, a woman she didn't know was attempting to get his attention. She put a hand on his arm and stepped between him and the woman.

"Hi. I've been looking all over for you. See any champagne around here?" She had no intention of drinking champagne, but she knew what the mention of it would suggest to him.

His eyes nearly doubled in size, and his Adam's apple bobbed furiously. "Not tonight, you don't," he said, forgetting the woman who wanted his attention.

"Well, what can I drink? I just got out of bed, and I'm thirsty."

"Come with me," Luther told her. "If I didn't know better, I'd think you arrived on a motorcycle."

She slipped her hand into his. "Don't you like how I look? The heels are kind of high, but other than that—"

"You don't look like yourself, but the effect is fantastic. It suits you."

"Thanks. I was a little worried about making such a drastic change. You deserve a kiss."

"Thanks," he said. "Unfortunately, I don't always get what I deserve."

She took the glass of white wine that he handed her

and lowered her lashes. "I'm not sure how I should interpret that statement."

"It doesn't need interpretation, Ruby. It's as plain as your face. Did a man bring you here tonight?"

"No. I checked in around noon, and I've been up in my room resting all afternoon. If Opal hadn't called me, I'd probably still be asleep. She said you were asking for me."

Luther set his wine on the bar and grasped her left arm. "Who's escorting you to the gala tomorrow night?"

"Good heavens, Luther. I didn't think I needed an escort in this group."

His frown would have suggested to anyone who didn't know him that he was either perplexed or searching for something elusive. But she knew him. And when he said, "Of course you do. At least half the people here are strangers," he let her know that he'd rather she wasn't unescorted among Lyman's basketball buddies.

"You want the job?" she asked him and, in order to appear less aggressive, added, "You can have glazed raspberries on your cheesecake."

His gaze warned her not to push the envelope. "The only compensation I'd ever want for escorting you is you. Make no mistake about that. Stay here. I'll be right back."

She watched him walk away. He was telling her something, but she had to be careful. She knew what she wanted, but wasn't sure about him. She couldn't let him think she was easy and not just because he was a man she wanted, but because he was Luther, and she cared about Luther's perception of her as a woman. Her manicurist had said you only have to let the man know you want him... But how the devil did you do that without cheapening yourself?

He returned with a plate of grilled shrimp on skewers and tiny quiches. "I don't think you should drink wine on a empty stomach," he told her. "This is likely to be a long evening. Besides, the shrimp are delicious."

"Thanks. Let's share this. I want room for the barbecue. By the way, did you see any champagne?"

"Plenty of it, but every bottle bore a sign that read, Not for Ruby."

"Really? Are you serious? Oh dear, I've ruined my good name."

"Of course not. I was just yanking your chain. Let's go to the dining room. They're already seating."

"You mean it's a sit-down barbecue?" she asked him.

"You bet, and the tables are breathtaking. Sorry, man. Find your own woman. This one's taken for now, tomorrow, tomorrow night and the next day and night."

She looked to her left and saw Trevor Johns looking like a whipped puppy. "Trevor, didn't I tell you when I came in here that I was with someone? I'm not going to leave him and go anywhere with you. Now please leave me be."

Trevor left them, but she could see that the man had

irritated Luther. "Are you with me because you wanted to avoid him? Is that it?"

She had learned that offense was often the best defense. "Luther Biggens, don't get my dander up. There must be at least half a dozen unattached men here. Do you think I couldn't be with one of them if I wanted to? I'm with you because I prefer to be with you and you seem to feel the same way."

"Did you put on that red shirt because I like you in red?" he asked with a sheepish grin.

"Trust me, I put it on because I knew you'd hate it," she said. "Come on and let's go find a table."

He took her hand, and she let him hold it while she struggled to make herself breathe regularly and to force her nerves to calm down. As they neared the head table, a waiter asked Luther for his registration number and, to her delight, he seated them at a table beside the bride- and groom-to-be. The large bowl of red and yellow roses in the center of the table emitted a mild, almost seductive perfume, and in the glow of the half dozen sixteen-inch tapered candles, the man who held her hand looked ever more certainly to be the man of her dreams. She wondered how she looked to him and whether her eyes sparkled with the happiness she felt.

"Did you know they were seating us together?" he asked her. She didn't, she told him, but since Amber had arranged the seating, she wasn't surprised. Pearl and Wade joined them, and she thought it interesting that Luther still held on to her. She pretended that there was nothing unusual about him holding her hand, and if Pearl or Wade found it exceptional, they didn't let on.

She had thought she was the one who cast the net. Now she wasn't so sure.

Chapter 7

"I'll walk you to your room," Luther told her shortly after midnight when the crowd began to thin. She'd been stifling yawns for the past hour, but hadn't wanted to waste a minute of the chance to be with him in that romantic setting when they were man and woman rather than pals.

She knew her smile amounted to a promise, and recognition of it seemed to flicker in his eyes. She resisted the urge to wipe away the telltale moisture that beaded her forehead. Besides, if he knew her nerves had begun a rampage throughout her body, maybe that would excite him.

She waved at Opal and D'marcus, looked around for her other sisters and their husbands and noted that they had left as had Paige and Lyman. "Would you like anything before we go?" Luther asked her.

"I'm fine," she told him, "unless maybe you're going to let me have some champagne."

She stared at him. How had she looked at this man for nearly thirty years and not realized how gorgeous he was? His grin began around his lips and spread to his eyes. Large brown eyes that twinkled like evening stars. She sucked in her breath, reached for his hand and said, "Never mind the champagne."

"If you didn't drink any champagne," he said, "that was your decision, not mine. I'll give you anything you want. All you have to do is ask."

If she hadn't been sober, that comment would have done the job. He walked with her to her room, took her key and opened the door. "Thanks for spending the evening with me. I'll call you tomorrow morning." He leaned down, kissed her cheek and left her.

With her mouth a gaping hole, she backed into the room, closed the door and collapsed on the bed. What had come over that man? Infuriated, she dialed the operator and asked for his room number.

"I'm sorry, ma'am. I can connect you to his room, but it's against policy to give out room numbers." She thanked the operator and hung up. She didn't want to talk with Luther Biggens on the phone; she wanted to punch him in the chest. She struggled out of the boots and kicked them across the room. Tugging out of those skintight leather pants only exacerbated her temper. She never wanted to see them again.

Damn him. She'd show him. Sweet as she'd been to him all evening, he could at least have kissed her good-night. But she hadn't wanted a mere kiss; she'd wanted him; and she still did. "All right, buddy," she said aloud, "you're not the only good-looking man at this party. Mama always said you shouldn't spend too much time blowing up a man's ego, and I think she was right." She jumped up and stamped her feet. How could he do this? He couldn't be stupid. She must have thrown that man fifty cues this evening. Oh, hell! She stamped her foot again. "I'll show him!"

Luther started toward the other end of the hall to his own room, thought better of it, got into the elevator and went back downstairs where he met Amber and Paul coming out of the bar.

"Where's Ruby?" Amber asked.

"She's in her room. I'm not ready to turn in yet." He didn't missed Amber's raised eyebrows or the censoring look Paul gave her, as if he knew his wife would have more to say on the topic.

"I'll take Amber upstairs," Paul said. "Wait for me right here. I don't want to spend an hour searching for you in this crowd."

He saw the flirtatious pout Amber gave her husband and figured that he didn't know the Lockhart women as well as he'd thought. Throughout the evening, Ruby had sent him invitations and, to make certain he understood, she buttressed them with innuendos. He intended to disabuse her of the notion that she had only to snap her fingers and he'd jump. He liked a woman who went after what she wanted, but he also liked subtlety in the way she did it. She'd had her fun pretending that their having made love to each other wasn't of any special moment, and then she'd rejected him in the most painful manner. Recently, she'd made it clear that she'd changed her mind, or maybe she realized that he meant something to her. He couldn't be sure. He suspected that she wanted what he'd given her that night, and she wanted it badly enough to be frank about it. But he couldn't be certain of that either.

He wasn't seeking revenge. But, for both their sakes, he meant to teach her a lesson. She couldn't turn him on and off like a faucet that never dried up. He refused to allow any woman to be that sure of him, no matter how much he loved her, and he loved Ruby.

He saw Paul approaching him, a tall and powerfully built man who wore self-confidence the way some women wore fine jewelry. That quiet dignity was the first thing that had attracted him to Paul when they'd served together as navy SEALS. Knowing that Amber had such a man for her husband gave him an immense feeling of happiness.

"Man, when these women make up their minds, they don't give a hoot about anything else, come hell or high water," Paul said.

"You could have phoned me and I wouldn't have waited for you. First things first, man."

Paul released a short laugh. "Not to worry. She'll be glad to see me half an hour from now. Let's go to the bar where it's more quiet." They did, and he ordered a vodka and tonic. "What are you drinking?" Luther ordered Scotch whiskey and club soda. "What's happening between you and Ruby?" Paul asked him. "Something is, and everybody knows it."

Luther couldn't resist a laugh, bitter though it sounded. "Everybody but Ruby, you mean."

"Uh-uh. She knows. I watched her all evening, and so did Amber. She's feeling a lot for you, and she's well aware of it."

"I've always let her twirl me around her finger, but our relationship was—"

When he hesitated, Paul interrupted him. "Your relationship is different now. You don't have to tell me how or when. I know it's changed."

"It has…for her. It's been this way for me since I was in my late teens."

Paul's whistle split the air. "You're kidding!"

"Not by a long shot," Luther said. "Get back upstairs to your wife, man. If a woman thinks she's not getting her due, whether it's a smile or a Valentine card, there's no reasoning with her."

"Tell me about it. You know that, and you're not even married?"

Ruby went down to the dining room for breakfast at seven o'clock. With luck, Luther would still be asleep. She walked in and looked around. Fewer than twenty people and not one of them suited her purpose. "How can you look so fresh at seven in the morning?" a male voice said as she picked up a tray on her way to the buffet table.

She spun around. Uh-oh. The great Craig Murphy.

"I hope you don't remember me," he said, grinning. "Because if you don't, maybe I'll have a chance to make amends for the worst boo-boo I've ever made. I was going to read this paper while I ate breakfast, but you'd be much more pleasant company."

She didn't respond to that, but collected what she wanted to eat and found a small table. As if he interpreted her move to mean that she'd like to sit with him at a table too small for a third person, he joined her with a smile.

"Am I forgiven? We're more than even you know, because I can never go back to that restaurant, and it's my favorite. Let me take that tray for you," he said, after removing the food from his own tray and placing it on the table. "Be right back."

"Where are you in the Lockhart hierarchy?" he asked her as he seated himself.

"I'm the eldest," she said. "What's your team, Craig?" She realized that she didn't really care, but it was a safe topic; most men enjoyed talking about themselves.

Both of his eyebrow shot up, and his eyes widened. "Detroit." Well, heck, she didn't follow professional basketball, so how was she to know he was a genuine hotshot?"

"I'm ignorant about a few other things, too," she said. "I only recently learned that a famous TV announcer never finished high school. And until a couple of days ago, I didn't know that a woman held the all-time best record for tennis matches won."

To his credit, he laughed. "What's her name?"

"Margaret Court. She's Australian."

As they were leaving the dining room together an hour later, her gaze captured Luther sitting alone with his attention on a copy of *USA Today*. He wasn't reading that paper, she thought. He'd seen her with a guy, and he was ready to make a big deal out of it. Well, she'd deal with it when she had to.

"Who're you going to the gala with tonight?" Craig asked her.

Giving him a taste of honesty, she said, "I don't know. I was supposed to go with a man who's sitting in the dining room reading a paper, but I suspect he saw me with you—"

"Added two and two and got eleven, eh? I've done that a few times. Pretend you didn't see him."

She had planned to let Luther know she didn't spend the night pining for him, but she hadn't intended to shoot herself in the foot. She avoided complicating things by refusing a date with Craig.

She spent the remainder of the morning in her room working out staff changes in the likely event that Marva Wright didn't recover sufficiently to return to Everyday Opportunities, Inc., as its CEO. She hadn't wanted to seem pushy, since she stood to gain if Marva couldn't return to work, but she couldn't continue doing Marva's work as well as her own, so she'd asked Marva's doctor.

"If she goes to that office again," he'd said, "it'll be a modern-day miracle. She'll be lucky if she's able to walk."

Shortly before one, she put on her string bikini and a matching wrap skirt that showed most of her thigh when she walked. She knew it was daring, but she was hunting big game, and she needed first-rate ammunition.

Luther hadn't called her, and she knew he was smarting for no reason. She'd spent a lot of time the previous night thinking about their relationship, and concluded that their problems were of her making. Further, Luther could be sensitive about his leg, and she'd done nothing to reassure him that the loss of his leg and foot did not diminish him in her regard. But, she didn't think it appropriate to give him that assurance just then; after all, it was one o'clock, and he hadn't bothered to acknowledge her existence.

She took the elevator to the indoor pool. Artificial daylight, wall murals that replicated sandy beaches and palm trees that swayed gently as if in a balmy trade wind greeted her startled gaze. White lounge chairs and sea-green cabanas around the pool added to its allure. She stood at the entrance, looking around. He wasn't there, but she knew he wouldn't miss the chance to show her he didn't care. He'd done it before.

"I hope you've got on more under that skirt than you have up top," Pearl said. "Girl, that bra top hardly covers your nipples."

"Yours would cover plenty," Ruby told her, "if I couldn't see right through it. Pluck the beam from your own eye, sis," she said and winked to let Pearl know how little concern she had for the amount of flesh she exposed, provided Luther showed up.

She sat on the edge of a big artificial boulder with a glass of lemonade on the floor beside her, looked toward the door and he walked in. She nearly sprang forward. Had he been pretending about that leg? She'd felt the plastic limb against her flesh the night they'd made love, but she didn't get a good look at it and now socks covered it. She stared at him. Luther without long pants. Luther wearing a yellow open-collared shirt and Bermuda shorts. She caught herself and took a deep breath. What a body that man had! With his flat, muscular belly, he looked good in that getup. She swallowed hard.

Images of herself thrashing beneath him floated through her mind, and she blew out a long breath, trying to gather her aplomb. Where had she been all this time? Surely he hadn't changed. And the women! Four of them latched on to him immediately.

She slid over to the lounge chair that rested beside the boulder, stretched out and closed her eyes. She had to get herself together. "I can't behave like those women," she told herself. "It's far too late for that."

When at last she opened her eyes, she saw that Luther was walking toward her, and the booming palpitations of her heart frightened her. As if to slow down her heart, her right hand went to her chest.

Mindless of all except the man approaching her, she wet her lips with the tip of her tongue. He took his time getting to her, and by the time he did, she had all but memorized his every moving muscle, from his biceps down.

"Why are you sitting over here alone?" he asked. "What happened to your breakfast date?"

Don't show annoyance. He wants to bait you. "I have no idea."

"There you are, Ruby," the voice of Craig Murphy sounded from over her shoulder. "I looked everywhere for you." She looked at Luther, fearing that he would act precisely as he did.

"Don't let me interrupt anything," he said, turned around and walked away.

"Did I mess up something?" Craig asked her.

"You did, but if it can't be fixed, it wasn't worth much."

"Now wait a minute. If the guy means anything to you, you shouldn't be so casual about this. No guy wants another one fooling around on his turf, and especially not with a woman like you. He seems like a nice guy."

She sat up and wrapped her forearms around her knees. "He *is* a nice guy, but he's giving me mixed signals."

"Uh-uh. That guy's no lounge lizard. He's straight. You're inviting mixed signals."

"How do you know he's straight. Do you know him?"

"I know a man when I see one. If he's the one who

was with you last night, I'd say he thinks a lot of you. You want him?"

She nodded. "Yes."

"Okay. This is my good deed for today. Get busy. It shouldn't take you an hour. Good luck."

"Thanks." *I was working on it when you showed up.*

She locked her gaze on Luther, who seemed oblivious to her presence. He looked in her direction, stared down at the woman who was trying to wrap herself around him and then glanced back at her. She continued to look at him, willing him to come to her, but he didn't move. He only gazed at her as if to say he knew she was there, but didn't care.

The hell with it! She kicked off her shoes, flung off the skirt, raced over to the pool and dived in.

He was not a foolish man, or at least, he'd never thought so. Luther Biggens was sensible. Everybody said so. But there were times—such as right then— when he couldn't overcome his stubbornness, not even when he knew that by not reversing his position he punished himself. Ruby wanted him to come to her, and she'd sent the great Craig Murphy packing in order to let him know it. He tried to focus his attention on the woman clawing at him, but his mind was on the seductive witch who reclined twenty feet away on a white lounge chair.

What the— She stripped off her skirt and exposed her nearly nude and luscious body. A gasp escaped him, and he pushed the woman away as Ruby dived into the water. He headed toward the pool, intent on giving her a tongue-lashing for hanging out her curves for all to see. Suddenly, he stopped. She hadn't surfaced.

Forgetting that he couldn't run and that he hadn't swum since before the accident five years earlier, he raced to the pool and dived in after her. God help him if he couldn't bring her up. His instincts kicked in, and he brought her to the surface.

"What's the matter? What happened?" The voices around him served as reminders of what could yet be a tragedy.

"Get back, everybody, and give him room." He heard Paul's voice and was grateful for the man's presence; if he needed relief giving her artificial respiration, Paul could provide it.

Silently praying, Luther opened her mouth, pinched her nostrils and began alternately to breathe into her mouth and count. After a minute, she spat out water and began to breathe.

She opened her eyes, looked at him and, to his amazement, her arms looped around his neck and then fell away as if she lacked energy. "How do you feel, sweetheart?" he asked her.

More alert now, she frowned. "What happened?"

"That's what I want to ask you. Did you forget how to swim? You dived into the pool and didn't come up."

"Oh! I remember. I had a cramp in my leg. I guess

I'd been lying here with my leg tucked under me, and I didn't realize it was half asleep. Maybe that was the reason. I panicked when I realized I couldn't come up." She leaned against him, as comfortable as if she knew she had a right to do so. "Who brought me up?"

"I did."

"B-but you aren't supposed to... Won't your prosthesis come off?"

He shook his head. "No. But I wouldn't have cared. You're safe, and that's what matters to me." The crowd moved away, though Opal and Amber remained beside them.

"Do you think she should see the house doctor?" Opal asked Luther.

"It wouldn't be a bad idea. He can check to see whether her lungs are clear, but I think she's all right."

"In that case," Amber said to Ruby, "I guess you feel like putting on some clothes. You look as if Michelangelo painted you and forgot the fig leaf. I'm not even *that* daring."

Ruby stared down at herself, saw that she still wore what passed for a bathing suit and let out a long breath. "Your name should have been Drama," she told her youngest sister. "Where's Pearl?"

"She and Wade haven't come down yet," Opal said. "I'll call them when the waiters begin serving the food."

"Thank you for bringing me up, Luther. I wish I hadn't jumped in. I know you don't swim anymore and I made you risk your life unnecessarily." She took his hand and looked steadily in his face. "You can't possibly know how sorry I am. If anything happened to you, I don't know how I could have handled it."

He saw the pain in her eyes, pain for him, but did that mean she accepted him as he was, or had today's happenings reinforced her misgivings about him?

"You're safe, and so am I. That's what matters, Ruby."

"You'd better make an appointment with the hairdresser," Amber said. "Half the women here will want their hair done if they get into that pool."

"You're right. I'm going to get a shower and change. I can't stand that chlorine on my body for long," Ruby said.

When Ruby stood, he detected wobbliness. "I'll go with you," he told her.

Her withering look brought a raised eyebrow from him. "That's what started all this," she said. "I'd better go by myself."

"But you're not quite steady," he told her, understanding now that when he didn't kiss her, and maybe when he didn't even make love with her the night before, he had annoyed her to the point that she'd decided to show him a thing or two.

"I'll go with her," Amber said to him. "Tell Paul I'll be back in a few minutes."

"He wanted to bring you up to your room," Amber said, her tone more like of a mother than of a younger sister. "Why didn't you let him?"

"I know you mean well, Amber, and maybe Luther

does, too, but I have to figure these things out for myself."

"Don't forget that with all those big-shot athletes there, Luther's the one who jumped in after you, although he wasn't the closest to you. I didn't know he could run, and I suspect he didn't either. Be careful, hon. Don't wait too long to do your figuring, and don't forget to make an appointment with the hairdresser."

She returned to the pool room and looked around. "Where's Luther?" she asked Paul, hoping she hadn't hurt him by refusing to allow him to walk with her to her room.

"He had to change." Paul's eyes sparkled and his grin suggested more than he said. "He'll be back in a few minutes. How do you feel?"

"Fine, except all of a sudden, I'm starving."

"That's a good sign. They've just begun serving food." He turned to walk away, looked back at her and said, "Stay out of mischief, now."

It had been years since Luther had felt so triumphant. He was as good as any man. At least eight of the country's top athletes had stood between him and a drowning woman, but it was he, a thirty-five-year-old amputee, who'd had both the presence of mind and the ability to rescue her. Only God knew what would have happened if he'd stopped and thought about it. But he hadn't, he'd gone in, and he'd made that leg remember when he'd dived for the fun of it, when he was whole and could swim with the best of them. He felt like shouting it to the whole world.

At least he got to tell his parents when his dad called.

"How are you, son? How's the party?"

"The party's fine. What's up?"

"Nothing special. Your mother had one of her premonitions, and she said there's danger around you, so I called to see how you are."

"Tell her I'm fine." He related to his father the events of the past hour and said, "How does Mom do this? Doesn't it make you nervous?"

"It's a gift, and it doesn't make me nervous. That gift's been a blessing more than once. She'll be happy to know you were able to surface after diving into the deep end of a full-sized swimming pool. Sometimes I think you and Ruby ought to get married."

He nearly dropped the receiver. "What? Why do you say that?"

"Well, she always worshipped you, and she didn't even have to whistle when she needed you, because you were always there. Her father and I used to say that nothing and nobody would separate the two of you, and I'm beginning to think we were right."

"We were children, Dad."

"I know," Jack Biggens said. "And now that you're adults, nothing has changed. By the way, did you know Ruby called Charles and chewed him out because he's taking you to court?"

"You can't be serious. She did that? That's more

than I did. I'm so used to coddling him that I haven't given him the tongue-lashing he deserves. How'd he take it?"

"She shamed him thoroughly," Jack said. "He's not so sure about it now. We'll see."

Luther stopped, dumbfounded, as he entered the pool area later. Applause erupted and every person stood. But he saw only one.

Ruby smiled at him, and frissons of heat shot through his veins, excitement washed over him and he had a sudden feeling that the world had stopped turning. He tried to smile, to encourage the warmth he thought he saw in her eyes, but he felt as if he'd become frozen in time. As if she knew he needed a jolt, she reached up and kissed his cheek. He laughed then, laughed to express the happiness that enveloped him.

"How's your leg?" Ruby whispered.

"It's okay. I think maybe I'll start swimming again."

"Be careful," she said. "Maybe you'd better check with your physical therapist."

"Humph. That brother doesn't know past sit-ups and push-ups. Who's going to the gala with you tonight?"

She seemed surprised by the question. "I thought you were."

Maybe she'd intended for him to accompany her, and maybe she hadn't. Her apparent surprise confirmed nothing. Females of the human species were born actors, and from birth to death, they exploited that God-given talent whenever it suited them.

"In that case, I'll knock on your door at seven."

Her right eyelid lowered slowly in a seductive wink. "I'll spend the afternoon anticipating that," she said, giving his heart a jolt.

Ruby answered his knock on her door at seven o'clock exactly and sucked in her breath as she stared at the picture of masculinity energy that loomed before her, mesmerizing her. In that black, satin-lapelled tuxedo, white-silk ruffled shirt and royal blue accessories, she thought he put all other men to shame.

"Like what you see?" he asked her with a grin that made her blood race.

"Absolutely," she said, embarrassed that she'd let him see her reaction to him. Reaching for levity, she added, "If I'd realized you were so doggone good-looking, I'd have had my way with you long ago." She meant it as a joke, but he didn't laugh.

"You still have plenty of time," he said. "I always knew you were beautiful, but the Ruby I'm looking at right now is…" He threw up his hands. "You look…so lovely and so…beautiful. I'm proud to be with you. And we'd better be going—you're temptation personified."

She noticed that, as they entered the ballroom, Luther put her arm through his, and she knew he was signaling territorial rights. Fine with her; that was precisely what she wanted him to do. Candlelit tables for two lined the room and, except for Paige and Lyman, couples could sit where they chose. An orchestra occupied one end of the great room, and a bar stood at the other end.

Luther chose to sit in the center of the room, and she was glad, because she enjoyed the glow from the massive, intricate chandelier that hung above them.

Before dinner Craig Murphy, resplendent in an Oxford gray tuxedo with red accessories, stood to introduce the engaged couple and to toast them. Ruby's gaze followed Craig back to his table where he joined the only blue-eyed blonde in the room. She didn't realize that her private laugh would be evident to Luther.

"Let me in on it," he said.

She told him, "I laughed because it didn't surprise me. I think he's probably a nice guy, but...well, I suppose he sees himself as exceptional."

"He's the big man these days, now that Jordan's retired. He obviously knows a pretty woman when he sees her."

At that point, Lyman walked out to the center of the dance floor holding Paige's hand and knelt before her. Ruby couldn't hear his words, but she knew what he said, and because she couldn't stand to watch the hot kiss that Lyman gave his bride-to-be, she lowered her gaze.

Luther's hand grasped hers, and her heart pounded furiously. "Look at me," he ordered. She tried, but couldn't, and she knew that he could see her lips tremble. "Why can't you look at me, Ruby?"

Don't let him see how you feel. His finger beneath her chin urged her, and she forced herself to look into his mesmerizing gaze, into eyes that burned with hunger and need. When she gasped, he stood and walked around the table to her, extended his hand and said, "Dance with me."

She'd been so focused on him that she didn't know the dancing had begun; indeed, the only music she heard was the tune that flowed wave on wave from him. Somehow, she managed to stand, and then she was in his arms.

"You're holding me too close," she said.

His grip tightened. "I'm not holding you close enough," he said, and began to sing softly the words to Luther Vandross's song, "Here and Now."

She missed several steps, but he didn't care. He was in a mood to let it all hang out. If she didn't know what they could mean to each other, he did, and he meant to open her eyes in any way he could.

"What will people think?" she said, but he got the feeling that she was pretending.

"Ruby," he said stepping back a bit and looking her in the eye, "I don't give a damn what anybody thinks. Other people don't know what goes on inside of me, and they can't heal me when I'm raw inside. To hell with what they think."

This didn't sound like the Luther she thought she knew, but still, when he brought her close to him again, she relaxed in his arms and enjoyed the contentment she felt. Inhaling the scent of his cologne and enjoying it, she stopped herself as her lips moved toward his neck.

I must be losing my mind. I don't act like this in public, she said to herself. The music stopped and she walked with him back to her table as the reggae music drew half the crowd to the floor.

"Man, do you mind sharing this beautiful lady for one dance?"

She looked up at Craig Murphy and considered telling him flatly no. Craig grinned a grin that she suspected usually gained for him whatever he wanted. "I deferred to you yesterday after she let me know that she was more interested in you than in me. How about it?"

"It's up to her." Luther looked at her. "I should dance once with the bride-to-be anyway, and I didn't want to leave you here alone." He looked at Craig and showed a grin that didn't reach his eyes. "Don't get comfortable with her, man."

The reggae ended, and she was thankful that she didn't have to dance a rollicking number with Craig. It would have seemed unfair to Luther, who could only dance one- and two-steps. The man used good judgment and didn't hold her close.

"Where's your girl?" she asked him.

"Dancing with one of my teammates. What's wrong with these people? Not one woman has said a word to her."

Ruby wondered if Craig didn't understand black women. "If I was with a white man, would you do your best to make him feel comfortable? When some of these good-looking brothers get rich, where do they spend it?"

"Touché. She and I have been together since before I was famous or rich, and I sure as hell don't plan to abandon her to please a bunch of idiots."

"Good for you. Why don't you marry her?"

"'Cause my mother would have a stroke."

"She won't do any such thing. If your wife is warm and kind to her and behaves like a daughter, your mother won't care what color she is. Quit pussyfooting around and do what's right."

The music ended and he walked her back to the table. Craig shook hands with Luther who arrived there at the same time. "Thanks, Ruby. I'm pretty certain that I'll take your advice. I suspect I only needed the right kind of encouragement."

"You're going to explain that, aren't you?" Luther said after Craig left them. She did, and he looked at her a long time before replying. "You gave him good advice. Sometimes it's easier to give it than to apply it in one's own life."

He said no to the waiter who brought drinks for the nth time. "There's a closed balcony off the third-floor lounge, more like a veranda. Want to go up there for a while? I imagine it's a bit quieter. But if you'd rather stay here—"

"I'm going with you," she said. "I haven't been up there. Is it nice?"

He looked at her and scattered her nerves with a wink. "You bet. What's more romantic, more seductive than a full moon on a cold starry night?" He stood and reached for her hand. "Come on. I promise you nothing but joy."

Chapter 8

I've wrestled sharks underwater, Luther reminded himself as he stepped off the elevator with Ruby and headed for the balcony. *If I did that, I can stay above the water, so to speak, with this woman. If I have to, I'll come right out and ask her if this prosthesis offended her. I'll make her look closely at it, touch it. It's who I am, and she can't like my face and reject any other part of me.*

"Why are you so quiet?" Ruby asked him.

"I don't feel the need to say anything. I'm content right now. I found this place yesterday morning, and I thought I would enjoy sitting here with you." He didn't intend for her to get too far from him, so he sat on a sofa that faced the windows, patted the space beside him, and she sat there. "How about going with me to see the ice sculptures in Kellogg Park?" he asked her. "Have you ever seen them?"

He noticed that she clung to his hand and that she sat as close to him as she could without actually sitting in his lap. "I'm ashamed to say that I've never seen them, except on TV, of course. I'd love to see them."

"Every January, people come from all over the world to look at those sculptures and to watch the artists chisel those intricate forms out of ice. They do it right there in front of those huge crowds," he said. "Let's go tomorrow. I've found that it's best to go at the beginning before it becomes so crowded that you can't see much."

"All right." She spoke very softly, and he wondered about that, because it sounded to him as if, consciously or not, she wanted to induce greater intimacy.

He released her hand, slid his arm around her bare shoulders and caressed her flesh. He'd spent the evening trying not to focus on her beautiful bosom that her dress barely covered, and his mouth began to water as the desire to pull her sweet nipple into his mouth slowly got to him. His blood pounded in his ears, and in spite of the increasing heat of his libido, he had a primitive feeling of protectiveness toward her.

He couldn't tell what she was thinking or feeling, for she remained as still as a windless winter night. The scent of her perfume teased his nostrils, and he suddenly remembered her own wild woman's scent, a musty odor that would always remain with him. God help him, he wanted her badly enough to take her and run away with her.

Somewhere nearby, an alto saxophone wailed the most lonesome blues he'd ever heard, and she chose that moment to lay her head on his shoulder, reach across him and clasp his free arm.

"Sweetheart, do you want to go to the club and listen to that music? I think it may be on the ballroom floor somewhere."

She shook her head. "I want to stay here with you." Her fingers stroked his cheek, and as if that weren't enough, he felt her lips on his neck.

"Ruby, do you know what you're doing?" Her answer was another kiss in the same spot. "Why are you doing this?" he asked her, hardly recognizing the guttural tones that escaped his lips. "Baby, I'm human."

"So am I," she whispered.

He couldn't let it get any further, because he hadn't brought any condoms with him, and as needy as he was, he didn't trust himself to withdraw in the heat of his passion. But he didn't want to discourage her either.

"Let's go back to the gala," he said. "I wouldn't want you to miss any of it."

"I don't care about anything or anybody in that place," she whispered. "I just want to be with you."

He moved her from him and stared into her face, looking for more than sexual desire, more than momentary passion, as tremors streaked through him and hope surfaced in his heart. "Don't play games with me, Ruby."

"I'm not. Can't you see that I'm not?"

He wanted to believe her, wanted that more than he'd ever wanted anything, but he didn't want the searing pain of rejection that she'd inflicted on him after loving him until he almost lost his mind. She whispered words that he didn't understand, strung out as he was by the pure feminine spice of her voice and the seductive scent rising from the pores of her satin skin.

"Kiss me," she whispered, her eyes sultry pools of desire.

Her hand grasped his nape and her lips parted. He stared into her eyes for a second, and then, helpless to resist her, he plunged his tongue into her. She sucked him in deeper and deeper, feasting as if starved, and moaning from the pleasure of it. He couldn't stand it, and his body rioted against its prison of denial until he could no longer restrain the tide. His attempt to break the kiss went for naught, for she clung to him, stroking his cheek and sucking on his tongue, shattering his will and bringing him to a full erection.

He broke loose as gently as he could. "Do you know where we are?" he asked her in an effort to introduce mental sobriety. "Honey, we're in a public place." The way in which she looked at him suggested that she neither comprehended his words nor understood why he'd stopped the kiss.

"Why didn't you kiss me last night?"

"I thought we finished with that. I didn't because it didn't seem warranted." He allowed himself a slight shrug in the hope of reducing the impact of his words. "I've about had it with these noncommittal kisses, much as I enjoy them. You just kissed me as if you wanted to eat me alive. Why?"

She looked away from him. He didn't want to corner her, but it wouldn't surprise him if the next time she saw him she blew him a sisterly kiss as if he'd never had his tongue in her mouth or buried himself deep inside her body.

"I didn't kiss you differently from the way you kissed me," she said, a little testily, he thought. "I didn't hold a gun on you and make you put your tongue in my mouth."

He let a grin surface around his lips, although he was certain that it didn't touch any other part of his face. "Maybe we'd better join the others."

"You join them. I think I'll turn in for the night."

"I'll see you to your room."

"Thanks, but it isn't necessary. Thanks for a pleasant evening, and I really mean that. Good night." She rushed away before he could stand up, and he let her go, but it would be the last time. If she initiated such an exchange with him again, he was going to make love with her, and when he finished, she would be his.

Ruby didn't take the elevator but raced up the short staircase to the grand ballroom. Immediately, she wished she'd taken the elevator when she glanced up and saw Trevor Johns approaching her.

"Hi, babe," he said, blocking her way and reeking of free liquor. "How 'bout a little bitty kiss?" He grabbed her and attempted to kiss her, but after struggling with him for a minute, she kicked his shin, and he released her.

"Must be the dress," she said to herself after she reached her room and locked her door. "A lot of screwed-up men around here, led by Trevor Johns. The one I want doesn't want to settle on me. He pleased me in bed, but I didn't please him." She'd give anything if she could laugh about it, but it hurt so badly that she thought she'd cry. If only she hadn't let herself get out of control with him on that balcony! Shudders passed through her as she imagined what Luther must think of her. *I don't roll over for men, but he'll probably never believe that.*

"What happened to you?" Opal's voice startled her when she answered the phone, because she'd thought the caller would be Luther.

"You know I can stand only so much of the whoopee stuff and no more," she said, summoning her best superior manner.

"I don't know any such thing. You left the ballroom all lovey-dovey with Luther, he came back alone, and you're in your room. You want me to believe Luther mistreated you? No way, sis. What happened? You two had been as tight as corn kernels all evening."

Ruby sat on the edge of a chair twisting the telephone cord around her wrist. "Opal, I'm tired. Yesterday, I nearly drowned. I barely slept last night, and I've been going nonstop all day. What do you want from me?"

"I was hoping you'd...well, open up and let me know what's going on. Luther looks as if he's just received a life sentence."

"I'm so sorry," she said, knowing that she'd just kindled Opal's suspicion, for even to her own ears, her voice sound like the subdued chirp of a bird that couldn't fly.

"Be careful, hon. Don't lose something precious," Opal said.

"I can't lose what I've never had, Opal."

"What did she say?" Pearl asked Opal as they huddled together in the women's lounge, where they'd gone ostensibly to repair their makeup and hairdos.

"I couldn't get a peep out of her. But I know one thing—she didn't sound any happier than he looks."

Pearl leaned against the marble counter. "I don't like it. At their ages, they ought to have sense enough to know how they feel about each other."

"Maybe one of them just can't step over that line from pal to lover. What else could it be?" Opal asked Pearl. "Amber swears that Luther loves Ruby, that he didn't deny it when she and Paul all but told him he did."

"Yeah, but Amber's such a romantic, she may have seen something that wasn't there. What are we going to do?"

"D'marcus said we shouldn't worry about it. He thinks you can always count on Old Man Libido to bring things to a head," Opal said.

"Lord, I sure hope he's right. Anyway, tomorrow we start to get back to normal, and they won't see each other all day and into the night as they have this weekend."

Opal let out a deep breath. "Thank the Lord. When do you start rehearsing with your new piano player? Wade told my husband that you're very pleased with him."

"Indeed I am," Pearl said. "He's so sensitive to my singing, and he plays so effortlessly that he makes me sound better than I am. That's something else to thank Luther for. Sometimes I wonder how we'd get along without him. My label likes my pianist so much that it's going to pay him to accompany me, and as a part of the deal, he gets a recording contract."

"I'm glad to hear it, Pearl. You've always had a wonderful voice." They went back to the party with thoughts on Luther and Ruby.

From where he stood near the bandstand, Luther saw Opal and Pearl enter the ballroom, both of them looking his way. He supposed that they were speculating about Ruby and him, and especially since Amber and Paul thought he and Ruby were more than friends. He didn't care how much they speculated so long as they kept their thoughts to themselves. And he hoped they didn't pester Ruby with advice and comments. He and Ruby would work out their relationship best if left alone to do it.

Ruby wanted him, or at least she behaved as if she did. But he needed more with her than the passion she didn't seem able to control. It had occurred to him more than once that she let herself go with him because she had always trusted him to take care of whatever went wrong in her life. Oh, hell! He was tired of trying to figure it out. One thing was certain: she'd changed from an ordinary, nice-looking, kind woman to a siren. Talk about late bloomers! He cut the whistle that almost flew out of him and walked over to speak with Paige and Lyman.

"This has been an awesome weekend. I've enjoyed every second of it, and I wish you love and happiness together forever." He leaned down, kissed Paige's cheek and then shook Lyman's hand. "You two throw a great party, and we'll all be talking about it for a long time. Thanks."

He went to his room then, and when he stepped off the elevator on the seventh floor, he didn't glance toward Ruby's room. "I've tortured myself enough for one weekend."

Half a dozen doors from Ruby's room, he entered his own, undressed, hung up his tux and prepared for bed. The message light blinked on his phone, but when he checked for messages, he didn't have any. He sat on the edge of the bed and dialed Ruby's room number.

"This is Luther. Are you all right?"

"More or less. What about you?"

"The same. Don't forget that you promised to go with me to Kellogg Park tomorrow."

"I haven't forgotten it. What time do you want to leave?"

The woman was a bag of surprises. He'd have sworn that she'd find a reason not to go with him. "I'm checking out at nine in the morning. That will give me time to go home, change and be at your place around noon."

"Great. Are you in your room?" He told her that he was. "Uh...well, sleep tight," she said in barely a whisper.

"And you do the same." When he hung up the phone, he groaned. What a way to say good-night to someone you loved as much as he loved her! He wished he hadn't called her.

He checked out of the hotel shortly before nine the next morning, and large snowflakes were dampening his favorite lizard shoes as he headed up the stone walk of Ruby's house. How many hundreds of times had he traveled that route? First with his father when he was barely able to walk. Luther knew that house as well as Ruby did. After ringing the bell, he looked up to gauge the elements and decided that they could expect a heavy snowfall.

Ruby smiled when she opened the door. "Sorry I made you wait. It's cold out there. Come on in."

He gazed down at her for a minute. Even though she reached his shoulder, she seemed so small in that big house. He remembered that she'd said she didn't like living there alone, and his heart went out to her. Without thinking of what he did, he reached for her and folded her into his arms.

"I don't mind waiting on you. You're always worth it."

When she stepped away and looked at him, her expression seemed plaintive. "If you mean that, I'm glad. I just don't know about you anymore."

He drew her back into his arms. "Our relationship has changed, Ruby, and the way in which we used to treat each other and understand each other won't always work now or in the future. We're more sensitive, and we hurt more easily." Instead of saying she agreed, she kissed his neck, and his demon libido raised its head.

"We'd better leave now, before we start something," he said. "Where's your coat?"

She handed it to him, and he breathed deeply in relief. They were not going to get into a clench every time they were alone together. They no longer knew each other, and he meant to repair that with their outing to Kellogg Park.

After he parked in a parking garage, they walked several blocks to the park. Noticing that she clutched herself for warmth, he asked her, "Are you cold already?"

"I'm always cold unless you're kissing me," she said through teeth that chattered. "But I never freeze, so not to worry."

He stopped walking and tied her long woolen scarf so that it covered her lower lip as well as her neck.

"Forget about fashion," he told her. "This thing is supposed to keep you warm."

He heard her mutter, "So are you," but pretended that he didn't. In less than a month, she had revealed aspects of her personality that he didn't know she had, and oddly enough, he liked this new and open Ruby.

He discovered that she liked the intricate carvings rather than the human figures and marveled that they had that in common along with so many other things.

"My favorite is this replica of the *USS Constitution,* with all the sails in place," she said of the ice-sculpted model of the first United States commissioned ship. "You'd get my vote for first prize," she told the sculptor, who beamed with pride.

"How'd you know that was the *USS Constitution?*" Luther asked as they walked on. "It wasn't labeled."

"Well, Commander Biggens, after the *HMS Bounty,* it's the most well-known of the tall ships, isn't it?"

"Right. You'd make a fine navy w...woman," he said and, seeing the delight that shone in her eyes, hugged her close. He'd almost told her she'd make a fine navy wife.

"Want to go ice-skating when we leave here?" he asked her.

"I haven't skated in ages," she said. "I'd love— Oh."

"What's the matter? Forget something."

"Uh…no. I mean, can you…? I didn't think you could skate."

Whenever they were together and he began to feel that they had a chance, something happened to dampen his spirits. *I'm not giving in to it this time,* he told himself. "Ruby, I can do practically everything I ever did. I wouldn't try to tap dance, fence or play football, and I'm careful about getting on ladders. If you ever have the courage to see how this prosthesis works, I'll be glad to show you." He realized that he probably came across as testy, but he was beyond caring about that. He wanted her to accept him as he was.

A frown marred her features, and she worried her bottom lip. "Why would I need courage? And why are you annoyed?"

He softened his voice. "Some people are unable to accept that many of us are not perfect physically. Imperfections in others repulse them."

She took his hand. "Surely you aren't talking about me. Come on. If we're going to skate, we'd better go."

What was he to say to that? They made their way through the park, enjoying the sculptures, till he noticed her blowing on her hands to warm them.

"You're cold. We'd better leave. I don't want you to get sick." He put an arm around her waist, walked with her to the exit and stopped beside a pillar that sheltered them from the wind. "I'll bring the car. Wait here."

"Thanks, but I'd rather go with you."

He noticed that she hunched over as she walked. "Are you sure you want to skate?" he asked her. "The rink's outside."

"Hadn't thought of that. I think I've had enough cold for today. Besides, I need to get ready for work tomorrow. Marva's husband told me that she won't recover sufficiently to come back to work, so I need to meet with him and work out something. Maybe a buyout of some kind."

"If I were you, Ruby, I'd let a lawyer handle this. What was her financial investment in the business?"

"Almost none. We worked in our homes until we got a large enough clientele. Then we rented office space, and the business paid our expenses. We spent maybe a couple of thousand dollars on office furnishings, maybe less."

"Get a lawyer, and save yourself a lot of grief," he advised as he parked in front of her house.

"Don't get out," she said. "The walk is slick with ice."

"If I—"

"No argument. Kiss me and let me get out of here. With the motor off, this car is already getting cold."

"Why don't you want me to walk you to your door? I always—"

"You said things are different with us now, and you're right. You always looked out for me, and now I have to look out for you as well."

"Listen, Ruby. That's nice of you, but it isn't what I meant. I was telling you that, when a man and a woman become intimate, when they exchange affection at the level you and I do now, there's more at stake than smiles between two friends. You can hurt me with little things, like not allowing me to walk you to your door. I can damn well negotiate the smattering of ice out there."

He got out of the car, walked around and opened the door for her, and when she didn't move, he asked her, "What's the matter? Do you want me to lift you out of there?"

She laughed. "I ought to say yes. Have you always been this bossy, or am I just noticing it?"

"Both." He leaned into the car and unhooked her seat belt.

"I'm going to kiss you for that." she said. "And one of these days, it won't be you who decides what's next—it will be me."

He took her hand and walked to the door. "If I remember, you did that once. Next time you decide to do it, consider the consequences." He unlocked the door with her key and steeled his will against the feminine entreaties he knew she'd lay on him. "You promised me a kiss."

Her eyebrows shot up. "When?"

It was his turn to show surprise. "A minute ago."

If deviltry had been her intent, the idea floundered somewhere, and her left hand went to the side of his face, stroking his cheek in featherlike touches, almost as if she hardly dared to do it. He reeled beneath the feel of her soft hand dusting his skin in what was surely a lover's touch. Didn't she know that she cared for him?

"Sweetheart, you promised me a kiss, and I'm waiting for it."

Instead of kissing him, she rubbed her thumb across his bottom lip, possessively, gazing at his mouth as she did so. "This lip is a troublemaker. It's downright tantalizing," she said as if speaking to herself. And, as if he were hers to do with as she pleased, she reached up and sucked his bottom lip into her mouth.

He heard his groan and couldn't stop it as she pulled his body to hers, parted her lips beneath his and drew his tongue into her mouth. He struggled hard for self-discipline and eased her away, but not before his erection pressed against her belly.

"Don't pour it on so thick, sweetheart," he said. "I'm just human, you know. Besides, I'd better get on home. I need to call Maggie, and I don't have her phone number with me."

He'd never known anyone's demeanor to shift so quickly. From molten soft one minute to feisty the next. He told himself not to laugh as he stared down at her standing there like an irritated bantam hen with her fists on her hips and her chin poked out.

"Who, may I ask, is Maggie?"

"Oh," he said with childlike innocence, "didn't I tell you I hired a housekeeper a couple of weeks ago? She's wonderful. When I get home after a rough day, I no longer have to cook. Sh—"

"Really! Does she live in?"

"Oh, no. I don't need a live-in housekeeper, at least not now."

"How old is she?"

He let himself give the appearance of one struggling to find the right answer, frowning with half-closed eyes. "Gee, I don't know. Maybe a young sixty."

Ruby's eyes began to narrow, but she didn't follow through with the gesture. "She must be good-looking, otherwise you would have asked her her age. Does she have a husband?"

At last, he laughed. He couldn't help it. "Sweetheart, Maggie's a widow."

"What's funny?" she huffed. "Widows are the neediest kind."

"You're wrong about that," he said, mainly to needle her. "Divorcees are needy ones. Trust me. Widows are grieving."

She folded her arms across her waist and kicked at the carpet. "I suppose you'd know."

He reached to her and tweaked her nose. "That's right. I would. I'll call you when I get home."

What a weekend! Ruby sat on the edge of her bed, tossing around in her mind all that had happened to her from the time she'd registered in that hotel until Luther left her a few minutes earlier.

He's attracted to me. Strongly, too. But what does it mean? And why do I go up in smoke when that man touches me? Damn, I'm not that needy!

She kicked off her boots and socks, pulled off her heavy Irish wool sweater and made some notes as to what she'd say to the lawyer when she called him the next day.

She answered the telephone, but released a long sigh when it wasn't Luther. Instead, her brother-in-law Paul asked, "What do you say we all get together for dinner at Joe Moody's Texas Ribs before Amber and I leave? Is tomorrow evening at seven okay? Your sisters are agreeable, and I'll see if Luther can make it."

She decided not to ask him why he had to invite Luther, for it occurred to her that people traveled in twos, that her three sisters were a part of couples, and she was the odd woman out. "Works for me," she said, feeling like a burden. "I'll be there at seven."

Why did they feel they had to pick a man for her? She was capable of getting one of her own. Thoroughly irritated, she hung up and went downstairs to the kitchen. She'd barely begun making a tuna sandwich when the phone rang. This time it was Luther.

"Did I disturb you? I was about to hang up."

At the sound of his voice Ruby could feel her heartbeat accelerate. "Hi, Luther. Did Paul call you?"

"He did. Are you going to join them? I thought I would. If you are, I'd like to drive by your house and take you with me."

"What time are we supposed to be there?" she asked him.

"Seven. I'll be at your house a few minutes before six. Can you be ready then?"

"I have a heavy schedule tomorrow, Luther. I think it would be best if I left directly from my office. An extra hour and a half at my desk when the office is empty would ease my work load. Would you mind?"

"Of course not. I'll be at your office between six-twenty and six-thirty. What are you eating for dinner?"

"A tuna fish sandwich, a tomato and some grapes."

"Are you serious? There's a small grocery store not too far from me. I'll be glad to get whatever you'd like and bring it to you. I'd be at your place in less than an hour."

"You'd do that for me in this hideous weather? Oh, Luther. I love you for that." Realizing what she'd said, she slapped her hand over her mouth. Why didn't he say something? In an attempt to cover up her remark, she said, "But I don't mind eating this. I love tuna salad."

As if he hadn't heard her weak attempt, he said, "I'd be happier if you didn't feel you had to give a reason for loving me, but I'll take what I can get. For now."

She ignored that. "Do you know attorney James Loder? I'm thinking of engaging him to help me get control of my company."

"Yeah, I know him. He's a good corporate lawyer. That job won't stretch him a bit." They spoke for a few minutes longer, and then he stunned her again when he said, "Good-night, love. See you tomorrow."

"Good night," she said, dissatisfied with her cowardice.

"I'd begun to wonder if you two were going to show up," Amber said, as Ruby and Luther joined them in the restaurant.

"Knowing how you love drama, we should have gone somewhere else instead," Ruby said as she hugged her sisters.

"Amber makes up her mind about something," Paul said, "and expects it to come true."

"At least she's a positive person," Luther said. "Some people make up their minds about a thing, and decide that since it wasn't on their agenda it can't happen."

"I hope you're not talking about anybody sitting here," Pearl said.

"Of course, he isn't," Wade said. "Let's say grace."

"But we haven't ordered yet," D'marcus said.

Wade laughed. "I wanted to change the subject, and I think I managed. You guys stay off Ruby's case."

"If they do," Ruby said, "it will be the first time in my memory."

"We don't order," Paul said. "When I made the reservation, I said we're having the barbecued sparerib dinner. That saves us at least an hour during which people make up their minds."

"It's too bad you and Amber live so far," Ruby said to Paul.

"No. It's a good thing," Luther said. "The first thing I noticed about Amber when I visited Paul and her in Moreno Valley was that she's no longer the baby. She's her own woman, and being away from her big sisters helped, although I'm sure that marriage played a major role."

They joked, teased and exchanged views on everything from politics to the state of fine art. Ruby noticed Paul remained quiet most of the evening. Something wasn't right, and she suspected that Luther's comment brought the matter front and center for Paul. As they were leaving, Opal and Pearl rushed ahead, sandwiched Luther between them, and walked elbow to elbow with him until they reached his car.

"What was that about?" Ruby asked Luther.

"Amber's giving Paul a hard time. She wants to enlarge their house and install a pool. Their four-bedroom house is already too big for them. Opal wants me to talk with her. Can you invite them over for coffee? It won't seem right if I do it."

"All right, I will. Paul," she called to him," why don't you and Amber ride with us instead of taking a taxi?"

Luther slipped an arm around Ruby's shoulder and tucked her closer as they waited for Paul and Amber to join them. "Listen, baby," he said, "when we get to the house, make an excuse to get Paul into the kitchen with you while I talk with Amber. He loves her, but he isn't going to let her run him into debt. "Too bad. I thought she'd matured."

"She has in some respects, but evidently she still feels that she should be pampered. It'll work out. It has to. Do the best you can."

"I'm going to tell her the bald truth," Luther said.

As they headed for 12025 St. Jean Street, Ruby wondered if she and Luther weren't settling into an affair. She wanted him, but as she sat beside him on that frigid night speeding through the Motor City to her big empty house, she knew with certainty that she loved Luther and wanted to marry him. In recent weeks she had realized that she wanted him, that she was strongly attracted to him and felt more for him that she had ever thought possible. She exhaled sharply and slumped into the seat.

"What's the matter?" he asked her. "Are you all right?"

"I'm fine. I just realized something, and it surprised me."

"Is it worth sharing?"

She shrugged. "Maybe one day soon."

Chapter 9

"Mind if I borrow Paul for a minute?" Ruby asked Amber after they removed their coats. "I'm going to make us some coffee. You two know where the cups and saucers are."

She and Paul headed for the kitchen, and Luther took Amber's hand and led her to the dining room. "Which cups and saucers do you think she wants?" he asked her.

Instead Amber collected four matching mugs. "Ruby can get so fancy, but coffee tastes the same whether you drink it from mugs or bone china."

He watched her line up the mugs on the coffee table in the living room as if she planned to use them for target practice. "That isn't the way I see it," he said.

No point in stalling; he had a minute, and he'd better use it well.

"Amber, why do you want Paul to spend a few hundred thousand dollars improving a brand-new house? He has a child to support and educate, and he'll have to support and educate the children you give him. Today, an Ivy League school education averages around forty thousand dollars a year. Not to mention the music lessons, tennis, swimming and on and on, and it all costs money. He will want his children to have the best, because that's the kind of man he is, but they won't have the best if he's waist-deep in unnecessary debts.

"You have a beautiful home, so don't break your husband's heart by showing him that no matter what you have, you're never satisfied. And one more thing. A pool is dangerous where there are small children."

"Be fair, Luther. The people out there live that way, so…"

"I thought you loved your home. It's beautiful and elegant. A man wants to know he can keep his woman happy. If you make him feel that he can't please you, you'll regret it forever."

"I hadn't thought about all this. You've reminded me that instead of thinking about what one person wants and needs, I now have concerns for the three of us, and I have to remember that that means looking way ahead." She threw up her hands. "Being a wife and mother is work, but you know…I love it. Thanks for the jolt, Luther."

About that time, Ruby returned with Paul, who carried the tray.

"Gosh, if I'd known Ruby was serving that, I'd have let Luther bring out those porcelain cups and saucers."

"What? What did she bring?" Luther asked. Surely she hadn't made—

Ruby must have deciphered his look of expectancy, for she shook her head. "I'm sorry Luther, but I haven't had time to make a cheesecake. Amber loves these little cakes, and I remembered that I'd stored some in a tin. Taste one."

He chose one covered with caramel and topped with a pecan, and tasted it. "Delicious. It isn't the equal of cheesecake, but it's almost there."

"How did Joachim react to that long trip across country, Paul?" Luther asked.

"Except for take off and landing, he seemed not to mind it at all. We thought of leaving him with the woman who used to be his nanny, but we decided to bring him with us when the hotel assured us that it had a roster of approved babysitters. We're very pleased with the service. Joachim liked her, and we've been free to enjoy ourselves."

"We can't stay too long, Ruby," Amber said, "because we have to get up early. We'll call you from California."

"That's right," Paul said. "Thanks for the hospitality, Ruby. And Luther, thanks for providing the transportation."

Ruby walked to the door with them, hugged Paul and kissed Amber. It always tugged at her heart to see her baby sister leave and head thousands of miles away.

"You and Luther behave yourselves," Amber said to Ruby as she and Paul headed down the walkway.

Luther locked his gaze on Ruby in an attempt to get her reaction and saw what could only be annoyance. So she didn't want her sister to think there was anything between her and him. He got a sinking feeling that she didn't want anyone to know that he was more to her than a pal, but damned if he was going to let her shove him into a proverbial closet.

"Sure you couldn't want something better for us, Amber?" he said and winked just before he draped an arm around Ruby's shoulder, pulled her to him and placed a fierce, punishing kiss on her mouth.

He let a smile dance around his lips. "Good night, sweetheart. I'll call you later." He didn't look back. He didn't have to. If she wasn't seething with anger, it was because she'd fainted.

What was that all about?

Ruby didn't know what Luther was trying to accomplish with that display, for although it may have appeared to Amber and Paul as a gesture of affection, to her it seemed as if he was either angry or using her to vent some frustration. She didn't intend to let him get away with it.

Sitting at her computer, she'd begun reading the

files on Everyday Opportunities, Inc., from its inception, but she couldn't get Luther's kiss out of her head. The telephone ringing further interrupted her focus.

"Hi, Ruby." Luther's voice sent a jolt of electricity through her body.

He continued, without a pause. "I think I succeeded in showing Amber that she's not being wise in pushing Paul because she knows he adores her. She told him in my presence that the changes she asked for in their house were too expensive and that she'd rather they saved the money for their children's education. Paul didn't look any happier the day they married than he did when she told him that. I think she's got it together now."

"Good," she said. "And what about you, mister? That trick you pulled as you were leaving doesn't suggest to me that you've got it together, as you put it. If you were angry with me, you shouldn't have kissed me, not that you had a reason to be angry."

"I can't imagine what you're talking about. You're not trying to pick a fight with me, are you?"

"Luther Biggens, if I was near you, I'd—I'd—"

"You'd give me a big hug and tell me how happy you are that I talked with Amber. Now, wouldn't you?"

"That's not the issue here, and you know it."

"Are you saying you didn't want members of your family to know what kind of kissing we do? Shame on you. At your age, you're entitled to do whatever you want to, so long as it's legal and decent. Don't think you can kiss me as if I were the last man alive and then get out of joint if anybody other than me knows about it."

"You aren't being fair."

"Yes I am, but take a look at yourself, and maybe you should have a talk with yourself, too, and figure out what you want. "

"I know what I want."

"You couldn't prove it by me. Good night."

The dial tone sounded in her ear like the death knell of her dreams. She hung up, but couldn't force her feet to move from that spot. He had effectively slammed the door on a relationship with her. She threw up her hands.

What did everybody want from her? She was supposed to be a role model for her baby sister, and Luther expected her to…to…

Oh, the devil with it. I'm not going to cry about it. And if he thinks I'm going to call him back, he'll learn something. I love him, but I won't grovel now or ever.

For a few minutes, she let her feelings have sway, and the tears cascaded down her cheeks. Then, disgusted with herself, she went into the bathroom, splashed cold water on her face, uttered a few choice expletives and said aloud, "That wasn't a pretty sight, but I feel a lot better."

The next morning, she felt sharp and alert when she called the lawyer, told him her problem and asked if he would handle the transfer of the company to her as sole owner.

"It shouldn't be difficult," he assured her, "provided Marva's doctor will certify the unlikelihood of her returning to work. Then I'll contact her husband."

She gave the lawyer the information that he needed and then telephoned Marva's husband, reasoning that she and Marva were not only business associates, but very close friends. "I wanted to warn you to expect a call from my lawyer," she told him. "If I continue doing both her work and mine, the business will suffer. Someone needs to work full-time at the job I always did. I was always the technician, so to speak."

"I appreciate what you're saying, Ruby. How can we place a value on Marva's contribution?"

"You can work that out with the lawyer. It's painful to me to lose Marva. We've been together from the start, and we've always had the same vision for the company."

"I know. I also know she won't get well enough to go back to that office, and I appreciate your trying to do the right thing."

After hanging up, she blew out a long breath, symbolic of the burden she'd just shed. "She was going to make some changes in the firm, and as always she lifted the receiver to call Luther and ask him what he thought of the idea, then she remembered their estrangement and hung up. "I could always rely on his judgment, but now… Okay. I respect my own good sense, and I'll use it."

The picture of Luther cuddling Joachim while the child investigated Luther's ears and nose flashed through her mind, and she shook her head in wonder. Memories of the softness and sweetness in the man tugged at her heart. He had so many ways that excited her and that she loved and hadn't noticed until after that night when he'd loved her until she hardly knew herself.

I am not going to let that man ruin my day. I've got work to do, and I'm going to do it. Get thee behind me, Luther Biggens.

But her day wouldn't go smoothly. She punched the intercom. "I'm leaving to keep my appointments, and I should be back after lunch," she told her secretary. Battling the slow and hazardous traffic made her late for her visit with the proprietors of Morning Glory Florals, and she arrived only to find a sign on the shop that read, Closed Due to Bad Weather. Such lackadaisical management no doubt accounted for the store's loss of revenues.

Back in her car, she phoned Louvenia's Books 'N Things. "We have an appointment at eleven," she said, "and I'm calling to find out if you're open."

"Yes, ma'am, Ms. Lockhart. We're here."

At the store, she sat in the back room surrounded by everything from books to soaps, to statues, to cheap drawings, to hip-hop CDs.

"You need to focus on one or two products," she told the woman. "This is a bookstore, but you have fewer books than candles and soaps. You can sell other things, but make the books front and center and put some order in this place. Mrs. Rimes, we've been over this a dozen times already, and you haven't made one of the changes I suggested. I don't see the point in continuing this. It's a waste of your money and my time."

"Maybe if you could send somebody here to get me started, I could keep it up. I don't have the kind of help that can do that, and I'm too busy doing other things. Please don't give up on me. This is all I know to do, and I just can't watch it go down."

"All right, I'll see what I can do, but you can begin by putting these books on the shelves." She pointed to the unopened boxes and the books scattered on the tables and shelves in the back room. "I'll call you in about ten days."

As she drove to the restaurant for lunch, she imagined that Louvenia Rimes's home resembled a pigsty, for she had never seen such disorder in a store.

"How'd it go?" her secretary asked when Ruby returned to her office.

She related her experiences that morning and added, "Both of those stores should be out of business by now. Only the Lord knows what's keeping them going."

"LeRoy's bored. Why don't you tell him what to do and let her pay him to do it?"

"The idea has merit. I'll look into it right away. Thanks." As she considered Julia's suggestion, which duplicated Louvenia Rimes's idea, possibilities for the growth of Everyday Opportunities, Inc., formed in her mind. The company had needed an edge, something extra, that one element that could spell success every time. She pushed the intercom. "Julia, would you please ask LeRoy to come to my office."

"I understand that you're bored, and that you'd like a more demanding assignment," she said to LeRoy a few minutes later. Young and enthusiastic LeRoy Murchison had been with the firm about a year.

He sat forward, almost on the edge of the chair and looked her in the eye. "Yes, ma'am. I didn't get a university degree in order to fish out small business from a telephone book. It's getting to me."

"Let that be the last time you suffer in silence. This job will not be boring." She told him about Louvenia's shop and her efforts to change it into a more profitable business. She handed him her analysis and list of recommendations. "Do you think you could implement these changes in two weeks?"

He nodded slowly and continued to read. "Suppose I see something here that should be altered. "

"Then you and I will have a conference. Convince me, and you can alter it. If you do a good job of it, that will be your new assignment. But, Leroy, it will mean learning how different kinds of businesses function. For the first year, you'll practically be back in school."

"Do I get a promotion?"

"And a reclassification…as soon as you finish this job. If you have problems, talk to me. I need to understand your experiences as you try to implement the changes I'm proposing."

"Sure thing. I'm going to enjoy this. Already, I feel like a different man. When do I start?"

"Tomorrow. Just remember to keep a record of your expenses."

After phoning Louvenia Rimes and getting her enthusiastic agreement, she set about restructuring her company. Who else among her workers was underemployed?

She went to the secretary's office and sat down, causing Julia to raise her eyebrows. "This afternoon, I want to see every employee in this company for fifteen minutes. I've already spoken with LeRoy. I'll speak with you last."

By the end of the working day, she knew where her company was going and how it would get there. She reached for the phone to call Luther and rejoice with him, remembered that they were on the outs, and, thinking that he probably wouldn't enjoy speaking with her, she replaced the receiver in its cradle.

If she needed something to show her how much a part of her life Luther had been and how much she'd relied on his friendship, this was it. She knew she had to find a way to get them back together, but he'd made it seem so…final. Just a polite 'Good night,' nothing more.

When she encountered LeRoy in the corridor the next morning, she almost failed to recognize him. After she passed him without speaking, she whirled around. "LeRoy?"

He walked back to her. "Good morning. I'm about to leave. I was on my way to your office."

The jeans, T-shirt, sweater and running shoes had been replaced with a smart brown business suit, beige shirt and green and beige striped tie. She looked down at his highly polished brown shoes, and said, "I'll have some business cards printed for you today."

His grin told her that he understood all that she didn't say. "You won't regret trusting me with this, Ms. Lockhart. I don't ever let myself down."

That was as much of a promise as she would need from anybody, and she told him as much. "Remember, I'll be here to help if you need me."

"Yes, ma'am. I'll call you tomorrow, and let you know how it's going."

She got busy, satisfied that giving LeRoy that assignment was the best move she'd made since she and Marva went into business. Everyday Opportunities, Inc., had become a complete service, she thought, with no small amount of pride.

Now, if my personal life were only going as well!

Luther squatted down beside the wall in his Dearborn showroom, and wiped away the paint from the carpet. His customers had reacted favorably to the changes in his Morningside showroom, and he meant to duplicate them in his other two stores. He unhooked his cell phone and held his breath for a moment before answering. It wouldn't be Ruby, because she could be as stubborn as he. He'd already decided that any future exchanges with Ruby would be at her instigation. However, he knew his weakness for her and that, if she needed him, he'd be there for her.

"Biggens. How may I help you?"

"Do you have a minute, Luther?" At the sound of his father's voice, he took a seat and relaxed.

"How are you, Dad? And how's Mom?"

"We're both fine. I want us to get together with Charles before this foolishness of his goes any further. I don't want my family's affairs publicized in court. It's ridiculous what he's doing. Can you come over around six tonight?"

"Yes, sir. I have a few things to say to Charles, and this will be as good a time as any."

"I hope you'll try to be gentle about it. See you this evening."

He hung up and called Maggie. "I have to go out to my parents' home this evening, and you may imagine that my mother won't let me leave without eating dinner. If you don't want to brave the cold, read something till I get there, and I'll drive you home."

"I do appreciate that, Mr. B. By the time I got here this morning, I felt as if I'd turned to ice. Give my regards to your folks."

He finished painting and looked around the showroom, hoping for a simple idea that would brighten up the place. It was just the thing that Ruby— No, he was not going to use that as an excuse to call her. Until she showed him that she took pride in their real relationship, showed him that he was more to her than a human heater, he was not going to risk any more of their sizzling scenes.

A grin danced around his mouth. With Ruby, what you saw was definitely not what you got. That sedate lady became a ball of fire whenever he got his hands on her. "Doesn't matter," he said aloud. "I need more than a tease or an hour of secret passion once in a while." A glance at his watch told him that, if he wanted to get to his parents home by six o'clock, he'd better hurry. He left the closing of the business to his assistant and headed for his parents' home.

"You're as beautiful as ever, Mom," he said when she met him at the door and hugged him.

"I don't know how much truth there is to that," she said, "but you know I love to hear it."

He hugged his father and his brother Robert and sat down. "Where's Charles?" he asked no one in particular.

"There you are," Charles said, as he entered the room carrying an armful of firewood. "I was hoping you'd chicken out."

"Let's make this short," Jack said. "Charles, your mother, sister, Robert and I will appear as witnesses for Luther in this stupid court case you insist on bringing up. You have no additional rights to those dealerships, because you voted to sell and you accepted your share of the amount to which we agreed."

"I was pressured to do it."

Jack leaned forward. "In other words, you've spent

the money foolishly, and you no longer have an income from the dealerships, so you're making this underhanded attempt to squeeze more money out of Luther. Nobody in this family pressured you."

Luther knew that his father's words were not affecting Charles, for his brother appeared not to listen. "I think I should warn you," Luther told Charles, "that the minute that judge bangs the gavel for the start of the trial, your college tuition dries up, and you'll have to leave school and go to work."

Charles nearly jumped out of his chair. "What do you mean? What's he talking about, Dad?"

Luther nearly laughed at the expression of satisfaction on his father's face. "He means that he will not continue to send you to the university if a legal indictment is the thanks he gets."

"But he doesn't—"

"He has paid every cent of your tuition as well as your room and board. You're so used to accepting largesse that you don't bother to ask where it comes from. Your brother deserves better from you, and you will not sue any member of this family in a court of law."

Charles looked from one to the other. "Don't look at me," his brother Robert said. "Dad is the reason why I haven't already knocked you down a few times myself."

Charles walked over to the fireplace, stared down at the flames and then stood with his back to them. "Everybody's on my case. Even Ruby called and blasted me. All right. I'll drop it."

Amidst the sighs of relief, Irma Biggens stood. "I guess I can put supper on the table now."

"I'm going out and bringing in some more wood," Charles said. "Mom likes to have a fire in the fireplace."

"Yeah," Robert said. "Mom is a dyed-in-the-wool romantic. She's the only woman I know who can't do without candles and flowers."

"Soft women are a joy to be around," Jack said. "That kind of woman can tame a man without trying."

"She's also the kind you fall in love with," Luther said.

"Yeah," Robert said with a half laugh. "There ought to be some kind of shield or something to prevent that, or at least to keep you from falling hard."

"Wishful thinking," Jack said, seemingly amused. "There is no cure for love. When it hits you, make up your mind to live with it."

"Tell me about it," Luther murmured to himself, but his father and his brother stared at him.

"Who is she?" they asked in unison.

"Dinner must be ready by now," Luther said, knowing they wouldn't question him further. He pretended not to notice how they cast furtive glances at him as they ate, and he hoped his mother didn't notice it, because she would demand to know why they did it.

He rejoiced in not having to oppose his brother in court, but he was glad to get away from his family's watchful and knowing eyes.

At home, he parked in front of the house, cut the motor and went inside. "Ready to go?" he asked Maggie when she came into the hallway.

"I know you ate at your mama's table, but I made some apple strudels, and I'm going to warm a couple and make a pot of fresh coffee, so you can have yours right now," she said. "It must be awfully cold out there."

It was, but he'd been in his warm car and hadn't felt it. He realized that she needed to look after him and didn't want anyone else to do it, including his mother. He laughed at the thought. If a man still needed a mother at the age of thirty-five, he could probably use a psychiatrist, too.

"You have to stop spoiling me, Maggie. I'm getting used to it."

"Oh, shucks," she said. "Everybody needs a little spoiling. And since I don't see any nice girls spoiling you…" She let it hang, as if he'd get her meaning without further elaboration.

She made places for them at the kitchen table, and they sat down to eat. She said grace at the same time as he put a forkful of strudel in his mouth, and she patted his hand. "All food should be blessed."

He didn't say, "Yes, mother," because he swallowed the words just before they slipped off his tongue.

"When are you going to tell me to fix one of my first-class gourmet dinners for you and a nice lady?" she asked.

There was no point in discouraging her meddling because she considered it her right. "I had hoped to bring her to meet you by now, but things aren't going too well with us."

She stopped chewing and placed her fork on her plate. "What's the matter? If she didn't lie, didn't do something disgraceful and didn't cheat on you, make up with her."

He leaned back in his chair and gave her his full attention. "Let me get this straight. Are you saying those are the only reasons for breaking up a relationship?"

"Don't put words in my mouth, Mr. B. I'm suggesting that anything else may be a misunderstanding. What do you think the problem is?"

"I need for her to accept me as I am, plastic prosthesis and all."

"Hmm. Does she love you?"

"I believe she does."

"Hmm. And she responds to you all right?"

"Oh, yes. That, she does. Absolutely!"

She drained her coffee cup, cleared the table and sat back down. "The problem is in your head."

"No it isn't. She doesn't want members of her family to know we have a relationship."

"Then you're not telling me everything. Have you known her long?"

"Since she was three and I was nine, and I've been in love with her ever since I was nineteen years old, but I knew I had to wait for her to grow up. Our relationship changed from friends to lovers about a month ago."

Maggie rubbed her chin as if deep in thought. After a while she said, "She probably always thought of you as her big brother, and now she's sensitive about the way she realizes she feels about you. If I were you, I'd expose her every chance I got. If you're sure you want her, you don't have a thing to lose by letting people know you're more to each other than buddies."

"I did that, and she acted out."

"Do it some more. She's not ashamed of you. No sane woman could be."

Maybe she was right, but he didn't plan to test it, at least not until Ruby made the right overtures to him. *But what if she's waiting for you to reach out to her?* his conscience needled. And wasn't he the one who'd said a curt good-night and hung up?

After accompanying Maggie to her door, he stood there until she opened it. "Thanks for the strudel and for your advice and confidence," he said. "It meant a lot to me."

"You're a blessing to me, Mr. B," she said, and he'd swear that her lips quivered.

Instead of going back home after dropping Maggie off, Luther headed for the officers' club. Maybe he could borrow a guitar and jam awhile with some of the men. It would beat thinking about his feelings for Ruby.

When he walked into the club, he realized that he should bring Ruby there. Perhaps then she would understand that to be disabled didn't prevent a man from enjoying a fruitful life.

"Seen Roger lately?" a marine asked Luther. "I hear he's in the big time, thanks to you. Somebody said he got a recording contract. Did he?"

Luther nodded. "That's what I heard. He's accompanying one of my friends, too."

"Have a seat, man," someone said. "Borrow Gus's guitar and let's jam a little." Luther looked at Gus, who told him, "I've been entertaining these guys all evening. You're welcome to use it."

Like leaves dropping from trees in late autumn, stress and cares fell away from him while his fingers danced over those guitar strings. Jazz had a way of giving him that freedom, lightening his spirit and blowing him away from things worldly. At last, the pianist struck the first cords of "Back Home in Indiana," and he closed his eyes and let the music enthrall him.

"You're blessed to be able to play like that," a retired admiral said. He hadn't realized that the old man stood a few feet away, watching while the group played.

"I'm blessed. Period. And I'm more aware of it here than anywhere."

"I know what you mean," the man said, and as he limped away, Luther could see that he wore a prosthesis on each leg. Yes, he thought. Not only Ruby, but a lot of people ought to visit this club.

He phoned her the next morning as he drove to

work, and the note of surprise in her voice was as he had expected.

"Hi," she said, after he identified himself.

"Hi. I was calling because I'd like you to go with me to the officers' club tonight. Will you?"

"Uh...sure. What time and what should I wear?"

"About eight o'clock, and street clothes will be fine. Thanks for agreeing to go with me."

"How've you been?"

He refused to engage in some banal small talk with a woman who meant to him what she did. "There's nothing new. We can talk this evening. See you then?"

"Okay. See you later."

He hung up, knowing he'd put her off. He'd have to find a way to make up for it without bringing their relationship to a head prematurely.

Chapter 10

Ruby walked rather than ran down the stairs when the bell rang at eight o'clock, although that action brought a laugh from her. Who was she fooling?

She opened the door, gazed up at his beloved face and said, "Hi. Want to come in? It's cold out there. I'll get my coat." She added the last so that he wouldn't suspect her of wanting to drag him into a clinch.

"Hi. We can leave as soon as you're ready."

She took her coat from the closet in the foyer and, instead of handing it to him as she would normally have done, she proceeded to put it on.

He stepped toward her and took it. "Let me help you with that."

Even with the cold air clinging to him, his nearness warmed her, and his aura enticed her to lean back into the comfort of his arms. She resisted the temptation, trying though it was, and moved away. She could feel his gaze upon her as she buttoned and belted her coat, but she willed herself not to look into his face.

"Don't you have something to put on your head?" he asked.

Although she hadn't planned to wear a hat, she recognized the question as a suggestion that sprang from his caring. "Excuse me a minute." She went up to her room and put on a red velvet beret. "I'm ready," she said when she came back.

He stood there looking down at her for what seemed to her like hours, and she shifted her weight from one foot to the other. Then she began to rub her arms. The movement of his Adam's apple was the only evidence he gave that he was as disconcerted as she. Finally, he took a deep breath and exhaled, turned to the door and opened it.

Mad enough to chew him out—mad because he'd fought himself and won while she watched—she locked the door and walked down the steps in front of him. She'd have given anything if she could have opened the car door and seated herself before he reached the car, but he'd locked it. As if he read her mind, he joined her where she stood at the front passenger's door, opened it and, with a firm hand, assisted her into the car. The devil had gotten into him, she figured, because he leaned in and fastened her seat belt, bringing his mouth as close to hers as it could get without touching and never looking at her.

"Have you ever seen a snapping turtle?" she asked him after he seated himself.

"I don't believe I have. Why?"

"If I'd been one a second ago, you'd be missing part of your lip."

His joyous laugh told her that his mood wasn't as dark as his manner. "Heavens, if you're feeling that evil, I'd better be careful. It wouldn't do my reputation one bit of good to have it reported that I checked into the hospital with half of a mouth due to a woman's bite." He laughed aloud. "I hope your bark is worse than your bite."

She wanted to ask him about his good mood and whether anything special had happened to make him happy. But with neither their camaraderie as friends nor their tenderness and passion as lovers governing their behavior, she didn't know how to react. As if he sensed her dilemma, he turned on the radio, and though "Cotton Eyed Joe" wasn't to her taste, it beat the silence that had become awkward, at least for her.

"Have you ever been in the officers' club?" he asked as he drove into the garage beneath it. When told that she hadn't, he replied, "You'll probably be surprised. I came here for the first time only recently, and I can't tell you the difference it's made in my life. I'm not sure I could have pulled you out of that pool if I hadn't spent some time here."

"What's different about it?"

He punched the elevator call button. "You'll see."

After he signed in, they checked their coats at the cloak room and, to her surprise, he took her hand and walked with her into a large room that was attractively decorated with masculine furnishings, Old Glory and the flags of the different armed services. Approximately thirty men lounged there talking, playing cards or sitting quietly alone.

"I want you to meet my friends," Luther said as they reached the old admiral who was reclining in an overstuffed leather chair eating chocolates from a box lined with gold foil.

The admiral stood as they approached. "Admiral Conner, this is Ruby Lockhart." The man extended his hand. "I'm delighted to meet you, Ms. Lockhart. We don't see enough beautiful women in this place. Good for you, Biggens." She hesitated when he introduced her to a man who extended the metal prosthesis that served as his right hand, but quickly recovered, smiled and shook the man's hand.

Luther stopped at a group that lounged near a piano, smiled and said, "Fellows, I want you to meet Ruby Lockhart." Some stood, and some didn't. So she took the initiative and walked to each one to shake hands.

"Are you going to play tonight?"

She looked around and saw the admiral leaning against the grand piano. He walked to her with an obvious limp. "See if you can get him to play," the admiral said. "I love to hear that guitar."

"I didn't think to bring it," Luther said. But the words had barely escaped his lips when a man said, "You may borrow mine, Commander."

Luther dragged a chair close to the group, while a man hobbled to the piano with the aid of crutches, nodded to the group and said, "Lover Come Back to Me." The old admiral limped to her and said, "Pull up a chair and sit down. I'd do it for you if I could."

Unable to resist, she said, "What...what's your handicap?"

"I've got two borrowed legs, and I'm damned lucky to have them. Most of the time, I don't think about 'em, because I don't even use a cane, but I can't pull that big chair over here for you, and that makes me sad."

"I'll pull one over for each of us," she told him.

"Thank you, my dear, and if you don't mind, would you please bring me that box of candy on the table over there. We can have some while we listen to these fellows play. They're good, you know."

She pulled the chairs forward and got the chocolates for the admiral, whose age she estimated to be close to ninety. The pianist slid his fingers across the keys in a fast riff, and the group joined him in a rendition of "Lover Come Back to Me" that, to her estimation, equaled any that she'd heard. And she considered herself a good judge, inasmuch as she had at least six recordings of the piece. As they played, she shook her head. She hadn't dreamed that Luther was so talented, and that he played so well and with such abandon.

He's in his element, she thought to herself, but the thought troubled her. He belonged among these men. He was at home among them, and she needed to know whether to attribute that to their common experience as servicemen or to their being disabled.

As he drove her home, she asked him, "Is that a club for disabled servicemen only?"

His head snapped around at the question, but he immediately turned his attention to the business of driving. "No. It's an officers' club. Some of the officers hang out in the second basement, down in the gym and around the pool, and some were probably upstairs reading or writing, maybe asleep. No card playing, music or loud noise is allowed up there. Most of the men who frequent the second floor are disabled, and they tend to give each other moral support."

"They were so cheerful. If I had the handicap of some of those men, trust me I wouldn't be smiling. One guy was hurrying home to his wife. He went to the club to let his buddies know he got married last weekend. Another has married and fathered a child since he lost his right hand and a part of his arm. Luther, I am never going to complain again about anything. Imagine a man who lost both legs and can't wear a prosthesis starting an Internet business and making a good living for himself and his four children."

"I told you that coming here these past few weeks has changed my outlook on life. I no longer consider myself disabled, Ruby. Not when I see how those men go about life as if they didn't have a handicap, accepting themselves as they are, marrying, raising families and working. I feel like genuflecting in their presence."

She wanted to ask why he had wanted her to see those men, to meet them and talk with them. If she were his fiancée, she'd know his motive; those men were as brothers to him, indeed, several had served under his command. But she wasn't engaged to him, and didn't see a likelihood that she would be. *I won't ask him. If I'm patient, eventually I'll know.*

"By the way," he said during a lull in their conversation. "Charles dropped the suit against me. We had a family conference and we spanked Charles thoroughly. He said you called and blasted him. Thanks for that."

"It's the least I can do, after everything you've done for me."

Luther parked in front of Ruby's house, got out, walked around the car and let a half smile float across his face when he saw her getting out of the car.

He walked with her to the front door and waited while she unlocked it. She stepped inside and looked at him.

"It's been an interesting evening, Luther. I know I'm supposed to take something from it, and I'll eventually figure out what that is. Good night."

"Thanks for coming with me tonight. I'll be in touch," he said. He looked at her for a long time, almost as if memorizing her features, before he said, "Good-night."

Ruby shut the door and went upstairs, muttering, "If he wants to punish himself, he's welcome. But he'd better not wait too long to get over whatever's holding him back." She'd just taken off her suit when the phone rang. A glance at her watch told her that it was a quarter past ten, so the caller had to be one of her sisters. "Hello."

"Hi, sis," Amber said. "Can you come out next weekend? Some of our neighbors are giving a garden party on Saturday to introduce me to the local women. These people drink from dusk till dawn, and we're not into that. Can you come?"

Ruby laughed. "Now that I'm the only one of us who's single, I can be called upon at the last minute to dash across the country, eh? Okay. I'll see you Friday night."

She found herself looking forward to it, despite all the work at the office.

On Friday she went to work with her suitcase in tow, worked until eleven o'clock, took a taxi to the airport and boarded the plane at twenty minutes after two.

"I'm a fortunate man to have such a beautiful seatmate," a deep, masculine voice beside her said. She looked up to see a tall, good-looking brother putting his carry-on luggage in the overhead bin.

I am definitely not going to spend five hours talking trash with this brother, she said to herself.

She looked over as he sat down, saw the ring on the third finger of his left hand and decided to put him in his place. "I'm going to sleep as soon as this plane takes off. I don't like flying out west, and I hate making small talk. Have a pleasant trip."

The man's head turned very slowly in her direction, and he saw only as much of her as his peripheral vision would allow. He held that pose until evidently satisfied that he had communicated his distaste for her and then crossed his knees, opened his paper and began to read as if *he* had dismissed *her*. She'd always thought it bad manners to snicker, but in this case it was unavoidable.

Nearly three hours into the flight, the plane encountered turbulence, and the ride became bumpy. Ruby's first thought was of Luther and how he would feel if the plane didn't land safely. She told herself that a man couldn't make love to a woman as he did to her if he didn't love her. So what was wrong with them? Why couldn't they admit to loving each other? He was holding something against her, and she'd give anything to know what it was.

At the moment, Luther was examining his reasons for cooling things between Ruby and him. They seemed to drift farther apart, and he didn't want that. He got a pad and pencil from the desk in his den, and listed what he liked about Ruby. On the other side of the page, he listed the things about her that displeased him. Reading to himself later, he shook his head in amazement. He had written in the first column: I love her face, smile, height, walk, figure; the shape of her breasts and the way they taste; her voice, laugh; her hands and the way they feel on my body; her intelligence, wit, sharp mind, independence; the way she responds to me; the way she made love to me; her cheesecake, honesty, loyalty.

What didn't he like about her? He listed two points: She doesn't seem proud to be with me the way I am of her, and I don't think she's ready to settle for a man with my disability.

He walked over to the window and stared out at the snowflakes as they hit the window pane and died there. The things he didn't like about her were things he couldn't prove. He only sensed them, and he could be wrong. They needed to sit together in a moment of truth and reach an understanding. He loved her, and he believed she loved him. Still, their relationship had gone nowhere.

He had never told anyone how he felt about Ruby, not even her. Maybe the two of them were guilty of plural ignorance. After thinking a long while about the possible consequences, he phoned his father.

"Hi, Dad. Where's Mom?"

"She's at her sewing circle. You need to talk with her?"

"No. I want to talk with you privately."

After a lengthy pause, Jack Biggens said, "I'm here for you, son. What is it?"

"I wouldn't tell you this, but I just can't get a handle on it, and it's getting worse."

"Start at the beginning."

"Ruby and I have always been pals, but I've been in love with her since I was nineteen. I waited for her to grow up, and I figured that when I graduated from the academy, I'd go after her. But she'd gotten involved with someone, and that left her bruised, so to speak."

"Go on."

"You're not surprised?"

"Not a bit. Go on."

"I escorted her to Opal and D'marcus's wedding reception, and later, something happened between us. She swears she was cold sober, and that she did what she always wanted to do. I only have to touch her, and she goes up in flames. But I get the impression that she's ashamed of a relationship with me, at least where her family is concerned. I kissed her in front of Amber and she was annoyed. I am also uncertain as to whether this prosthesis repulses her. Right now, we're barely speaking. A couple of nights ago, I took her to the officers' club and let her see disabled servicemen leading useful lives."

"What was her reaction to that?"

"I don't know. She told me she knew she was supposed to learn something from it, and that she'd figure it out."

"I see. Does she know you love her?"

"She may have guessed, but I haven't told her."

"And she hasn't told you how she feels. Right?"

"Right."

"It doesn't take an Einstein to figure this out, son.

Stop playing it safe. With women, you have to take a chance. They see themselves as vulnerable in regard to men, and they are. Tell her how you feel. When she knows that you love her, she'll be ready to tell the whole world. A woman like Ruby doesn't respond to a man as you say she responds to you unless she loves the man."

"And suppose she really can't stand this artificial limb? Then what?"

"I don't lay much store by that, son. I have a feeling that's in your head. Has she ever seen it in broad daylight? I mean is she aware that you can hardly distinguish that thing from your flesh unless you touch it?

"I want you to open your mind, sit her down in a quiet place, preferably your home, and talk with her. Choose a time when there isn't a chance that you'll be interrupted and when you have plenty of time. Nothing this important should be allowed to slide along unattended. Take matters in hand."

"Thanks. Why aren't you surprised?"

"Because her father and I always said that nothing would separate the two of you, that you loved each other and would eventually realize it."

"You're kidding."

"When did I ever joke about something this serious?"

"I'd as soon you didn't share this with Mom yet. She'd be calling Ruby and inviting her for every occasion she can think of."

"I won't. You said it was private, and I'll treat it that way."

He hung up, rubbed the back of his neck, and the dampness on his hand let him know that he'd been perspiring. Never before had he gone to his father with anything so personal; not even when he faced wearing a prosthesis for the remainder of his life had he shared his pain and trepidation with anyone. He'd smiled as if it didn't matter as long as he could walk upright without a crutch of any kind, and he discouraged sympathy as being unwarranted. Yet, the hurt went deep each night when he pulled it off and each morning when he put it on.

He had avoided meaningful attachments to women because he couldn't bring himself to share that part of his life. But after that fateful night when, at last, he'd held Ruby in his arms and buried himself in her body, the choice was no longer his. He had loved her, but from that moment on, he also needed her.

"I can't go on this way, having her and not having her. I'm going for it, and if I lose, I lose." He opened his bedroom window and let the frigid air shock him out of his dark mood. "It may take a while, but I'll teach her to accept me as I am."

Ruby sat on the deck of Paul and Amber's modern home sipping a piña colada as the cool evening breeze kissed her face. She found the salty air refreshing and began to appreciate Amber's affection for life near the Pacific Ocean.

"It's more than the weather here," Amber said. "We don't live on top of each other as people do in big cities. I love the space and the privacy and, with this low crime rate, I think it's a good place to raise a family." She paused. "I'd better check on Joachim."

Alone with Paul, Ruby asked him, "Uh…Paul, I need to ask you something in confidence."

"Sure. What is it?"

"It's about Luther and me." She scrutinized his face for a reaction, saw none and continued. "We… uh…got together the night of Opal and D'marcus's wedding reception. It was so sudden, and I precipitated it. Afterward, I was ashamed because I didn't know what he thought of me. Next time I saw him, he froze me out. Then, he rescued me from that pool, and we became pretty tight, but after that night he, you and Amber were at my place, everything just went to pot."

"Of course, there's a lot more to it than that, Ruby," Paul said. "I saw Luther kiss you that night at the reception, and yes, you invited it. I saw that, too. Luther is not a frivolous man. Far from it. And you're not the person I knew two months earlier. You've bloomed into a beautiful and appealing woman, so whatever happened between you two was a good thing. Does he know you love him?"

She shook her head. "I don't know how he feels about me, so I've never told him."

"I see. Why were you annoyed when he kissed you as we were about to leave your house?"

"He was angry with me."

"Angry because you didn't want Amber and me to know what was going on? We already knew, Ruby. You can't keep a thing like that a secret unless you avoid the company of other people. Let me tell you something. A man has to know that his woman is proud of him admires him, and wants the whole world to know that he's her man. A man's ego is in his woman, his kids and his work. I've known Luther as my commander, my friend, and I've seen him under fire, risking his life for others. There isn't a finer human being. Amber has told me what you sacrificed for her and her sisters. I think you and Luther are well suited. Handle it with care."

She wanted to ask him how to bridge the gap between them, but Amber floated back to the deck. "This is the perfect evening for a cookout, honey," she said to Paul. "Why don't I make some hamburgers and you grill 'em out here. I have some big, Spanish onions, mushrooms and green peppers. Ruby, stop drinking that highball. We're going to have beer with supper, and I don't want you to get a headache."

Ruby stared at her sister. Since when had Amber become a take-charge woman? If marriage did this for a person… She raised her glass. "Here's to Paul, the magician." Amber stared at her, and Paul bubbled up with laughter.

He filled a glass with beer and raised it. "I'll drink to that, Ruby."

"Let me in on it," Amber said. "I didn't hear anything funny."

Paul draped an arm around Amber's shoulder. "Not

to worry, love. That was Ruby's way of saying you've grown into a mature woman, and I concur."

"In that case, you should be toasting me with champagne. Who ever heard of a beer toast?" Amber asked him.

Can I have that with Luther? Ruby wondered. *Is happiness with the man I love too much to ask for?* She put her drink on the table and turned aside. If only she could talk with him, touch him. Did he have any idea how she hungered for the feel of him inside of her? She looked around and saw that Paul watched her, and she smiled when he gave her the thumbs-up sign.

"Let me see your dress for the party," Amber said.

Ruby rose immediately, anxious to prevent a slide into melancholy, and went up to the guest room. She'd hung the lavender chiffon on the closet door to release the creases.

"It's gorgeous," Amber said. "I'm so glad you're wearing colors these days. I was scared you'd bring something gray or navy. You looked so good in that red dress and later at Paige's engagement weekend because you wore colors. Wear this for him. He'd love you in it."

She hoped Amber noticed that she neither commented nor questioned the identification of "him." As she thought back on it in bed later that night, she remembered Paul's words, "A man has to know his woman is proud of him." What was wrong with her that she couldn't acknowledge to her sisters that she loved

Luther Biggens? Would she do so if she knew he loved her?

I wish I could understand myself. In my work, I know who I am and where I'm headed, but when it comes to this love business, I'm in left field. Where was I all those years when I was supposed to be growing up?

Two evenings later, sitting in Opal's kitchen sucking on a sparerib, Ruby said to her sister, "Now I understand what got into Amber. The garden party was at the home of one of her neighbors, and let me tell you, that sister laid it out. It was a catered affair with tuxedo-clad waiters, a band, caviar, smoked salmon, imported cheeses, lobster and any kind of liquor you cared to stone yourself with. The house was something out of *Better Homes and Gardens*."

"Rich, huh?"

"Either rich or heavily in debt for the rest of their lives. The place was a shrine to conspicuous consumption. What's more, everything looked as if it had never been used. I kept wondering what part of the house she and her husband lived in. But Paul and Amber have a lovely home, too, in a beautiful setting, and our little sister has become completely domesticated. It's wonderful to see."

Opal helped herself to a barbecued sparerib. "That's wonderful. When she and Paul were here for Paige's engagement party, I could see that they're very happy. Now, dear sister, what about you?"

Ruby pitched the bone into the garbage can. "Me?

I'm fine. In a few days, I'll be sole owner of Everyday Opportunities, Inc., and I'm expanding our services. Life is good."

Opal was undeterred. "Seen Luther since you got back?"

Ruby did not want to discuss Luther. "Why would I? I just got back this morning. And since I took the red-eye flight back last night, I need to get home and go to bed." She stood, signaling her intention to leave. "Thanks for those delicious spareribs."

Opal hugged Ruby. "I'm glad you stopped by. When you feel like talking, I'm here."

"You're a peach," Ruby said, dodging the issue. "I'll call you." As she drove home, she vowed not to discuss her relationship with Luther until she had talked with him. It wouldn't be easy, she knew, because it seemed that her family had decided they were more than friends, or at least her sisters wanted them to be. It wouldn't help to talk with them. Paul had given her all the advice she needed.

"I have to be patient," she said to herself, "and I will be."

The next morning at work, she had a call from her lawyer. He and Marva's husband had come to a deal for the consulting firm. "I think it's a good offer. You reimburse your partner for all of her capital investment and for the cost of her labor before the company earned money. After the company began earning, she was compensated as a part of the cost of doing business. Nonetheless, you have to buy her out, and we've estimated that as one half of the company's net worth, or half of the company's current bank account minus bills due. I think it's fair."

She had expected much worse, but didn't tell him. "All right. Can I pay it monthly?"

"Wright suggested payment within six months. Can you manage that?"

"I think so, but I'll have to check with my accountant. I'll get back to you tomorrow morning. Thanks for a good job."

After she called her accountant, she left her office and drove to Louvenia's Books 'N Things. She wasn't checking on LeRoy, but she needed to see precisely the effect of her plan for that store before she offered similar suggestions to another client.

When she pulled up in front of the shop Ruby observed the sparkling windows and inviting display. Inside, the store appeared organized and inviting.

"This is wonderful," she said to LeRoy. "And so are you." LeRoy had surpassed her expectations. Even in her plan for the store, she had not envisaged such a remarkable outcome.

Satisfied that her company could become the best of its kind in the region, she went on to her next appointment. But she didn't have that sense of euphoria that she should have had after seeing those striking results of her company's work, because she didn't have Luther to share it with.

I'm going to get over it, dammit. My life is not

*going to revolve around a man who can go for days
without saying a word to me.*

Who was she fooling?

Chapter 11

"I tell you, Pearl, it's no use. I couldn't get a peep out of Ruby. As soon as I mentioned Luther, she folded up and went home. She was always so open, and you could talk to her about anything, no matter how personal." Opal had called to discuss Pearl's upcoming benefit concert at the Lakeview Baptist Church, but as usual the topic switched quickly to Ruby's love life.

"Think about it, Opal. She willingly talked to us about *our* problems and affairs, but when did she ever discuss *hers*? Certainly not with me. She was smitten with that one guy—what's his name—and she got into a blue funk about him and stayed in it for weeks. But whenever you asked her if anything was wrong, she grinned and said, 'Nothing. Why do you ask?' Don't you remember?"

"You're right, and she's doing the same thing now. Pearl, I am not so stupid that I don't know when a man and a woman have something going. You saw how they were after he got her out of that pool."

"I saw how they were the night of your wedding reception, too," Pearl said. "I don't get it. They're so much alike that they should get along beautifully."

"Maybe that's the problem. I never thought Luther was stubborn, but we may not know him as well as we think we do. You know what happens when Ruby finally puts her foot down."

"Sure I do," Pearl said, "but when Cupid gets to work, things change."

The evening of the concert, Ruby sat in an aisle seat in the second row from the stage, fidgeting in turn with her coat, her hair and the concert program. She knew Pearl could sing, but what if the pianist didn't show up. Or maybe her sister would get a sore throat. She just couldn't seem to stop worrying.

When a man took the seat beside her, she turned to him.

"Oh, my goodness! Mr. Biggens! How are you?"

"How are *you?* You look…well, fantastic. It's been a while since I saw you." Luther's father seemed to train his gaze and the focus of his concentration on her, and immediately she thought that the man did not seat himself beside her by accident.

"I didn't see Luther anywhere," he said. "Isn't he coming?"

She looked him straight in the eye and made certain that nothing resembling a smile flashed across her face. "Mr. Biggens, I last saw Luther several days ago, and he didn't mention his future plans." She knew it was a smart aleck answer, and the censure in his eyes told her that he didn't like it.

"I'm sorry, Mr. Biggens. I didn't intend to be rude, but…well, life's a mess right now." Both of his eyebrows shot up, and she'd never been more grateful than when she saw Roger Perkins struggle on two crutches to the piano and sit down.

She was barely aware that Jack Biggens patted her hand in comfort when a hush descended over the crowded auditorium. Roger flexed his fingers and began to coax from that concert grand a medley of tunes by American composers. "That man can really play," she said to Jack.

Roger positioned the microphone so that he could speak to the audience. "As you know, Duke Ellington wrote a lot of spiritual music and presented sacred concerts throughout the world. This is the theme from 'New World A-Coming' by Duke Ellington."

"I didn't know that," she said to Luther's father. "Did you?"

"I knew he wrote sacred music, particularly in his later years," Jack said, "but I hadn't heard this. It's remarkable," he said, speaking above the deafening applause.

"Yes, it is." She looked around the vast auditorium hoping for a glimpse of Luther, but didn't see him. The audience began to applaud again, and she looked toward the stage to see Pearl appear in a bright green evening dress. A few minutes later, her sultry, dulcet tones brought a hush to the room as she sang, "My Lord, What a Morning." Ruby wiped the tears from her cheeks and marveled at the beauty of her sister's voice.

"She has a wonderful gift," Jack said. "What is it? What's wrong, Ruby."

"Nothing. I guess I'm overjoyed. I'm so happy for her."

"Yes, I know," Jack said. "This is the first time you've seen your sister in concert, and it's one of those occasions that you want to share with someone you love. I wish Irma were here, but she has a terrible cold. You get my meaning, don't you?"

Of course she got it, but she wasn't taking any hints, just as she didn't intend to discuss Luther. She looked at Jack, smiled and turned her attention to the concert. Later, she went backstage to her sister's dressing room.

"You were wonderful," she said. "If only our parents could have been here. You're going to be as big a name as Sister Thorpe and Mahalia Jackson." She looked at Opal who stood between D'marcus and Wade and the thought flashed through her mind that her three sisters had the men they loved and wanted and that, if she wasn't careful, she'd have to settle for being sister and auntie. She prepared to leave, kissed her sisters and turned toward the door just as it opened and struck her.

"Hi, all," Luther said. "Pearl, that was a fantastic debut." He swung around. "Say, I'm sorry. I'm— Ruby! Good heavens, did I hit you with that door?"

"Hi, Luther. It's okay. I—I'm fine." But she wasn't, and she could barely avoid holding her right shoulder. She flinched when he grabbed her right arm.

"It isn't all right, and you aren't fine. The door hit your shoulder. Didn't it?"

She looked into eyes filled with compassion, and worked hard at keeping her composure. "I'm all right. Honest." But she knew he wouldn't let it rest, and he didn't.

"I'll walk with you to your car," he said and slung his arm around her waist. "I'll see you all later."

"I'm fine, Luther. You needn't worry. I'm all right."

"That may be, but I want to be sure you aren't too sore to drive. The truth is, we probably ought to stop by the emergency room and make sure it isn't dislocated."

"You're not serious," she said. "I don't need to go to a hospital."

"Does it hurt still?" he asked, and she wanted to lean into him and soak up his tenderness, but she was tired of letting him fling her up on a cloud only to dangle there indefinitely.

"Thanks," she said, "But it will be all right." His arm tightened about her, and she didn't know whether to respond to the Luther who had always looked after his little buddy or the man who drove her wild in bed.

He walked with her out into the bracing winter night, a night in which the still air heralded the coming of snow. He didn't hold her and she had an urge to thank him for that. "I'm parked right around the corner," she said. "You really don't have to go with me."

He stopped walking, and when he gazed down at her, she knew he had taken exception either to what she said or the way in which she said it. His next words confirmed the accuracy of her thoughts.

"I wanted to walk with you to see you safely to your car, but I'd be the last man to impose myself on a woman." He wheeled around, evidently forgetting his prosthesis, for he nearly tripped.

"I didn't say that. Luther, for goodness' sake."

She hadn't seen him walk that fast since before he had sustained that terrible wound in Yemen. "Luther, please wait! Don't..." He didn't stop, so she didn't finish the sentence, didn't beg him not to widen the gap between them. She took a few steps behind him, turned and headed to her car. "I'm sure I've made a lot of mistakes with Luther, but chasing him was not and will not be one of them," she said to herself, taking a meager measure of satisfaction where she could find it.

She sat in the car for a time before turning on the ignition and moving slowly away from the curb. "If this thing doesn't come to a head soon, I don't know how I'll be able to stand it. I miss my friend, and I want my lover."

* * *

"That was pretty quick." At the sound of his father's voice, Luther stopped in the act of opening the door of the lodge where he expected to rejoin Ruby's sisters and their husbands.

"Yeah. I looked around for you when I got here. Where were you sitting?"

"I had a seat in the second row beside Ruby."

"It's a good thing I didn't find you. She didn't want me to walk with her to her car." He related the incident in which the door had hit her shoulder. "I wanted to be sure she could drive safely."

His father looked into the distance. "And you took her word for it? You believed she didn't want you to walk with her to her car?"

"Wouldn't you have?"

"Definitely not. When your mother says to me, 'That's all right, hon, I can do it,' I use my own judgment. She's an independent woman who doesn't like seeming a burden to me."

Luther threw up his hands. "After almost forty years? How the devil are you supposed to have a relationship with women if they don't tell you the truth?"

He couldn't see what his father found amusing enough to laugh about. "They don't lie, son; they expect you to divine the reality of the situation. You'll see tears streaming down their faces, and they'll tell you they aren't crying. Go figure."

Suddenly, he remembered Ruby sitting on a high stool in Pearl's kitchen swinging her long legs and telling him that she went to bed with him because she wanted to and had always wanted to.

He shook his head, thoroughly perplexed. "And sometimes they tell you a truth that's so stunning you don't believe it?"

"Yep," Jack said. "If a man tells you he understands his woman completely, you're listening to a liar. Still, if you're willing to give a hundred percent to a relationship, you'll come out ahead, because it won't be long before you know whether she, too, is willing to give full measure."

Jack took Luther's arm. "I'm parked right down the street here. You know, I don't think Ruby's one bit happy. When Pearl was singing 'My Lord What a Morning,' Ruby cried, and she was not smiling through those tears."

"Don't tell me that, Dad."

"It won't hurt you to hear it." They stopped at Jack's car. "Come see your mother first chance you get."

"You always tell me she wants to see me or that I should come see her, but you never include yourself. Why?"

"Twenty years from now, I'll be old enough to lean on my son. Right now, I'm not. Good seeing you, son."

Luther walked on to his own car, thinking how lucky he was to have Jack and Irma Biggens as his parents.

As he drove home, he pondered his father's words. Had he dropped the ball by walking away from Ruby earlier? She'd called him, but he was too annoyed to turn back. He had listened with his ears and not with his heart.

He drove up to his elegant, modern house where not a light shone, and, in its ghostly loneliness, it stood sadly dark and silent in the moonlight. His gaze took in the sleeping trees that made his environment so much friendlier from spring to early autumn when they hung heavy with green leaves, but which now, in their winter nakedness, brought a dreariness to his life.

"If I'm in the dumps, it's nobody's fault but mine," he said aloud, restarted the car and drove into the garage. He entered the house through the kitchen and, as usual, he saw cookies on the kitchen table and a note that led him to the refrigerator and glass of milk that Maggie had covered with plastic wrap. He had told Maggie that she shouldn't spoil him, but he enjoyed it, particularly on this evening when her thoughtfulness helped to dispel his loneliness.

He enjoyed the homemade oatmeal-raisin cookies, drank the milk and made his way up the stairs. A glance at the telephone in his bedroom and the sight of the red light flashing weakened his knees. He checked his messages and sat down, his heart thumping loudly, and his fingers shaking so badly that he could hardly dial the phone number.

"Hello, Ruby. This is Luther," he said when she answered. "You called me." He made it a flat statement not a question, and he didn't begin with small talk. He'd had more than enough of their shadow-boxing with his life. "Talk to me, Ruby."

"I called you because I don't want you to feel that you impose yourself on me. That isn't possible, Luther."

"Why didn't you want me to see you to your car? There's no way that door could have avoided hurting you. Furthermore, unless you've taken a strong pain-killer, your shoulder hurts right this minute."

"Yes, it hurts, but not too badly. It isn't that I didn't want you to walk with me. I did want you to. I didn't want you to walk that far with me and then walk all the way back to your car."

He leaned forward and rested his elbows on his thighs. Was this the time for brutal honesty? And if he voiced his thoughts, what would it net him? He decided not to risk it. Instead, he said, "That may be true, but it isn't the whole truth."

Her silence lasted so long that he wondered if she'd put the phone down and gone away. "Are you still there?"

"I'm here. Luther, I...I can't take any more of these clinches we get into. They leave me miserable."

He wasn't sure how he should take that. "Do you want us to be casual friends, to see each other only by chance encounter?"

"I need some consistency. I'll be an emotional wreck if this continues."

"Now, look here, Ruby. I don't want this call to end with us fighting, but you check that word, *consistency*, in the dictionary. You'll kiss the hell out of me when we're alone, but you didn't want your sister to hear me call you sweetheart. And tonight, you didn't want your family to see us leave together. If you think I'm some milquetoast that you can stash away in your proverbial closet and bring me out to play with when it suits you, you can forget it, baby."

"You…Luther, you're making me angry."

"Funny. As close as you and I have been for the better part of my life, I didn't know you had a temper until after I made love with you. I wonder why that is."

"I always had a temper, but you always catered to me, so why would I have gotten angry with you?"

"Let's not change the subject. What is it going to be, Ruby?"

"I'm surprised that you think I'm the one with the answers. I'm not, and you ought to know that. When you left me tonight, I sat in my car thinking how much I missed you."

"Did you figure out which Luther you missed?"

"I didn't have to figure it out. I know. I think I've always known. Thanks for calling, Luther. I couldn't have slept knowing that I hurt you. Good night."

He needed to think about that long and hard. "Wait a minute. What do you mean by that cryptic remark?"

"You think it's cryptic? You should hear some of *your* comments. Good night, Luther, and thanks for returning my call."

"Good night, love." He didn't know whether she heard it, because the dial tone sounded shortly after he said the word *love*. It could be wishful thinking on his part, maybe, but he felt uplifted. Her softness had always made him conscious of himself as a man, always gave a boost to his self-esteem, and no other woman did that for him. She hadn't previously called him expressly to make amends or to satisfy herself that she hadn't hurt him in some way, and there had been times when she could have. He recalled that she had made other gestures in his interest, including her reprimand of his brother Charles.

He had to decide two things: would he regret it forever if she slipped out of his life, and did he want his children to call her mother? It seemed to him that the answer to both had been settled long ago.

His hope for the future persisted throughout the next thirty-six hours. After days of no sales, thanks to the continuing cold and snowy weather, his dealerships sold a total of five cars that day, and when he got home that night, the odor of chicken and dumplings perfumed the house.

"Have you been talking with my mother?" he asked Maggie. "This house smells the way it does when she cooks chicken and dumplings."

"Maybe that's because we both know how to cook," she said, her face aglow with joy. "Comparing my cooking to your mama's is some compliment, Mr. B. Your mail is on the coffee table. I waxed the table in the foyer, so I can't put the mail there till I polish that table a few times."

"Thanks." He went into the living room, looked at the mail and opened a letter from Amber.

"Dear Luther. We thought you'd like to have a picture of your godchild. We told him to wave at you. Hope all's well. Amber."

After looking at Joachim's picture for a long time, he went to the kitchen and showed it to Maggie. "This is my godchild. He's about ten months old, but he looks as if he's a toddler."

She wiped her hands on her apron, took the picture and examined it. "He isn't so big, it's his facial expression that does it. That's a smart child."

"Heavens, I hope so. I'd hate to have a backward godchild."

"Don't let that thought take up space in your mind, Mr. B. What you want to be thinking about is when you gonna get some kids of your own. A man like you ought to be a father, Mr. B. I know I'm talking out of turn, but I feel toward you like I would my son. Running behind little kids ain't something you want to do when you're fifty."

He looked down at her and a smile floated across his face. "Why didn't I know you'd use this occasion to get on me about getting married?"

She rolled her eyes. "I sure would love to meet that woman. She's got more self-assurance about you than I'd have." Her hands went to her hips and she gazed up at him. "You must work awfully hard at staying single, 'cause you're a looker, and women in this town couldn't be that slow." She threw up her hands. "I do declare."

He grinned, because he thought that would be nicer than outright laughter. "I need to send my godchild a nice gift. What should I get him?"

She seemed to consider the question for a while, and then she said the obvious. "Since you don't know what he has, call his mama and ask her what he needs."

"That's the problem. I'm sure he doesn't *need* anything." When Maggie treated him to a withering look, he let the laughter roll out of him.

"Ask her anyhow," she said, in the tone of one thoroughly exasperated. She cocked her head to the side and gazed up at him. "Mr. B, you meddling with me?"

She grew on him daily. "You could say that. You're easy to tease."

"Supper's ready," she sang out, and it occurred to him then, that he was a central figure in the life of a widowed woman who lived alone, but whose joy it was to do things for others, and that Maggie delighted in making him happy.

"I'll be there as soon as I wash my hands, Maggie. The fantastic odors coming from that kitchen are making me hungry. You know, this place smells just like a home." He headed upstairs to wash his hands, for he knew that if he didn't get out of Maggie's way, she would start on her favorite lecture.

"I made you some apple turnovers," she said after he filled himself with chicken, dumplings and turnip greens. "We can have some of them and coffee for dessert."

He spoke softly, saying the words without weighting them. "You always encourage me to get married, Maggie, but you make things here so comfortable for me, that I could ask you why should I. Your cooking is fantastic, you keep this house in pristine order, you're good company—when you aren't minding my business—and you're even my dinner companion. In addition, you feed us for sixty-three percent less than I spent feeding myself."

She put her fork on the side of her plate, stopped eating and gazed at him, her facial expression more serious than he had ever seen it. His heartbeat accelerated rapidly, for he feared she might say something about leaving him.

"Mr. B, I was married for thirty-six years until my husband passed away. It wasn't perfect by any means, but it let me know that no housekeeper, no matter how good she is, can substitute for a loving relationship with that one woman who is everything to you and who shares your life. I'm certain that nothing on this earth could be like that." She looked down at her plate as if deciding to continue. "Don't you ever think about it?"

He wondered why it was so much easier to discuss his private affairs with Maggie than with his mother, and it occurred to him that it might be that his mother tiptoed around his feelings, and Maggie didn't bother with such niceties.

"Of course I do, Maggie. Every day. I told you about her once. I have a feeling that it will come to a head soon. It has to, because I can't continue with her this way."

She left the table and returned with the apple

turnovers and coffee. "It'll work out, because I'm going to call the Lord's attention to it every time I pray."

"Thanks." He tasted an apple turnover, and looked toward the ceiling. "This is just as good as Ruby's cheesecake, and I didn't think anything could equal that."

A satisfied look settled on her face as she too tasted the result of her labor. "Who's Ruby?" She held up one hand. "No, don't tell me. She's the object of your affection. Right?"

"To put it mildly."

"I'll teach her how to make these, provided she won't think I'm meddling in her business."

He laughed at that. "Wouldn't you be doing just that?" He got up and took his plate to the sink, rinsed it and put it in the dishwasher.

"If you do that," she said, "what are you paying me for?"

"I forget sometimes. Hurry up. I'm calling a cab for you, and it'll be here in fifteen minutes. It's too cold to stand out there waiting for public transportation. I'd take you home, but I have a few things to do."

"The Lord's gonna bless you, Mr. B."

"You just be sure and get those prayers in."

Luther rushed up the stairs and dialed Paul and Amber's phone number. "This is Luther," he said when Amber answered the phone. "Thanks for these pictures of Joachim. He's growing like a weed. How's Paul?"

"We're all fine. Paul hasn't come home yet. It's not quite five here."

"I want to send Joachim something, and I'd like to know what he needs or what you'd like him to have. Don't tell me not to do it. Godparents are supposed to give their godchild a christening gift."

"He doesn't need anything. He's just started crawling fast, and Paul's talking about getting tennis racquets."

"He'll settle down. Proud fathers are known to be nuts. I think I'll just open a bank account for Joachim. That seems to me preferable to wasting money on something he doesn't need."

"That's a wonderful idea, Luther." He heard her clear her throat and guessed the direction of her next words. "Uh, when did you last see Ruby?"

"The same night on which I last saw Opal and Pearl. Why?"

"Oh, Luther. For goodness sake, don't be oblique. You know very well why I asked you about Ruby. Nothing gets past us, Luther. Opal, Pearl and I know something's going on between you and Ruby, and we know when it started, or at least when it started to show.

"So I don't see why the two of you insist on pretending you're just buddies. Buddies don't do heavy French kissing. Besides, Ruby's in love with you, and you can't walk around pretending you don't know it."

"What are you talking about?"

"You heard me. If she won't tell you, I will. I'm getting tired of this nonsense."

He got up and walked as far as the telephone cord would permit, retraced his steps and began walking faster and faster from his night table to the foot of his king-sized bed. "Don't tell me anything like that, Amber, if you don't know what you're talking about. I know you're dramatic, but this is not the occasion to display it. Give me some evidence. Did she tell you that?"

"She didn't deny it, Luther. She loves you, and you love her, and she hurts in one part of Detroit while you hurt in another part. Good grief, Luther, if you don't know how to make her confess it, talk to Paul."

He didn't need advice from Paul as to how to work things out with Ruby. "I may be lacking in some respects, Amber, but that is not one of them."

"I know, but we'd all be so happy if the two of you would stop playing games with each other."

"Trust me, Amber, we're not playing games. What's Joachim's social security number?" She told him. "All right, I'll open the account and send you and Paul the papers." He said goodbye, hung up and fell back across the bed. Could Amber possibly be telling him the truth? He knew Ruby was attracted to him, because he could make her melt with almost no effort, but loving him was another matter. Could he risk assuming that Ruby Lockhart loved him? At the very thought of it, he rolled over on his belly and gave in to the tremors that shook him.

I'm going for it. I have everything to gain.

Chapter 12

Ruby bundled up that morning. With the temperature hovering around zero and the wind howling like a wounded dog, she put on layers of clothing, snow boots, a parka and her beaver coat. She put gloves beneath her mittens, and hoped she'd be able to drive. She laughed at herself when, finally in the warmth of her office, she began to shed the layers.

She'd just settled behind her desk when the secretary called, "Your lawyer on two, Ms. Lockhart."

Her hands shook as she lifted the receiver. "Ruby Lockhart speaking."

"I have great news for you. You are now legally the sole owner of Everyday Opportunities, Inc. It's signed, sealed and in my hand as we speak."

"I'm so pleased. I can't tell you how glad I am that it's over without a court fight. Send me the papers and your bill."

"Right," he said. "It's been a pleasure to work with you, Ms. Lockhart."

She dialed Luther's number, but when she realized what she was doing, she hung up, closed her eyes, covered her face with her hands and slumped in her desk chair. She needed him. How had they ever gotten to the place where they weren't there for each other? She shouldn't have made love to Luther, but if she hadn't she might never have known how a woman was supposed to feel in a man's arms. What was wrong with him? He'd lie if he said he hadn't enjoyed it. She flung out her arms. *Oh, I don't know whether he did or whether he was pretending as I once did with someone. Lord, if I could only stop thinking about it.*

A few minutes later, she met LeRoy in the corridor carrying a brown bag from the delicatessen next door. "It's hell out there," he said. "Cold, windy and damp. We're in for a heavy snow, at least according to the weather forecast."

"When? My heating oil must be getting low, and delivery isn't due for another four days."

"You'll probably be all right. The snow isn't due for two days," he said. "Thank God my rent includes the heating bill."

"Don't mention heating bills, LeRoy. That big old Tudor house of mine eats fuel the way a wolf consumes meat."

When she reached home later that day, she wished she had left the thermostat higher, for she couldn't feel much difference between the temperature inside her house and outside of it, but with fuel so low, she hadn't dared leave the heat up. She put a kettle of water on to boil and went up to her bedroom to change into heavy pants and a sweater.

If Ruby worried about the inclement weather, so did Luther. He left work early and went home to Maggie.

"I'm going to drive you home now before the traffic worsens, and if it's snowing when you wake up tomorrow morning, don't come in."

"But, Mr. B, I haven't cooked anything for you. Oh, the pantry, refrigerator and freezer are full, but I haven't had a chance to cook."

He walked up to her and put a hand on her shoulder. "Maggie, I cooked for myself for years before you began spoiling me. Now get dressed. We have to stop at the supermarket."

"You think we're going to have a storm sure enough?"

"Absolutely," he said and winked at her. "My dad's big toe is acting up. That's a better weather predictor than a meteorologist."

She stared at him for a second and then laughter poured out of her. "You go 'way from here, Mr. B. I do declare."

After taking Maggie shopping and on to her apartment, he went home, spread salt on his driveway in case of snow, heated a frozen pizza in the microwave, got a can of beer and went to the living room to watch television while he ate it. Damn! He'd become so used to having Maggie for company at dinnertime that intense loneliness enveloped him.

"This is no good," he said aloud, and although he didn't want to do it—or so he told himself—he dialed Ruby's number. She didn't answer her home phone or her cell phone, and he had to assume that she was at one of her sisters' homes. He had no intention of calling either of them and asking for her. As it was, they seemed to have welded him to Ruby, and as much as he wanted her with him, her family wouldn't be the instrument that brought it about.

"What the heck! I may as well get a good night's sleep."

He awakened the following morning to the sound of wind howling so fiercely that his bedroom window rattled. He slid out of bed. He attached his prosthesis and hobbled over to the window and released a sharp whistle. Snow barely covered the sidewalk in front of his house, the street and the tree limbs, but it fell so hard, he couldn't see the street or the nearest house.

"Looks as if we're in for it," he said to himself, and reached for his robe. He raised the thermostat and called the managers of his showrooms and told them to remain closed. After eating one of Maggie's delicious scones and washing it down with two cups of coffee, he crawled back into bed and set the alarm for ten-thirty. What was the advantage of a blizzard if you couldn't stay in bed longer than usual?

At about nine o'clock, the ringing of the telephone beside his bed awakened him. "Biggens speaking."

"Hi, Luther. It's Ruby." He bolted upright in bed. "Are you all right?"

Her voice sounded far less confident than usual, alerting him and filling his head with all kinds of possibilities, none of which comforted him. "I...I don't think so. I'm not getting any heat and the thermometer in my dining room registers thirty-eight. When I called the oil company, a man told me that day after tomorrow is the earliest that he could promise delivery, and then, only if it's stopped snowing."

He pulled the covers up to his shoulders. "Pack what you'll need for two or three days. I'll be over there in forty-five minutes."

"I don't think you can see enough to drive."

"Don't worry. I'll be there shortly." He slid out of bed and took special care doing it. Call it a premonition, but something told him that the day would be his, that it would either be the beginning or the end of what was most precious to him. He was sorry for the circumstances in which she found herself, but he intended to make it the answer to his prayers.

Luther need not have worried about Ruby's reaction to his suggestion that she stay at his house during the emergency, for she had called him hoping that he would invite her to do precisely that. She peeked out of the window, saw him park, raced down the stairs with her small suitcase and flung the door open before he rang the bell.

"You're right; it's cold as the devil in here," he said, picking up her bag and holding out his hand for her key.

"It's sweet of you to do this, Luther. Things haven't been too good between us lately, but…I knew you'd help me if you could."

He didn't look at her when he said, "My pleasure, Ruby. I'll always be here for you. You know that." He locked her door and put the key in his pocket.

Luther's silence as he drove to his home almost unnerved her, but she pressed her lips firmly together and didn't comment on it. Instead, she focused on the sound of the grainy snow striking the windshield, the crunching of snow beneath his tires and the poor visibility. She told herself that Luther had to concentrate on driving, and that they might have three days in which to talk.

At last, he drove up to his house, into the garage, stopped and cut the motor. But instead of getting out of the car, he leaned back and closed his eyes. Two or three minutes passed, and she could stand it no longer.

"Are you sorry you brought me here, Luther?"

"Definitely not. Why? Are you sorry you came?"

She hadn't expected that question. "No. But you've been so quiet I thought maybe—"

He interrupted her. "Don't even think it. Let's go in," he said. He reached in the backseat for her suitcase, got out and went around to her door. "I hope you don't mind my taking you through the kitchen."

She hadn't been in his kitchen, so she stopped and looked around. "This is a supermodern kitchen, Luther, and…my goodness, you're neat. I always thought bachelors were messy."

"Some of them may be. Come on, I'll show you to your room, and I want you to feel at home and to behave as if you are home."

"Is it the same room I had before?" she asked him, and when his eyebrows shot up, she realized that she had surprised him. Feeling suddenly wicked, she said, "Did you think I forgot I spent the better part of a night here? I'd remember that if I woke up after twenty years in a coma." Having dropped that bomb, she walked past him without looking at him, climbed the stairs, turned to her left and went directly to the guest room that she had used briefly on that momentous night.

When she didn't hear footsteps behind her, she strode back to the landing and looked down at him. He stood like a statue, staring up at her with his knuckles pressed against his hip bones.

"I'm sorry," she said, enjoying the fact that she'd discombobulated him. "Had you planned for me to sleep somewhere else?"

"Don't overdo it, Ruby," he growled. "I haven't yet achieved sainthood, and you'd be wise to remember that."

She whirled around, went back to the guest room,

flopped down on the bed, kicked up her heels and flung her arms out wide. "Lord, let it snow. Please let it snow."

A few minutes later, the sound of what she presumed was her suitcase hitting the floor outside her room startled her, and she perched on the edge of the bed, her heart pounding like the hoofs of a runaway thoroughbred.

"Did you have any breakfast?" Luther called to her.

"Not a thing," she called back. "Come in."

He ignored the invitation. "I'll get you something to eat. It'll be ready in about fifteen minutes. Your suitcase is here at the door."

If he was planning on being big brother to her for the next few days while she slept a dozen feet from him, he had a surprise coming. "Thanks," she called to him. "I'll be there in a minute." She got her suitcase, changed into jeans that were much too tight and a red cowl-neck sweater, replaced her boots with a pair of sneakers and tripped down the stairs, happier than she'd been since the night he'd taught her what it was to be a woman.

"I can set the table," she said, "if you tell me where everything is."

He turned the bacon, and she wanted to tell him that two people shouldn't consume half a pound of bacon, but she didn't. "You're my guest, and you're not expected to work."

She contemplated doing nothing for three days,

didn't like the idea and said, "If I don't have anything to do for three days, I'll go nuts and take you with me."

"I doubt that. The flatware's in that drawer, plates are in the cabinet beside your head, and we can eat in the dining room or here in the kitchen."

She set the table in the kitchen. "I believe in simplicity," she said.

She wondered at his frown until he said, "I suppose those jeans you're wearing represent simplicity."

"Don't tell me you noticed."

He stopped scrambling eggs and stared hard at her. "In all these years, I never realized that you've got a wild streak. You believe in being reckless, too?"

"When I think it'll pay off, yeah. In all these years—as you put it—I never felt free and liberated as I do now. My sisters are married, and they don't need me for a role model. Look after those eggs before they get tough as leather."

After censuring her with the look one gives a bad child, Luther turned his attention to the eggs. He put a platter of eggs and bacon on the table along with toast, butter, jam, and orange juice. "No instant?" she asked when he placed the coffeepot on the table.

"Instant is not coffee, and I drink coffee. I don't like anything that isn't real and unadulterated." He reached for her hand and said the grace. They ate, hardly speaking until he said, "Do you play poker?"

"Who me? I don't know the first rule. I can play black jack."

He refilled their cups with hot coffee, took a sip and leaned back in his chair. "Every four-year-old can play black jack. Well, if you can't play cards, I suppose we'll have to play house."

"House? What's tha...?" She slapped her hand over her mouth and thanked God for her dark skin that hid the flush of heat burning her face. A grin settled around his mouth and slowly encompassed his whole face as his eyes sparkled and laughter poured out of him. She stared at him. Did he have any idea how handsome he was? He winked at her, and she could feel her eyes narrowing.

"You're too cute for your own good," she said, getting up from the table and taking her soiled dishes to the sink.

"Thanks. You don't often compliment me."

"That's not what I meant, and you know it."

"I'll do that," he told her, and cleared away the remains of their breakfast and turned on the dishwasher. His elbow brushed her nipple, and when she gasped, his head snapped around, and she could see the hot want in his eyes.

Something had to give, and she wondered what they'd do next. He didn't keep her guessing. "Let's go outside and see how the snow's coming along. I want to feed the birds, too."

Electricity shot like live sparks from his fingers to hers when he took her hand and led her to his glass-enclosed, heated back porch. He felt the sparks and the tension, too, she realized when he stopped and gazed down at her with an inquiring expression on his face. He opened the porch door with difficulty, owing to the snowdrift leaning against it, and put seeds in the bird feeder.

The blast of cold air sent shivers through her, and she rubbed her arms for heat. Couldn't he see that she needed his arms around her, that she needed him to warm her and love her?

But her tongue did not betray her feelings. "You must spend a lot of time here," she said, observing the television, radio and CD player, and the comfortable living room–like seating arrangement. She sat beside him on the big leather sofa.

"It's my favorite part of the house. In summer, I often sleep out here, and I ate out here frequently until Maggie came to keep house for me. I told her to stay home until this emergency is over."

He turned on the radio and tuned it to a station that offered commercial-free, easy-listening music. "Let's talk, Ruby, and I mean open and honest with no holds barred. This may be our last chance to straighten out whatever it is that's wrong between us. I can't be your buddy, your pal any longer. I'm tired of the pretense, the on-again-off-again passion between us. I hate it."

The chill that enveloped her had nothing to do with the temperature of the room. "I don't understand what you're saying."

"I thought our relationship had finally gotten on the right track—well almost—and then you showed me that you didn't want your family to know that our feelings for each other had changed, that we were lovers, that—"

"That isn't true. You—"

"Oh yes it is. You got uptight when I called you sweetheart when Paul and Amber left your house with me. I was mad enough to shake you."

"I know, and you didn't kiss me, you bruised me." She took his hand, and at the touch, frissons of heat plowed through her. He saw her reaction, and a blaze kindled in his eyes.

"I never know what to expect from you any longer," Ruby said, still holding his hand. "It's like I don't know you as I once did." She didn't want to talk; she wanted what only he had given her. Without thinking, she moved closer to him, and the warmth of his body began to heat her blood.

His gaze, sweet and gentle, drew her even closer. "I told you that the relationship between us had changed, Ruby, and that comments and actions that once amused us, or that we formerly ignored, would have significance now, because we're not buddies but lovers. Lovers can hurt each other as no one else can."

She closed her eyes and rested her head against the sofa, as visions of him kissing, caressing and loving her played in her mind's eye. Without thinking, she parted her lips and rimmed them with the tip of her tongue. At his gasp, she opened her eyes and stared up at him, caught, like a deer in headlights, with his eyes hot and stormy, passion exposed.

She'd never wanted anything as she wanted him at

that moment. Unconsciously crossing and uncrossing her legs, she grabbed his arm and her fingers dug into his flesh. "Luther, I—"

She stopped short when a loud crash startled her. "My Lord! Somebody must have gotten killed."

"Don't worry. I'll see what it is. Stay here."

Damn the luck! In another second, she would have been in his arms, and he would have made her tell him why she had made love to him that night. He went to the front door, and saw the drivers of two SUVs and a US postal truck standing outside their vehicles gesticulating. None appeared to have been hurt. His conscience clear, he headed back out to the porch to deal with the business at hand.

Ruby hadn't moved. He sat in the spot he'd just vacated and took her hand. "Nobody seems to have been injured. If that crash hadn't occurred right then, only God knows what you and I would be doing this minute. Would you please look at me." She turned so that he could see her face. "I'm asking you for the very last time, Ruby. Why did you make love to me?"

"I—I wanted to. I mean—something happened to me that night. You were different, not my friend, but a living, breathing and stunning man that I wanted. I'd wondered what it would be like with you, and I wanted to...well, you know."

"No, I don't know. Talk to me. I've had a lot of pain about this. Tell me."

"Please believe me that it wasn't the champagne.

That only gave me the courage to do what I wanted to do."

"Okay. Why did you run away almost as soon as it was over? You can't imagine how that hurt me."

"I didn't mean to hurt you. I was so ashamed of myself."

He jerked his hand from hers. "You were ashamed of having me inside you? Is that what you're telling me?"

"No. I was ashamed of the way I acted. I mean I couldn't control...oh, I don't know. I was afraid of what you'd think of me."

He grabbed her shoulders. "Are you telling me the truth?"

"Yes."

"Look at me, woman! All this time, I thought you left either because I didn't satisfy you or because my prosthesis disgusted you. Talk to me!"

Her eyes widened and for a second her lower lip drooped. Then she said, "Didn't satisfy me? Until that night with you, I didn't know how I was supposed to feel. I burst into orgasm so many times that I hardly had energy enough to walk when I left you. I thought you weren't...that I didn't please you. I've nearly gone crazy wanting you ever since."

He thought his heart would fly out of his chest. "Ruby, I've been deeply in love with you since I was nineteen years old, and for over sixteen years, I've wanted you and dreamed of how we'd be together." She braced her hands against his chest, widemouthed and trembling, but he didn't stop. He couldn't, because the words tumbled out of him.

"When I finally had my place inside of you, I felt as if the whole world was mine. You suited me so perfectly. Yes, you were uninhibited, wild if you want to call it that, but that hour was the happiest of my life. I could hardly contain the joy I felt."

She couldn't wait any longer. Pounding his chest, she said. "Listen to me, Luther. I'm crazy in love with you. I don't know when it happened—"

He interrupted her. "You love me?" He stared at her as if she were an apparition. Then, as happiness suffused him, he locked her to his body, but when he felt her erect nipples, he eased her from him. "Amber said you loved me, but I didn't believe her."

"Oh, Luther, why do you think I jumped into that pool? You came in there looking like a brown Adonis, and all those women crowded around you and you hardly looked my way, so I jumped into the pool to get your attention. Unfortunately—"

"Don't go into that. It's in the past. I need your honesty about one more thing." Her eyes, wide and trusting, brought to his mind the Ruby who had so adored him when she was a little girl.

"What?" she asked him and added, "Now that I know you love me, nothing you say or do is going to keep you from me."

"You're a beautiful, desirable woman, and you attract men easily. There was a time when I could have offered you a whole, a complete man, but..." He made himself say it. "How do you feel about this prosthesis that I have to wear for the rest of my life? I take it off at night before I go to bed and put it back on the next morning."

She frowned as if she didn't understand his question. "I don't know. I've never seen it. I didn't notice it when you wore Bermuda shorts to Paige's pool party. Show me what it looks like."

Was she serious? He looked at her. Yes, she really wanted to see it. He pulled his right pant leg up above the amputation so that she could see where the prosthesis joined his flesh.

"Does it hurt there?" she asked, pointing to the spot where the artificial limb was attached to his flesh.

He didn't shift his gaze from her face; he wanted to know what she felt, and her words might not convey that. "It did a couple of weeks back because that padding wore thin. Otherwise I don't think about it."

She stroked the plastic limb. "Whoever makes these is clever. It looks almost exactly like your leg. No wonder I didn't notice it. You thought it disgusted me? Don't you know that any part of you is precious to me?"

She kept her gaze locked on him, and he couldn't pretend that what he wiped from beneath his eyes were not tears. He pulled her onto his lap. "Oh, sweetheart, I want to tell the world that we love each other."

She stroked his cheek and then rubbed his bottom lip with the pad of her thumb. "I love this lip, but it's my undoing." Suddenly, she sucked it into her mouth. "If I can't get you into me any other way…"

He plunged his tongue into her mouth, in and out, simulating the act of love, and her hot blood began to pound in her loins. "I need you," she moaned.

"And I need to give you what you want, what we both want," he said, as she straddled him and pinned him to the sofa.

His belly rumbled, and she sat up. "Oh, goodness. Does this mean you're hungry?"

"Looks like it." He had never been able to make love when his stomach was empty. "It's almost one, and I am starved. I'd better fix us some lunch. I'm gonna need all the energy I can get."

If he'd asked her, Ruby would have told him that food was as far from her mind as Detroit was from the North Pole. "What can I do to help?" she asked.

He splintered her nerves with a wink and a wicked grin. "Not a thing. Go watch television and tell me what's happening."

She went back to the porch, tuned the TV set to a cable news channel and sat down to watch. How could they have been so far wrong about each other? She knew he cared, but she hadn't dreamed that he loved her. Imagine! Luther Biggens had loved her since she was a teenager, but had waited for her to grow up. During that time, she went to the University of Michigan and he went to the Naval Academy; he went overseas as a commissioned officer; her mother died; and she took care of her three sisters, had an affair and became disillusioned. He came home to recover from the loss of his leg and, although he remained friendly, he showed no interest in her until that miraculous evening.

"Luther, come here! Hurry!"

He opened the kitchen door. "What is it? What's the matter?"

"Look. It's Dashuan Kennedy. The police have him in handcuffs. Him and his trainer have been arrested for trafficking in steroids."

"Thank God, Paul got Amber away from him," Luther said. "He'd have ruined her life."

"Yeah. We don't always know what's good for us or what can be our ruination. Just think of the years that you and I lost."

He leaned down and kissed her nose. "Everything in its own time, sweetheart. Be ready to eat in ten minutes."

"It's a good thing I'm not hungry," she said to herself. She wanted to call her sisters and tell them of Dashuan Kennedy's apprehension, but the day belonged to her and Luther. After a few minutes, she went inside. He'd set the table in the dining room.

"My goodness! When did you do this?" she asked when he brought the food into the dining room.

He put on a stern face. "Look at me, miss. Would I give the woman I love a crummy lunch?"

She grabbed his hand and urged him closer. "Bend down. I need to kiss you."

His eyes darkened to obsidian, and then his irises seemed to light up like the blaze that heated her insides. "Better not. If you do, we won't get any lunch, and I need to eat, because I'm hoping to need energy," he said with a grin. He poured a glass of wine for each of them and sat down.

With her hand in his, he bowed his head and said, "Dear Lord, I thank you for the blessing of this woman's love that I so often thought would never be mine, and I thank you for giving us this day together. Amen."

"You don't like it?" he asked after they had been eating for a few minutes.

"It's delicious, but I'm too full to eat much."

He continued eating for a while and suddenly drained his glass of wine and looked at her. "Are you going to drink your wine?" She nodded and drank the remainder of it.

He looked at her, unmasked, his emotions bare. Shivers coursed through her. "Luther! You're tearing me up."

Luther stood and held out his arms to her. "I want to know if we can find again what we had the night after Christmas."

He took her to his room, sat her on the edge of his bed and knelt before her. "You are the only love my life has ever known, and I will never be truly happy until you are my wife. I will love you as long as we both live, and I will take care of you and our children. Will you marry me?"

She hated crying, but joy overcame her. He'd shattered her control. As tears met beneath her chin, she brought his head to her breast. "Yes. Yes. I thought we'd never get together. I love you so much, and I want to be your wife and the mother of your children.'

His tongue slid along the seam of her lips, and when she opened to him, he plunged into her, sending shock waves throughout her body. She pulled him deeper and, immediately, her nipples hardened and began to ache.

"Take this thing off me," she said, tugging at her sweater. He pulled it over her head while she tugged at her tight jeans. Finally she kicked them away, and he stood and stared down at her until, fired by the heat of his gaze, her body began to twist and turn of its own volition.

"What do you want?" he asked in deep guttural tones.

She fumbled at her bra, unhooked it and offered him her breast. He pushed her to her back, straddled her, pulled the nipple into his mouth and began sucking it. She rubbed his hand over her other nipple. She'd waited so long to feel like that, so long to have him inside of her. The rough fabric of his jeans against her naked skin gave her a feeling of wantonness, and she reached down to caress him.

"Wait a minute, baby. I need some protection for you." He sat on the edge of the bed, pulled off his clothes and stood. She sat up, pulled down his shorts, fondled his penis, and then sucked him slowly into her mouth. As much as his body cried out in pleasure, he told her to stop.

"You didn't like it?" she asked, afraid that she had offended him.

"I loved it." He lifted her, and covered her body with his own. When he looked down at her and smiled, she took his breath away.

"Be patient," he said when she started panting and her hips began to roll. But her hands swept up and down his back, squeezing and pinching his buttocks. How she adored him, as his lips cherished her eyes, ears, cheeks and mouth. She thought she'd explode from the heat he built up in her. But he did not linger there. She held her breath until at last his mouth was on her breast, and when he sucked the nipple into his mouth again, she cried out.

He didn't ignore the other one, but stroked and sucked it until she began to undulate wildly beneath him. "Luther, please just get in me. I'm on fire for you."

"Good. That's the way I want you." His tongue twirled around in her navel, and then he kissed, nipped and licked the inside of her thighs until she couldn't stand the tension.

"Luther, I feel like I'm going to explode."

He said nothing, but spread her legs wider, kissed her and buried his tongue into her. Screams poured out of her when he started sucking. When she thought she could stand no more, his finger slid into her, and she thought she'd go insane from the sensations he created.

"I can't stand it," she said. "Please get in me."

He moved up her body slowly, as if he relished every second of it. "Take me."

She grasped his penis with both hands and led him home.

"Look at me, don't close your eyes. I want you to know who's loving you," he said as he eased into her.

"So good," she moaned.

He accelerated his pace, and she hooked her legs around his hips and met him thrust for thrust. She felt as if she'd been sucked into quicksand. Her whole body quivered for release and then she exploded into ecstasy. She flung her arms wide and gave herself to him.

"You're mine. Mine, do you hear?" he shouted and gave her the essence of himself.

After a long while, he said, "What will we do with your house?"

He didn't think he'd ever seen a smile sparkle as hers did. "Sell it and split the money four ways. Can we call my sisters and tell them that we're lovers, and that we're getting married Valentine's Day?"

Happiness suffused him and he laughed aloud. "Sure, but why Valentine's Day? That's almost three weeks away."

"It'll take me that long to get ready. I want a formal wedding."

"And I want you to have whatever pleases you."

"Oh, Luther. I love you so much, and I'm so happy."

His arms tightened around her. "I can't express how I feel this minute, but I know I'll love you forever."

Could they have a new beginning?

Pride
AND
Consequence

Favorite author

ALTONYA
WASHINGTON

When devastating illness strikes him, Malik's pride causes
him to walk out on his passionate life with Zakira.
She is devastated but dedicates herself to their business.
But when Malik returns fully recovered, Zakira is stunned...
and still angry. Now Malik will need more than soul-searing
kisses to win her trust again. He will have to make her
believe in them...again.

**Available the first week of November
wherever books are sold.**

KIMANI
ROMANCE ™

The Knight family trilogy continues...

to love a
KNIGHT
WAYNE JORDAN

As Dr. Tamara Knight cares for gravely injured
Jared St. Clair, she's drawn to his rugged sensuality and
commanding strength. Despite his gruff exterior, she can't
stop herself from indulging in a passionate love affair with
him. But unbeknownst to Tamara, Jared was sent to save
her. Now protecting Tamara isn't just another mission for
Jared—it's all that matters!

"Mr. Jordan's writing simply captures his audience."
—*The Road to Romance*

*Available the first week of November
wherever books are sold.*

KIMANI™
ROMANCE

www.kimanipress.com

KPWJ0431107

The stunning sequel to *The Beautiful Ones...*

feel THE fire

NATIONAL BESTSELLING AUTHOR
ADRIANNE BYRD

Business mogul Jonas Hinton has learned to stay clear of gorgeous women and the heartbreak they bring. But when his younger brother starts dating sexy attorney Toni Wright, Jonas discovers a sizzling attraction he's never felt before. Torn between family loyalty and overwhelming desire, can he find a way to win the woman who could be his real-life Ms. Wright?

"Byrd proves once again that she's a wonderful storyteller."
—*Romantic Times BOOKreviews* on *The Beautiful Ones*

*Available the first week of November
wherever books are sold.*

ARABESQUE®

www.kimanipress.com

KPAB0221107

Love can be sweeter the second time around...

USA TODAY Bestselling Author

KAYLA PERRIN

Midnight **D**REAMS

Betrayed by her husband, Jade Alexander resolved
never again to trust a man with her heart. But after
meeting old flame Terrell Edmonds at a New Year's
Eve party, Jade feels her resolve weakening—
and her desire kindling.

Terrell had lost Jade by letting her marry the wrong man.
Now he must convince her that together they can make
all their New Year wishes come true...

"A fine storytelling talent."
—the *Toronto Star*

*Available the first week of November
wherever books are sold.*

ARABESQUE®

www.kimanipress.com

KPKP0251107